IN THE DEAD OF NIGHT

ERIK CARTER

SEVERN RIVER
PUBLISHING

Copyright © 2024 by Erik Carter.

All rights reserved.

No part of this book may be reproduced in any form or by any electronic or mechanical means, including information storage and retrieval systems, without written permission from the author, except for the use of brief quotations in a book review.

Severn River Publishing
SevernRiverBooks.com

This is a work of fiction. Names, characters, businesses, places, events and incidents are either the products of the author's imagination or used in a fictitious manner. Any resemblance to actual persons, living or dead, or actual events is purely coincidental.

ISBN: 978-1-64875-677-1 (Paperback)

ALSO BY ERIK CARTER

Silence Jones Action Thrillers

The Suppressor

Hush Hush

Tight-Lipped

Before the Storm

Dead Air

Speechless

Quiet as the Grave

Don't Speak

A Strangled Cry

Muted

In the Dead of Night

Tell No Tales

Unspoken

Dying Breath

Stealth Tactics

Dale Conley Action Thrillers

Stone Groove

Dream On

The Lowdown

Get Real

Talkin' Jive

Be Still

Jump Back

The Skinny

No Fake

To find out more about Erik Carter and his books, visit

severnriverbooks.com

1

Haugan, Montana
The 1990s

Vigilante assassin Silence Jones hadn't been himself lately—in the chin area especially.

Usually, his jaw was impeccably sculpted, thanks to the facial reconstruction surgery performed years earlier by his employers, the Watchers. But for the past three days, a ledge of prosthetic skin and bone had stretched out into eternity from beneath Silence's lips, like a stubbly Olympic diving board, a chin that would give Bruce Campbell or Dick Dastardly a run for their money.

It was hyper-realistic, indistinguishable from genuine flesh...

...aside from the long slice running straight through it, courtesy of a knife fight a few hours earlier.

That's why Silence kept trying to conceal it.

He sat in a cracked vinyl booth at Highway Hangout, a greasy spoon diner on the side of a truck stop off I-90 in rural Montana. Staring out the dusty window to his right, he saw nighttime fog and a line of parked trucks, their lights flickering in the persistent rain, remnants of the earlier downpour.

The air inside the diner was thick with the scent of fried food, coffee, and cigarette smoke, and Silence detected Salisbury steak in the mix. The steak—along with mashed potatoes, gravy, green beans, and a roll—was that day's dinner special. Highway Hangout was the kind of place where every creak of the door elicited a momentary hush and wary glances from the regulars. As one of those glances landed on him, Silence propped his elbow on the table and placed his fake chin in his hand, hiding it with his large fingers.

Silence's employers, the Watchers, were a covert and illegal group dedicated to fixing flaws in U.S. procedural justice via their cadre of assassins, like Silence, whom they called Assets. Their extensive reach and infiltration across all levels of American infrastructure—from the highest federal offices to small-town governments—granted them access to technologies unknown to the public, sophisticated prosthetics among them. In the past three days, no one who saw Silence's enlarged chin had offered even a flicker of doubt to its authenticity, despite it being composed of silicone skin with a foam latex core.

Hell, *Silence* hadn't even been able to tell it was phony when he leaned in close to his reflection in the hotel mirror the first night in Montana. He'd scrutinized every detail. Inspected. Poked and prodded. And found no evidence of fakery. If not for the numb, lifeless feel of the silicone under his fingers, he would have thought the Watchers had once again surgically altered his appearance. Remarkable.

But no matter how extraordinary the prosthetic flesh was, it was no match for a Bowie knife.

A few hours earlier, Silence had trapped one of Maddox's enforcers—tall and broad with a menacing glare and a thick beard framing his face, tattoos peeking out from under his red flannel sleeves—in the isolated parking lot of a rundown motel. This was just before the downpour, and the sun had been slowly sinking below the mountains, casting a dim glow over the neglected section of the motel property. The fading light created ominous shapes on the cracked and chipped pavement, exposing the desolate atmosphere of the forsaken location.

Suddenly, the other man realized he was trapped. In a flash, a massive

Bowie knife appeared in his hand, and he lunged at Silence with lethal intent.

Silence darted to the left, avoiding the strike. His Beretta 92FS was in its shoulder holster, weighing heavily against his ribs, but he couldn't use the gun now. Not here. No matter how shitty the motel behind him looked, it was operational. There were people in the vicinity.

So he improvised.

Lying within arm's reach, at the edge of a pile of random, deteriorating objects spewing out of a propped-open door, was a broken shovel. He grabbed it. An impromptu shield.

Metal clashed against metal. The opponent might have been a ruffian by profession, but to this point Silence hadn't suspected the man had any professional training. Now, with the speed of the attack, with the handling of the blade, it was clear the man was more skilled than Silence had wagered. Silence, however, had *world-class* training, and with those honed reflexes, he parried each swipe of the man's knife, the strikes ringing in the air.

Another block.

Another.

Then a particularly vicious and unexpectedly on-target swing came right at Silence's face.

In one swift motion, he leaned back and deftly dodged the oncoming Bowie knife, a trained reflex that was honed from countless hours of practice and years of real-life encounters.

But he hadn't fully accounted for his prosthetic chin.

The razor-sharp blade sliced straight through the silicone and into the foam core. Silence felt it—a sharp jolt that registered not as pain but realization.

Regaining his focus, Silence saw the goon's arm arch wide for the latest attack, leaving him vulnerable. Silence brought the shovel forward, right into the man's forearm.

The man's face twisted in surprise as he stumbled back, off balance. Seizing the moment, Silence pushed forward, disarming the goon with a torquing of the shovel's handle.

The knife clattered to the ground.

And, after Silence's swift leg sweep, the man joined it.

The bearded behemoth landed hard on the cracked asphalt. He grunted at the impact.

Now the Beretta could come out. Silence pulled the weapon, aimed it at the man's head.

"Talk!" Silence said in a booming growl. The bruiser had eluded Silence for half the day, an annoying delay to the investigation, and Silence wouldn't waste any more time getting the intel he needed.

But the forceful use of his voice brought a shot of pain to Silence's throat. Years earlier, an incident had almost taken his life and left him with a permanently damaged larynx. Now, his throat was a patchwork of scar tissue, making speaking a painful experience. He had developed techniques to minimize the discomfort—such as using short sentences and swallowing frequently—but the pain never truly went away.

The man on the ground looked up at Silence, fear in his eyes.

"I ... I'll tell you," he stammered. The goon cleared his throat before he continued. "Maddox is gonna be at Highway Hangout tonight. There's something going down, like a big shipment coming through or something."

The man stared fearfully at the gun pointed at him, his body trembling. But Silence kept his finger off the trigger. Though this man was suspected of aiding Maddox in heinous deeds, there was no solid evidence to support it. The Watchers abided by their colloquialism—they had to be "three hundred percent sure" before sealing someone's fate.

This man hadn't earned a death sentence.

But there was a mountain of incriminating evidence against the man's employer, Maddox.

Iron-clad proof.

Fully aware of the lingering threat the man posed, Silence didn't turn his back as he left the guy quivering on the pavement.

A few moments later, peeling down I-90 in the Infiniti Q45 that had been his ride for the duration of the Montana mission, Silence touched his chin. The slice was straight and surgically thin. That part was good. It wasn't a twisted gash. But he could tell immediately by touching it that the cut was long and deep.

He glanced into the rearview mirror as he applied a bit of pressure. The cut opened up, revealing the porous foam interior, an inch and a half deep. When Silence released his grip, the quasi-wound sealed itself back up, but not entirely. There was still a visible marring, a bloodless cut, that surgically precise line.

This line on Silence's chin was the reason he'd been shielding his face for the last twenty minutes since entering Highway Hangout. As he stared out the window into the foggy fueling area, his gaze shifted to the reflection staring back at him from the murky window pane. He hardly recognized the man in the glass.

Not only was the fake chin absurdly large, it also had a sprinkling of incredibly lifelike whiskers that perfectly matched Silence's real ones. He'd spent the last few days carefully trimming his facial hair to match the stubble beard of the prosthetic. Along with his attire—a well-worn trucker's jacket layered over an oil-stained plaid shirt riding above a pair of soiled Wranglers—the chin added to his new aesthetic, giving Silence a gruffer, more weathered appearance. Colored contact lenses masked his dark brown eyes, now a bold blue.

Silence rarely did undercover work like this. His voice was not only painful, but it was also growling and crackling and hideous to behold—too distinctive for most false personas. It was even more uncommon for his undercover missions to require physical alterations. But he'd been through it before. In his previous life—before the facial reconstruction, before his throat had been ruined, before he was conscripted into the Watchers, and before he'd taken the name Silence Jones—he had been a police officer named Jake Rowe. On his final assignment before the disaster that changed his life forever, Jake had been undercover, wearing colored contact lenses to mask his brown eyes and hide his identity.

Jake's contact lenses had been bright green.

In Silence's current mission, the contact lenses were bright blue.

Both times, Silence and Jake had found themselves staring at reflections, questioning who the hell was looking back at them.

Silence sensed something.

Someone staring at him.

Again...

It was the one person in the diner who had noticed the cut on his chin: that damn kid.

When Silence's fiancée, C.C., was still alive, she had said Silence had a natural gift for reading people. Although he didn't necessarily agree with all of C.C.'s hippie-ish musings, Silence acknowledged that she was correct about his ability to read others. So despite the suspicious glances thrown his way when he'd first stepped into Highway Hangout, Silence discerned that the scrutiny wasn't due to the long incision on his oversized chin.

Except for the scrutiny of one individual's gaze.

Even in the dim lighting of the diner and despite Silence's efforts to hide his face, a boy on the other side of the room had quickly noticed the distinct line on the prosthetic chin. Kids have a way of picking up on things that adults miss. A young boy, around the age of four, sat on one side of a booth, his parents on the other. The boy had turned entirely around to get a better look at Silence—just his ketchup-smeared fingers and bright eyes and mop top peaking over the cracked vinyl cushion.

After Silence had taken his seat and begun his routine of inconspicuously resting his chin in his hand, the boy couldn't take his eyes off the odd marking. One of the boy's parents eventually scolded him, telling him to face forward. But for the last several minutes, the kid continued to risk admonition, occasionally turning around to catch another glimpse.

And there it was again.

That little face peaking over the cushion.

All right, all right.

With a cautious glance to ensure no one else noticed, Silence decided to sate the boy's curiosity. Making eye contact, he carefully extended his fingers over his chin. He pulled, stretching the gash to an unnatural width, revealing the foam rubber innards. The kid's eyes widened in a mix of shock and fascination, his expression quickly shifting into an impish grin.

Silence responded with a rare, small smile of his own.

And an even rarer wink.

Giggling, the boy whipped back around and disappeared behind the seat.

Silence pressed the chin back together.

A subtle shift in the diner's atmosphere drew Silence's attention. Hank

Maddox, the man Silence had been trailing for three days, moved across the space, having emerged from the door in the back that led to the convenience store and trucker showers. Maddox was average in height and build, but there was something about his face that was not so average, something in the depth of those rugged features that suggested a veiled cunning. He had sun-squinted eyes and leathery skin, lined from years on the road. A thick beard peppered with strands of gray. Nose slightly crooked from a past injury.

Maddox was more than a mere blip on the criminal radar; he was a vital node within the ruthless Los Sombra cartel. His operations stretched far beyond the borders of Montana, as he not only dispersed the Mexican narcotics throughout the northern United States but also played a pivotal role in surreptitiously crossing them into Canada, thereby extending Los Sombra's influence across three countries. The intelligence was unequivocal: Maddox exploited his extensive network within the trucking industry to transport the illicit drugs seamlessly.

His tactics included extortion, torture, and murder.

The Watchers were three hundred percent certain of this.

With one hand still covering his chin, the fingers of Silence's opposite hand unconsciously traced the edge of his coffee cup. His eyes never left Maddox, watching as the man approached a booth, bent over without bothering to sit, and held a hushed conversation with the rough-looking trio of men finishing their Salisbury steaks. A few seconds later, Maddox straightened and continued through Highway Hangout, going for the glass doors.

Silence waited.

When Maddox pushed through the door and the bell jingled faintly above him, Silence slid out of his booth. He tossed a twenty-dollar bill on the table—payment and tip for his eighty-nine-cent cup of coffee—then followed Maddox's path through the diner. The bell chimed again as he stepped out into the foggy night.

The chill nipped at Silence's face, everywhere but that insulated chin of his. Heavy drizzle immediately dampened his hair, his shoulders, and made the parking lot before him a glistening Edward Hopper show of shadow illuminated by glowing orbs of automotive lighting—red and amber—in a hazy atmosphere of diesel-tinged fog.

Silence stalked after Maddox, going for the rows of trucks, many of which were idling, rumbling, like beasts at slumber. I-90 played a gentle vehicular melody in the background; the highway was just visible in the mist, its pole lamps and the streaks of headlights and taillights.

Maddox went for the front of the truck that Silence had been trailing—the one with B8N453 on the door. As the creep disappeared around the front of the truck, Silence quickened his pace, minding the crunching noise of his boots on the asphalt, and approached the rear. The trailer doors were open, revealing darkness within. Grabbing the metal handrail, he pulled himself up and inside. His eyes adjusted to the dim interior; his senses went on high alert.

The trailer's interior confirmed his suspicions: it was a cache of illegal bullshit. Row after row of neatly stacked boxes and bags stretched before him, each one meticulously labeled and organized. These were not the haphazard collections of a small-time operation; this was the hallmark of a sophisticated and extensive narcotics enterprise. The boxes—some wooden, others cardboard—showed evidence of powder-filled plastic sacks within. Silence found one of the sacks peeking out of a crack in a wooden crate. He pierced the sack with a fingernail, touched his finger to the white powder within, dabbed it on his tongue, tasted, spit.

Cocaine.

Silence's attention sharply shifted as two figures emerged from the misty truck yard, slipping into the trailer's open back to join him. At first glance, they blended with the fog, almost ghost-like, but as they stepped closer into a patch of dim light, their truck driver disguises became visible, hallmarks of Maddox's operation. Stained caps. Worn jackets. Faded blue-jeans on par with those of Silence's disguise. They advanced toward Silence, a menacing presence behind their ordinary façade.

The goons made their move, fast and hungry. But Silence was faster. He dodged a clumsy punch, answering with an elbow strike—hard and precise—to the first goon's jaw.

The second came in, knife first, a dull gleam in the half-light. It was another damn Bowie knife. Silence stepped aside, and in one quick movement, he had the guy's arm, twisting it. The knife fell to the trailer floor.

Silence's boot struck the man's gut, cutting short his scream. The guy flew back, hit a crate, and didn't get up.

The first guy bounced back, coming at Silence full throttle. Raw aggression. Blind fury. Silence watched the guy come at him. Waited. The man lunged, throwing a punch that was more amusing than lethal. Silence stepped aside; he'd read the guy's angle before it even formed.

Another swing. Another dodge. Silence was patient, letting the guy tire himself out.

Then Silence struck. One clean hit. Precise and efficient, right where it needed to be—the solar plexus. The guy's eyes went wide with shock, his forward momentum turning against him. He crashed to the floor in a heap.

Silence looked down at him, the guy's chest heaving, his fight spent. The other guy, too, was done for. Silence stood over them. Waited for movement. Waited for a latecomer to join them from the open doors to their rear.

No one appeared.

Silence sprang into action again, leaping out of the back of the trailer and reemerging into the drizzle and mist. He pulled his Beretta from its shoulder holster and advanced cautiously. The gun's suppressor was already screwed into place. The dense fog made it difficult to see as he neared the tractor, moving slowly and ready for Maddox to make a sudden attack.

Three more paces, and he was to the cab. His boot clanked on the diamond-plate step bar as he climbed up the passenger side, flung open the door, and found...

Nothing.

Maddox wasn't there.

Whipping around, Silence caught sight of his quarry. Maddox was sprinting toward the edge of the parking lot, where an idling car awaited, its taillights bleeding red into the fog. One of his trucker-disguised men stood by the driver-side door, urging Maddox to hurry with broad swipes of his arm.

Without hesitation, Silence took off after Maddox, his boots pounding the wet pavement, splashing puddles. The looming presence of I-90 served as the perfect escape route for Maddox. As headlights of passing cars flickered dimly in the mist, they revealed that the traffic was sparse, which only added to the possibility of Maddox getting away if he got to the waiting vehicle. Silence's Infiniti was on the other side of the lot; by the time he could get to it, Maddox and his man would be long gone.

Silence would have to do things the old-fashioned way.

He sprinted harder.

The chase was a blur of motion, Silence's relentless pursuit closing the gap. At high speed, the raindrops became pinpoints, stinging his cheeks, blinding his eyes. Ahead, Maddox cast frantic glances over his shoulder. Silence pressed on, unyielding, the Beretta firm in his hand.

Maddox was almost to the car, a few yards away, when Silence made his move. He lunged forward with a burst of speed, closing the distance. The tackle came hard and fast, and Maddox yelped in surprise. They collided first with each other, then with the ground, a whirlwind of limbs and grunts, rolling across the wet asphalt.

Using their momentum, Silence maneuvered them away from the main parking lot, steering the struggle toward a secluded corner past one of the trucks, where a stack of wooden pallets lay forgotten. There, Silence gained the upper hand. He rolled to his feet, caught hold of Maddox's shirt, and yanked the scumbag up, throwing him against an upended pallet. There was the crack of breaking wood. Maddox squirmed, but Silence's grip was unyielding.

Maddox's mouth stayed shut, but his eyes flickered with a mix of recognition and confusion—the look of a man who knew that eventually someone would come to kill him but couldn't figure out why it was this trucker he'd never met, never even seen prior to a few days earlier.

...this stranger with piercing blue eyes and a chin that stretched out endlessly.

Instead of speaking, Maddox fought for his life, lunging forward with the desperation of a cornered animal.

Silence sized him up. Maddox's punches were wild, the kind you see from guys more accustomed to scaring people than fighting them. Silence was different. His moves were crisp, no show, just business: jabs and hooks, each one landing with purpose.

When Maddox threw a clumsy right, Silence was already moving. He ducked, smooth and fast, and came up with an uppercut to Maddox's ribs. The guy gasped, winded, but swung again, a left cross this time, desperate. Silence stepped aside, just a quick shift of weight, and countered with a straight right. It connected. Maddox's head snapped back, his feet stumbled.

The fight was quickly becoming a disaster for Maddox. His punches were slower now, even easier to read. Silence's eyes narrowed. He moved in fast, a left jab to the nose, a right to the temple. Maddox wobbled, his arms useless.

Without a word, Silence leveled his Beretta. Maddox's eyes widened; there was fear there, raw and real. Silence's trigger finger squeezed. The suppressor-muffled gunshots pulsed through the air, reverberating off the pallets, the trucks.

Crack! Crack!

A double tap to the face.

Standing there, Silence watched Maddox slump down the damaged pallet, clothes snagging on broken boards, blood chasing after him, until he collected on the ground with a gentle thump. Silence glanced left, right. There were a few shouts of concern from the distance, but no one had seen anything; no one was moving in his direction.

As Silence stole a glimpse around the stack of pallets, he saw that the car that had been waiting for Maddox was peeling away at the end of the parking lot, tires screeching as it went onto the frontage road and headed for the interstate. The loyalty of Maddox's man had been paper-thin. Shocking.

Another glance left. Another right. Satisfied, Silence put the Beretta away and walked off, vanishing into the fog.

2

Three weeks later.

It wasn't the best neighborhood Indianapolis had to offer.

Trash and broken bits of furniture. Buildings with peeling paint, boarded-up windows. Shabbily dressed people. Rot and desolation suffused the nighttime air.

Every city had these forgotten corners, and Grant Beckwith knew their ubiquitous shadows all too well. These areas had been his domain for years.

Tonight, Beckwith leaned against a crumbling brick wall, awaiting his employer's arrival. This wasn't just another new job, one he'd accepted two weeks earlier, but a necessity imposed by a past that was always one step behind, ready to redefine the course he'd been forced to tread. Each of Beckwith's life choices—every horrible, God-awful decision, often conceived in a desperate bid for survival—had now converged at this moment at a shithole side of Indianapolis, Indiana.

Beckwith scanned the alleyway. In the dim light were the silhouettes of trash cans and dumpsters, their contents spilling onto the ground. There was the distant whine of a police siren, and when it faded away, footsteps.

Tap, tap, tap.

Quiet at first, growing louder as they approached, echoing over the brickwork and pulling Beckwith back to the present. He tensed, watching as the figure drew near.

A scarred man in a stylish suit breezed in his direction.

Even in the weak lighting, the dichotomy of Colin Lennox's face was striking, unsettling. One half, caught in the flicker of the lights, showcased classic good looks: blond, youthful, chiseled, and coolly handsome, with a sparkling eye—dark brown—that glinted with vitality.

The other half, however, told a different story. A story involving fire.

Lennox's scarred flesh was a landscape of knotted burns and rough textures, extending about a quarter of the way across his face and halfway down his throat. His eye was milky and lifeless on this affected side of his visage, contrasting the lively sparkle in the opposite eye. A trio of deep furrows stood out in the scar tissue on his neck, as though he'd been slashed by a lawn tool or the claws of a three-fingered beast.

"Beckwith," Lennox began.

That voice…

It was as distinctive as the man's visage.

Beckwith had come to identify Lennox's utterances as serpentine, the voice of a snake. All breathy and hissing. The voice had an edge to it, the kind of edge that told you it had been rebuilt from something broken. Though powerful, it was just quiet enough that you had to focus your concentration to hear it. The voice came from a place of ruin—much like the man himself—caused, no doubt, by the fire that had created the scarring on his neck, including those three deep and twisted fissures.

"I have a task for you," Lennox hissed. "Something … delicate. There's a junkie, a loose end, who knows too much. He's threatening to spill our secrets."

He slipped a folded piece of paper into Beckwith's hand.

"You know what to do," Lennox said, nodding toward the handwritten address.

Beckwith nodded and said nothing. He'd quickly learned that showing any response was a vulnerability Lennox could exploit. No follow-up questions. He didn't need the details; the implications were clear. The junkie, whoever the hell he was, had signed his own death warrant the moment he became a liability to Lennox.

A twinge of dread as Beckwith pocketed the paper and met Lennox's stare. This wasn't just another task; it was a clean-up mission. The stubborn remnants of Beckwith's conscience protested, but he pushed them back down. In Lennox's world, hesitation was not an option. It was kill or be killed...

...literally, in this case.

"Understood," Beckwith said.

A sparkle in Lennox's functioning eye married up with a slight rise in his ringmaster smile.

"Good," he rasped.

Lennox retreated, disappearing back into the night, the tap of his dress shoes fading away.

Beckwith took a deep breath and looked at the address. Two blocks away. The night air smelled of rain and decay. He shoved his hands in his pockets. As he walked, Beckwith's thoughts churned. He had done many questionable things in his past—things that haunted his sleep—but this... this was different.

This was something he'd only done once before.

And that had been instinct. Self-defense, even if the circumstances were questionable.

Yes, that was different.

This time, Beckwith was setting out with the *intent* of killing someone.

He double-checked the address and approached the apartment building. Lichen-infested brick. Dangling wires. Shattered windows. As Beckwith stepped past a hunched-over figure clenching a paper sack of consolation, he hesitated at the entrance, fingers hovering over the handle. A moment passed. Then he pulled the door open and stepped in.

He was immediately assaulted by the stench of mold—damp, stagnant, and somehow both alive and dead. Doors with mismatched labeling lined the narrow hallway. Beckwith's footsteps echoed on the linoleum floor and stopped when he found 3B. This was the place.

He rapped sharply on the door, which was a couple of inches ajar. No response. The quiet sound of a TV buzzing came from within. Beckwith detected the faintest shuffle of movement inside. He leaned his ear closer. There it was again—the soft sound of someone trying not to be heard.

Beckwith shouldered the door, and it swung open with a creak. The apartment was a pitiful sight—a single, dim lamp barely illuminating the space; a three-legged sofa, angled sharply with its handicap; scattered newspapers; a card table with no chairs. But Beckwith's focus was on the figure he glimpsed slipping through a back window, scrambling onto the fire escape.

Cursing under his breath, Beckwith didn't waste a moment. He spun on his heel and retraced his steps, hurrying back down the hallway. The building seemed to spit him out as he exited back into the night. The drunk on the steps hadn't budged.

Beckwith scanned the surroundings. A woman leaning against a doorway, watching the street with wary eyes. A stray cat slinking over the top edge of a fence. An abandoned Chevy, its windshield spider-webbed.

And ... there!

He spotted the junkie darting between the shadows, trying to put distance between himself and the inevitable. Beckwith bolted after him.

As he rounded the corner of the apartment building, Beckwith saw the junkie sprinting toward the maze of alleys and parking lots. Beckwith quickened his pace, his boots pounding against the pavement.

A flash of that earlier unease resurfaced—Beckwith's resistance to the life he'd sought to leave behind for years.

Years...

Yet here he was, merely two weeks into a new job, immersed in the very existence he had tried to escape. In fact, he was deeper in it than ever before, threading through the worn back alleys and crumbling parking lots behind a neglected apartment building, chasing a man in order to kill him, embarking on the dark task at the behest of a scarred and hissing man he'd met less than a month prior.

He veered left, past a rusted dumpster. A disheveled man in a stained shirt, clutching a can of beer, looked up in surprise.

"You okay, buddy?" he slurred.

The guy was so similar to the passed-out man back at the apartment steps as to be comical—that is, it might be humorous if Beckwith was in any mood to laugh.

Beckwith, without a word, drew his Browning Hi-Power pistol. The drunk scuttled off, eyes wide.

Turning another corner, Beckwith slowed, moving silently, his boots barely whispering against the gravel. Amidst the distant city hum, he caught a faint sound. Someone was trying to move stealthily nearby. Slow, cautious footsteps on the asphalt.

Identifying the source, Beckwith leaped around the rotten wood fence, coming face to face with the junkie. The man was a malnourished type of thin with greasy and matted hair. His clothes were stained rags. Track marks covered his inner arms. Trembling hands. Sunken eyes that darted nervously.

The physical decay made it impossible to pinpoint the guy's age, but he was clearly young, nowhere near thirty.

Maybe not even twenty...

The junkie's voice trembled. "Oh, no! Please..."

Beckwith, suppressing another pang of reluctance, ignored the plea, tightening his grip on the Browning, which he noted was quivering in his hand.

"You're ... you're with Lennox, aren't you?" the junkie said.

Beckwith nodded.

The junkie shook—his lower lip first, then his entire body. "Please, I don't wanna die, dude."

"I'm ... sorry," Beckwith said.

Hearing the reluctant conviction in Beckwith's response, the junkie had a sudden urge of survival-forged confidence and lunged at Beckwith.

His swings were desperate and erratic. Beckwith quickly moved to the side, avoiding the man's wild punches that sliced through the air. He blocked and dodged the frenzied assaults.

A moment of this, then Beckwith countered. He caught the junkie's arm, spinning him around, then twisted both of the man's hands behind his back. One leg in front of the junkie's knobby knee. A thrust of the hips. And then they were on the ground.

The junkie took the brunt of it, screaming as he smacked into the wet asphalt facedown. Beckwith had the guy's arms contorted into a knot. He put the Browning to the back of the man's head.

"I'm sorry," Beckwith said again, this time hoarse and quiet.

Crack!

The gunshot roared through the brick and concrete surroundings, off the rotten wooden fence and the chain-link one on the opposite side of the lot. A woman yelled out. And a man, too. A dog barked.

Beckwith stood up and looked at the body. Blood poured from the back of the junkie's head, gathering in a rapidly expanding pool, dark in the night, glistening obsidian. A siren sounded in the distance.

Beckwith blinked.

And took off running.

3

The next morning. One hundred fifteen miles away. Cincinnati, Ohio.

It was the second time in less than two minutes that Silence had watched the man die.

Wet skin. Bangs plastered to his forehead. Brown eyes opened wide, bloodshot, pupils dilated, registering pure desperation as the man gazed directly at Silence. He was Caucasian, twenties, athletic build, medium blond hair. Sweat patches ringed the armpits of the man's wrinkled dress shirt. He was seated on a metal folding chair.

With a shaking voice, the man said, "My name is Special Agent Colin Lennox, FBI. I've been undercover in Indianapolis for two and a half weeks, since November 3rd."

Lennox raised a hand, revealing a Smith & Wesson 459 9mm pistol. It shook violently.

"Jordan Havelock has asked me to take my life, and I've been given the great honor of a special ending, one different from the ending that the others will have in a few minutes, one that will make a statement."

He paused. Blinked. Shoved the gun's barrel beneath his chin.

"Listen carefully. My investigation is complete, and my findings are simple: Jordan Havelock is a great man."

The pistol shook even more violently, the barrel pressing into the fleshy underside of Lennox's chin.

Then it fired.

Crack!

A red spray of blood and bone erupted from the side of Lennox's face. His body fell forward, teetering over the edge of his chair, but before it dropped to the floor...

...it stopped.

Locked in place. Frozen in time.

Lines of static crossed the screen, pulsing gray-and-white video noise over the color image, one line at the top of Lennox's drooping torso, the other running across his shins.

Silence leaned away from the television, and the springs of the cheap mattress on which he was sitting squealed with his weight.

"You'll have noticed the teeth that flew out in the blood spatter," the woman to Silence's left said in a matter-of-fact tone.

"Yes," Silence said, his single-syllable reply coming as a crackling grumble.

Upon hearing Silence's unsettling voice for the first time, strangers couldn't help but react to it, unable to control their shock.

But the woman beside Silence gave no reaction. She was no stranger to the bizarre voice. She knew Silence well—in many ways, she knew him better than anyone else in the world—and she'd heard him speak innumerable times.

Silence turned to her.

Doc Hazel was seated at a round laminate table on one of a pair of wooden chairs, the red fabric of its cushion faded and threadbare, barely clinging on. She wore a power suit, its skirt terminating well north of her knees, revealing copious amounts of her bare, crossed legs. Petite. Severe. A face full of angles nearly as sharp as those on Silence's. Her brown hair was pulled into a tight, professional tail.

The VCR remote sat in her right hand, finger still on the pause button. She looked back at Silence through a pair of smart, expensive eyeglasses, her face blank. It was Doc Hazel's standard expression—robotic and overtly impersonal.

They were in a ramshackle motel. Peeling walls and a musty smell. The sort of place that offered by-the-hour lodging in addition to traditional overnight stays. Though Silence and Doc Hazel had rented the space for wholly professional reasons, the upstairs neighbors had clearly taken full advantage of the pricing structure. The thumping and screaming had started five minutes earlier. Occasionally, the ceiling creaked.

Love was in the air.

Even at ten o'clock in the morning.

"With the gun shaking like it was, Lennox's shot went through the *side* of his face," Doc Hazel said, flicking her eyes toward the screen to stress her point, "not directly up through the skull. Those missing teeth are part of the reason behind his rumored hissing voice. But not the only reason."

She pressed a button on the remote, and the lines of static pulsed. *FAST-FORWARD* appeared in the upper lefthand corner of the screen. For a long time, Colin Lennox was motionless.

Then he moved. A twitch of his right arm.

Doc Hazel pressed another button, and the message in the corner said *PLAY.* The static lines disappeared. Time returned to its normal pace.

Lennox, groaning with agony, pulled himself off the concrete floor, blood pouring down his half-destroyed face and his soiled dress shirt. He stumbled off the screen. The concrete room was now empty.

Both Silence and Doc Hazel leaned closer to the television, their eyes fixed on the timestamp in the upper right-hand corner of the screen, watching the seconds tick away.

Five seconds since Lennox exited.

Eight seconds.

Eleven seconds.

Bang!

A tremendous roar registered as distorted auditory mayhem through the speakers, and the image rocked sideways—the room turning on end as the camera dropped to the floor—for just a split second before white static filled the screen. The speakers hissed.

Doc Hazel stopped the tape.

"Lennox didn't make it out of the building before the explosion," she said. "He survived, but not without consequences; he was badly burned on the left side of his face and neck, damaging his voice box." As she leaned back in her chair, she fixed her eyes on Silence's throat. "In that way, you two are similar, except Lennox is rumored to sound like a snake, not a garbage disposal."

She looked at Silence as though awaiting a response. Perhaps she was trying to get a rise out of him. Perhaps she was simply oblivious. Either way, Silence said nothing.

"Lennox was medically retired from the Bureau," Doc Hazel continued. "And then ... he vanished for two years. Now, if the report is to be believed, he's back. And if that same report is to be believed, and Lennox is doing what he's said to be doing, then you're to eliminate him."

"Yes, ma'am," Silence said.

Doc Hazel nodded.

She was one of Silence's many superiors. Specifically, she was among the Watchers' Specialists, the organization's lifeblood, the people who provided the copious logistical and technical needs.

Mission assignments typically came to Silence directly via his boss, Falcon, who was not a Specialist like Doc Hazel but a Prefect, a higher-ranking official. Sometimes, however, practicality and circumstance dictated that Doc Hazel provided Silence's briefings before sending him into the field for another round of righting wrongs.

It was an efficient practice since Silence had frequent appointments with Doc Hazel, who served as his Watchers-mandated mental health professional. He had never asked for counseling, but his employers rarely considered his wishes. Despite Silence's reluctance, Doc Hazel's presence had become a constant in his life, one of the few things that remained unchanged and dependable.

Even so, Doc Hazel's introduction to this latest assignment was particularly puzzling because of a recent email conversation Silence had held with Falcon.

The upstairs neighbors' tempo increased.

Thump. Thump. Thump.

The screaming grew louder, too, and a single word came through audibly out of the primal din. It was a name.

Carl!

Silence squinted at the frozen snow pattern of white static on the screen for a moment, considering Colin Lennox. He and Doc Hazel had watched the man's suicide attempt two times—once with no discussion and a second viewing for deeper analysis. But after witnessing the man's death twice now, Silence still didn't understand why he was being given the Lennox assignment after Falcon's recent email.

He turned to face Doc Hazel again.

"But Falcon..." Silence said and swallowed, one of his frequent attempts at lubricating his wretched throat. "Wants me—"

"Yes, he wants you to take a sabbatical," Doc Hazel said, "because of your Montana mission's after-action report. But first, he needs you to complete the Colin Lennox mission because of a special connection you might have to the Code Red."

Silence spun around on the mattress to face her, rocked by the news. There were two outrageous parts to what Doc Hazel had just said: that the Watchers were under a Code Red...

...*and that Silence had some sort of tie to it.*

Doc Hazel nodded sadly, a bit of emotion showing through the robot act. "That's another reason Falcon had me get you the Lennox mission instead of doing so himself—face-to-face, minimizing the chances of a leak. We're under a Code Red. The Watchers have been breached."

Silence's trained mind shifted gears to assess this new threat.

A Code Red...

The words alone sounded wicked. They meant a crack in the supposedly impregnable walls of the Watchers' clandestine and illegal organization. The revelation hit like an uppercut, hard and fast, somewhere just above the belt. The Watchers operated in the deepest shadows, relying on anonymity and secrecy. Breaches to their system were devastating.

Doc Hazel turned and glanced at the stack of paper beside her on the grimy table. Silence noted that the text was gibberish. He recognized the gibberish—a code language, one of the Watchers' many added security levels during a Code Red.

"Someone's been siphoning our databases. It's believed..." Though Doc Hazel's stony facade didn't waver as it had a moment earlier, she had to stop for a beat. "It's believed the individual is *selling* the information, Suppressor."

Suppressor was Silence's codename. He also had the numerical title Asset 23 and its shortened form, A-23.

Silence leaned forward, his mind racing with questions and twisted hypothetical situations. An insider, one of their own, turning against the organization was a scenario the Watchers had always prepared for but had rarely materialized.

"Leads?" Silence said.

Doc Hazel shook her head. "None. The information has been pulled from several databases in different locations, each time circumventing multiple electronic security frameworks. So the Captains are taking no chances. Communication protocols are at Level Zero, and we're operating on a completely need-to-know basis until the leak is plugged."

Silence nodded, turned away from her, stared straight into a bare spot in the matted carpet.

Any breach in Watchers' secrecy could lead to catastrophic consequences. Though the group's mission of correcting procedural injustices was righteous, it was also illegal. That meant every Watcher—from the Captains at the top to the Prefects to the Specialists to the Assets—were criminals, risking imprisonment. Many of the Specialists and *all* the higher-brass, the Prefects and the Captains, were government employees; consequences for *those* individuals could be particularly daunting.

Silence had only experienced a Code Red once. It had been one of the most challenging periods he'd faced while working with the organization.

And this time, the Code Red was somehow connected to Silence himself...

Silence swallowed before speaking again, driven as much by apprehension as by the need to lubricate his ruined throat.

"My tie to Code Red?"

He could have worded the question more clearly, but Doc Hazel was accustomed to his broken, abbreviated English—another of Silence's techniques to help with his throat condition.

Doc Hazel pulled her attaché case from the grimy table, sat it on her lap, and reached inside.

VROOM!

A tinny electronic noise broke the stillness of the motel room, jarringly loud.

Doc Hazel froze, face still down-turned toward the open bag. Slowly, her hazel eyes lifted to meet Silence's gaze, wide with a mixture of shock and embarrassment, a vulnerability seldom seen.

VROOM!

The noise repeated. This time, Doc Hazel, with a slightly flushed face, reached into the bag and extracted a small, bright red race car figure on a keychain. It looked as cartoonish as it sounded.

With an attempted casual shrug, failing to hide her unease, she flicked a switch on the toy, silencing it, then quickly stuffed it back into her bag. Her hands reemerged, now holding a file folder.

Silence blinked.

The whimsical toy seemed so at odds with the person he knew Doc Hazel to be. But the truth was, he didn't really know her. Not at all. He wasn't supposed to know her, wasn't allowed to.

Was she a mother? Did the toy belong to a child of hers? Maybe not hers, maybe a nephew or niece. A godchild, possibly. Silence's mind wandered through possibilities. A gift, perhaps, for a husband or boyfriend.

Or it could simply be hers. Maybe the real woman, the one behind the Watchers façade, simply had a fondness for fast cars.

She opened the folder, acting as though a two-inch, vroom-ing race car hadn't just emerged from her attaché case. But Silence knew he'd just glimpsed a sliver of the hidden world behind Doc Hazel's meticulously maintained mask.

Reading from a printout inside the folder, Doc Hazel said, "Do you remember your second assignment, Suppressor? The Richard Keane mission?"

Of course Silence remembered it.

His second assignment as an assassin had been a *true* assassination: the murder of a U.S. State Department official.

A guy doesn't forget something like that.

"Richard Keane, high-ranking U.S. diplomat," Doc Hazel said, her eyes dancing behind her glasses as she continued looking over the printout.

"Treason. Keane sold out his country." She paused. "There's almost some irony to that, considering the Watchers operate through treasonous activities."

"Yes," Silence agreed.

The idea of the Watchers' sanctimonious treason was just one of the many maddening hypocrisies he'd contemplated over the years.

"You eliminated Keane in his home," Doc Hazel said.

"Yes," Silence agreed.

Waiting in Richard Keane's home office.

Crouching in the corner, behind a tufted red leather armchair, entirely concealed in the shadows.

A click and then a hum and then a gentle, warm breeze—the house's heating system cycling back on, pumping air from the vent on the opposite wall.

Moonlight puddled on a carpet atop hardwood flooring. The carpet was thick and luxurious, spotless, and smelled brand-new.

The tick-tick-tick of Keane's wall clock.

Struggle. Violence. Awful death.

Family photos on the recessed shelves behind the man's desk, a few feet away from the computer he'd used to sell America's secrets.

"Out of the seventeen leaks we've uncovered, three relate to the Keane mission," Doc Hazel said. "The remaining fourteen are unrelated—lists of criminal records, three decryption keys, supply manifests, one of our low-tier bank accounts, surveillance data, and a few mission details spanning the globe and several decades. The only connection among any of them—and it's a glaring one—are the three transmissions about Richard Keane."

"What was in..." Silence said and swallowed. "Transmissions?"

Doc Hazel shook her head as she flipped through the paperwork. "Nothing important. In fact, it's all public knowledge with FOIA requests. Biographical info on Keane: his education, DOS assignments, things like that."

Silence exhaled. His overactive mind went to work, trying to decipher what he'd just heard. In his previous life as Jake Rowe, C.C. had taught him several methods to calm the tempest of his restless brain. But there were times like this—learning that his illegal vigilante justice organization was under attack from the inside, with the only clue being a tie to Silence's second mission years earlier—when no meditation or breathing techniques could help.

Doc Hazel brought her attention away from the file, glanced at Silence, and smirked, clearly picking up on Silence's mental consternation.

"Don't get hung up on your past mission, Suppressor," she said. "Specialists are already at work reanalyzing the Richard Keane matter—as best they can with Code Red protocols in place. We need to keep you focused on your *current* mission: Colin Lennox. So let's knock your session out of the way and get you back out in the field."

4

Ugh.

The session.

Silence groaned.

In response, Doc Hazel froze while rummaging through her attaché case, hand hovering mid-air over a folder. She shot him a look—that of a superior chastising an inferior.

Assets were tools, instruments of death that were used for righteous murder, individuals who had been criminals themselves but were yanked out of the judicial system, had their records erased, and were forced to commit righteous killings until they paid off their debts.

As such, the Watchers higher-ups—in another demonstration of befuddling hypocrisy—respected the hell out of their Assets but at the same time treated the assassins like shit, keeping them in their place, running them ragged, using and abusing them.

And sass sure as hell wasn't tolerated.

Doc Hazel stared at Silence for a long moment. Finally, she returned to her bag and found what she'd been looking for: a manila folder. She placed it on the table, then eased back into her chair, crossing her long legs.

She stared at Silence once more, not saying anything, just offering a few sterile blinks of her hazel eyes.

Doc Hazel's *hazel* eyes...

Just as Silence was barred from other Assets' identities, he wasn't to know the identities and backgrounds of anyone in higher positions. For the longest time, Silence had held the suspicion that Doc Hazel wasn't an actual mental health professional—neither a psychiatrist nor a counselor. The fact that her eyes were hazel-colored was almost like a sneering joke, another one of the Watchers' gleeful attempts at toying with an Asset, keeping him on his toes, not letting up on him.

Doc Hazel continued to stare.

And since he was already in trouble, Silence flicked his eyes toward her attaché case and back to her, letting her know he hadn't forgotten about the lil red car on the keychain. This small insight into her world, a fragment of knowledge about a Watchers higher-up's real life, lent him a bit of power in this charged situation.

"Vroom," he said.

Doc Hazel narrowed her eyes at him.

Above, the neighbors had progressed to the second act, their tempo increasing.

Thump-thump-thump.

Yes, Carl! Oh, yes! Give it to me!

The ceiling creaked.

Finally, Doc Hazel said, "Let's begin, Suppressor. Lie down and tell me about this AAR that Falcon's concerned about. Tell me about Montana. How did that mission make you feel?"

Dammit! Feelings again. She always wanted to talk about his damn feelings.

Silence didn't respond

But with a sigh, he obliged Doc Hazel's command and lay down, stretching his six-foot-three length over the bed, feet hanging off the end. He crossed his arms over his stomach in quintessential shrink-visit style and tried not to think about the comforter beneath him. A few years ago, he'd watched a *Present Day* television special investigating the cleanliness of hotel rooms using blacklight technology to reveal hidden moisture stains. The exposé had revealed that motel bedspreads harbored most of a room's dried-up bodily fluids.

Aligning with these thoughts, Silence's eyes went to the popcorn texture of the ceiling above; he detected faint movement in rhythm with the neighbors' festivities.

"The Montana mission," Doc Hazel insisted. "Tell me about your AAR."

"Mission successful," Silence said and swallowed. "AAR indicated as much."

Persistently, but without changing her clinical tone, Doc Hazel said, "You know the field to which I'm referring."

She was right. Silence *did* know the field she was talking about, the one at the very bottom of the AAR form.

He'd slipped a personal note into the miscellaneous section of his after-action report to vent his frustration about the prosthetic chin and colored contact lenses. He'd contended the physical alterations were an erasure of his identity, saying that the Watchers had already annihilated his former identity, Jake Rowe, and now they were trying to retool his new one.

It had been a rare instance where Silence allowed his emotions to surface, a departure from his usual stoicism. Now, lying there, he felt even stupider than he had when immediate regret washed over him the moment he'd submitted the AAR.

"Didn't like..." Silence said and swallowed. "The prosthetic."

"Yes, I gathered as much." There was the scratching sound of Doc Hazel's pen going to work on her notepad. "But how did the prosthetic make you *feel*?"

"Pissed off."

The pen-scratching sound came to a sudden halt.

Then a sigh from Doc Hazel.

"Be more substantive with your responses, please. Specifically, I'm talking about this line you wrote," Doc Hazel said. When she continued, her voice said she was reading from her materials. "'Joining the Watchers has left me with a partial identity, forced upon me and only exacerbated by the damn prosthetic chin.'"

She stopped there. A moment of quiet, just the ever-more-intense thumping emanating from the ceiling Silence was staring up at. He rolled his head over to the side of his pillow and found Doc Hazel staring at him.

He looked back at her. Blinked.

"Using the word 'damn' in an official report. Classy, Suppressor," Doc Hazel said. "But I frequently stress the need for you to vent your frustrations, so I suppose it's all right. The important thing is, Falcon's concerned about you. Especially because of your debt." She searched through her papers. "When you joined, Falcon didn't give you a standard number of kills to complete before we release you from your service. Rather, your debt is to reach out to Falcon one day with an explanation of—and I quote—who you are and what you're all about."

Every Watchers assassin was a former criminal who'd committed a heinous act, typically murder. The Watchers considered these individuals' crimes to be not only justifiable, but actually righteous. In Silence's case, he was conscripted as an Asset after his fiancée, C.C., was beaten to death and he'd gone on a killing spree, taking down C.C.'s murderers. Upon joining the Watchers, each Asset was given a debt in lieu of prison. To earn their freedom, they were required to settle this debt, typically by completing a set number of assignments.

But when Silence joined the Watchers, Falcon gave him an unorthodox debt. Silence was instructed to find himself, to figure himself out after a long period of soul-searching. When that theoretical soul-discovery occurred, he was to reach out to Falcon and explain it.

The problem was, it had never happened. And it seemed like it never would.

In fact, as far as Silence could tell, the closest thing he had to an identity was *Suppressor, A-23*.

The Watchers had stripped him of his prior identity—wiping Jake Rowe off the face of the earth—and built him a new one.

But they were constantly poking at that new identity, never letting it fully settle in.

"Suppressor, you're burnt out. It's obvious," Doc Hazel said. "But don't forget, you have an identity outside of 'Watchers Asset.' We've been working on it together for years, envisioning a life for you after you've paid your debt."

Silence didn't respond.

He rolled his head back to an up-facing position and stared at the ceiling.

Thump-thump-thump!

"Tell me about your beach," Doc Hazel said.

This was a sporadic yet ongoing component of their sessions: Doc Hazel instructing him to describe the beach-life-post-Watchers fantasy she'd coaxed out of him a few years back, a notion of what life would be like for Silence someday in an indeterminate future when he was no longer an Asset.

And it pissed Silence off. He hadn't wanted to concoct the fantasy; she'd forced him to. It was a silly exercise. Nonsense. Touchy-feely bullshit. C.C. would have appreciated it, true, but it was still touchy-feely bullshit.

So Silence continued with his petulance.

"The Emerald Coast," he said, referring to the beaches back home in his part of Florida. "The whitest sand..." He swallowed. "In the world."

"Suppressor..." Doc Hazel said, a bit of antagonism flavoring the word.

Silence exhaled. "Fine."

He closed his eyes and tried to find the image he and Doc Hazel had developed over the last several years. When he did so, C.C. spoke to him. Her voice visited often—usually in times of high stress or when he needed a little more coaxing to probe into the deeper parts of himself.

Stop being an ass, C.C. said in his mind. *This is a good exercise Doc Hazel has provided for you. Someday, this assassin's life of yours will be over. You need to be prepared—spiritually, if in no other way.*

Silence's inner voice offered C.C. the same single-word response he'd externalized to Doc Hazel: *Fine.*

His eyes moved behind his closed eyelids. Searching the dark.

And he found it.

He began, his terrible voice sounding remote. "Small beach house," he said and swallowed. "Isolated."

"Isolated," Doc Hazel repeated. "So this is a very different beach than the bustling tourist spot in your home city of Pensacola?"

She'd offered it up as a question, but it was strictly rhetorical. She knew the answer already. It was one of many repetitions she put forth when they discussed the beach fantasy.

"Yes. Away from chaos of world," Silence said, omitting a couple of instances of *the* from the sentence—more of his broken English. He swallowed and continued. "Little more than a hut."

"A hut," Doc Hazel said, repeating him once more. "But inside, the home will meet your style standards: hut on the outside, *GQ* on the inside. Correct?"

Again, she was being rhetorical. She knew the details as well as Silence. So he said only, "Yes."

A significant component of this beach fantasy Doc Hazel had developed from kernels of sentiments buried in Silence's subconscious was the notion that the house would be small and humble on the outside but decked out in a chic modern aesthetic inside.

In this way, the fantasy was quite like Silence's actual home in the East Hill neighborhood of Pensacola. The Watchers had afforded him a humble starter house when he'd first joined the organization years earlier, but Silence had never moved, staying put to remain close to his blind neighbor, Mrs. Enfield. He watched over the old woman.

And her cat Baxter.

But Silence had significantly transformed the interior of his modest East Hill house, giving it an appearance that echoed a contemporary designer aesthetic. The decor was a sleek combination of blacks, whites, silvers, and grays, accented with streaks of glass and brushed metals. Oversized plants were strategically positioned around the space, complemented by several abstract-design pieces.

The interior of the beach hut in his fantasy was much the same.

Doc Hazel whispered, "Go on."

In his head, C.C. echoed the encouragement. *Go on, love.*

Silence's eyes moved quicker. When she was alive, C.C. had taught him to visualize, and he'd gotten so good at it he could practically live in another place, another time.

He felt the sea breeze. Tasted it. The salt air. Warm. Whistling through the gap in the propped-open door.

"It's peace," Silence said to Doc Hazel. "No missions." He swallowed. "No threats. No shadows." He swallowed. "Sun. Sand. Quiet. Waves."

As he spoke, he was there. Somewhere. A simple home. One-bedroom. Right on the beach. Palm trees and undergrowth created a shadowy area past his door. He looked through the window. The surf and sand were right there, just past the swaying palms, bathed in sunlight. Not the brilliant, bone-white sand to which he was accustomed. Different sand. Darker. Some place ... different. Somewhere. He didn't know where.

The breeze was warm. The day ahead was empty and open and peaceful. He smelled the sea.

Yes, love, C.C. said. *That's it. You're there now.*

And as if working in tandem with the phantom voice of the dead woman inside Silence's head, Doc Hazel said, "Very good. Excellent work, Suppressor. You can open your eyes now. And sit up."

Waves. Gentle waves breaking a few yards away.

Seagulls talking to each other.

The smell of charcoal and something delicious being heated.

Silence opened his eyes.

He sat up and slowly swung his lengthy legs off the bed to face Doc Hazel, who was allowing a small smile to rest on that clinical face of hers.

"You struggle with identity. Not just since Montana. You *always* have," she said. "But don't think so hard about it. Life's all about finding your true self, Suppressor, constantly letting go of who we were and stepping into who we're becoming."

She did this often, becoming suddenly sage and kind, putting aside the cold exterior for a moment of warmth. This only strengthened Silence's belief that she was playing a role, putting on a performance.

Silence nodded.

Doc Hazel's smile dropped. Stone-faced once more.

"Falcon is concerned about you," she said. "That's why he's offering you the one-year sabbatical after this mission. He thinks you need a break, a chance to clear your head. We've demanded a lot of you over the years, and Montana pushed a button. Even Falcon recognizes that. Consider twelve months off a token of our appreciation." She paused. "But Falcon's convinced you won't accept our generous offer."

Silence didn't respond.

Falcon had phoned him with the offer before Silence took the private jet from Pensacola to Cincinnati. The notion had stunned Silence: a year away from the Watchers, from the life he knew. It was an unprecedented proposal.

A break from the relentless pace of his missions, the constant danger, the weight of the decisions he was forced to make—it was an appealing thought, to be sure.

Yet the idea of stepping away, even temporarily, felt foreign, almost uncomfortable.

He looked at Doc Hazel, her face a blank mask.

"I'll consider it, ma'am," Silence said and swallowed. "But tell me about..." Another swallow. "Colin Lennox first."

5

In the alley, Beckwith stood with his hands shoved deep into his pockets, head lowered. Short, ragged breaths. The overwhelming quiet was broken only by the sporadic hum of the flickering streetlamp above. Despite the forecast of a sunny day ahead, the morning's dark, gray sky kept the lights on, casting pulsating shadows that danced across the ground.

His hands trembled—not with fear, but with an acute awareness of what they'd done the previous evening. Beckwith had killed once before, but that had been a long time ago, a memory he'd pushed deep into the recesses of his mind, a past he'd vowed to leave behind. Yet here he was, in the alley, having crossed that line once more.

...at the behest of a charismatic man he'd met only two weeks ago.

The reality was suffocating.

A nearby broken window caught his reflection, and instantly, a phrase came to mind: *How can you look at yourself in the mirror?*

How indeed?

The reflection revealed nothing worth a damn, just an ugly middle-aged man. A road map of a face, all those highway lines forged by hard years and harder choices, stories he'd rather forget. Eyes like shards of dull stone—lifeless, empty. A prominent, diagonal scar on his chin. Three-day stubble that couldn't hide the grim set of his mouth.

The reflection showed a murderer.

Somehow, foolishly, for all these years, Beckwith had tricked himself into thinking he'd eluded that title: murderer. It was a sort of denial—"repression," a shrink might label it—but there were certain titles that, once attributed, could never be removed.

Murderer...

Murderer.

Now, there was no denying it, no repressing it, no more late nights of reassuring himself that his younger version had gotten into a bad situation and survival instinct had set in.

Less than twelve hours ago, this ugly middle-aged man had set out to kill a person and completed the task.

Murderer.

And, no, Beckwith *couldn't* look at himself in the mirror.

He whipped away from the reflection and pulled his hands from his pockets, glanced down at them. Still shaking. He rubbed them together. Still shaking.

Beckwith's phone chimed in his pocket. He didn't need to look; he knew it was Lennox. Right on time, but not as expected. They were supposed to meet there, in the alley. Clearly, Lennox was tied up with preparations for tonight's event, too busy to bother with a face-to-face, but he wouldn't explain to Beckwith the switch from a meeting to a call. Lennox's pawns—even Beckwith, one of the two top pawns—didn't get explanations. That's how Lennox operated.

Pulling out the phone, Beckwith saw Lennox's number on the multiplex. He flipped the phone open.

"Beckwith," came Lennox's snake voice. He'd asked nothing, only said Beckwith's name, but a clear question was hidden in the greeting.

Beckwith shoved his free hand back into his pocket and said, "It's done."

He could almost feel the piercing gaze through the line. His mind's eye watched as the perpetual grin on Lennox's scarred face grew wider, toothier.

"Excellent. I knew you had it in you," Lennox hissed. "Ya tough shit. That's why I chose you. I needed one confidant, one bruiser. Your mother would be proud, huh? Her son, the enforcer, my right-hand man."

Beckwith's grip on the phone tightened. The mention of his mother hit hard, a calculated jab from Lennox. Beckwith opened his mouth but couldn't respond. Somehow, Lennox picked up on this, only giving it half a beat before he continued.

"Aww, are you sad, Grant?" The voice slithered into a mocking tone. "Is that what I'm picking up on? Sadness? Don't you worry. The man you killed was suicidal, like they all are. You did him a favor. We just … sped the process up for him." Lennox snickered. "The man couldn't keep our secret; he had to die." A pause. "I'm good at keeping secrets, Grant. Wouldn't you agree?"

"Yes. I'm grateful for what you're doing for me." Beckwith's voice was steady, but his words came out forced. "For keeping my secret."

Beckwith didn't think it was possible to feel any more worthless than when he glimpsed his reflection moments earlier. But now, standing there with the phone pressed obediently to his ear, he sank even lower, realizing how futile the situation had become. Colin Lennox owned him now. Utterly worthless.

"You're quite welcome," Lennox said. "And I'm trusting you with a secret, too. You're one of just two people I've entrusted with the whole plan for tonight."

"Not the *whole* plan."

The line fell silent, crackling with static. Beckwith's muscles tightened, bracing for Lennox's venomous retort, which would be laced with implicit threats. He could picture Lennox on the other end, weighing each word, shaping his reply with precision. Beckwith cursed himself for questioning his new employer.

But when Lennox spoke again, the serpentine voice was smooth and even.

"Just remember, Grant, you're in this now. You're in deep." A pause. "And I'm the sole owner of your little secret." Another pause. "Next task: go to the house."

"What house?"

"*The* house."

"Oh."

"Wait. Outside. Out of sight. He'll be there eventually. A shadow of a man. Like a specter. Tall. Broad. Follow him."

"But I don't understand what—"

Beep.

Lennox was gone.

Beckwith stared at the phone, let a moment pass, then snapped the phone shut. The alley was quiet again.

His own words came back to him: *Not the* whole *plan.* Beckwith knew the program for tonight's gathering—Lennox had spelled it out, step by step. But Beckwith sensed an underlying current. There was more to this than what was on the surface, a final play of Lennox's, something big and unseen.

Whatever it was, Beckwith's gut told him it was going to be awful.

6

Silence reached forward and took the full-page photograph that Doc Hazel was sliding across the table in his direction just as the upstairs neighbors were finishing up.

Thump-thump-thump-thump-thump!
Oh, yes! Shit, Carl! YES! CARL!
THUMP!

The ceiling shook.

The light fixture rattled.

Then all was quiet and still.

Doc Hazel lowered her gaze from the ceiling, bringing her attention back to Silence. She exhaled.

"Meet Nathan Fuller," she said and pointed at the photograph. "He believes Colin Lennox's little club isn't what it appears to be."

The image, enlarged to fill an entire page, was a black-and-white still from a security video camera. Even with the minor distortion from enlargement, the picture retained enough clarity to discern the details. The camera must have been high quality, one of the new digital Rondache models, perhaps.

"Fuller's been shouting into the wind, begging for someone to believe him," Doc Hazel said. "The story he's peddling ... it's out there, and the authorities just brushed him aside, labeled him a crank. Fuller thinks Lennox's isn't leading a suicide-prevention self-help group, but the entire opposite: a Jim Jones-style mass suicide cult."

Silence studied the image. Nathan Fuller was in his mid thirties, Caucasian, disheveled and weary. He stood at a convenience store checkout counter, shelves of snacks and a line of coolers behind him. He was purchasing cigarettes. The harsh fluorescent lights cast a sterile glow on his corporate-amalgamated white shirt and nondescript tie. The shirt was unbuttoned at the top and wrinkled, sleeves rolled up to the elbows. Fuller was short and plain with an insignificant physique, hair a matted tangle, haven't-slept-in-days lines creeping around his eyes and mouth.

It was the image of a man who was coming unraveled.

Fuller's unraveling had an obvious cause: he was accusing Colin Lennox of the same misconduct that Lennox, as an FBI agent two years earlier, had investigated against another man.

Silence set the photo down.

"People accused Jordan Havelock..." Silence said and swallowed. "Of the same thing..." Another swallow. "Fuller is accusing Lennox of."

Doc Hazel smirked. "Exactly."

She thumbed through her folder, pulled out a small stack of newspaper clippings and magazine articles, and handed them to Silence. He placed them on top of Fuller's photo.

"You're right," Doc Hazel said. "Two years ago, people claimed Jordan Havelock's anti-suicide group was actually a cult leading his followers to mass suicide. The whole thing turned into a media circus."

"I avoid..." Silence said and swallowed. "Media circuses."

In the modern world, media frenzies were becoming more and more common. This was something that had worried C.C. deeply while she was still alive. It had troubled Jake Rowe as well. It still troubled Silence.

"I know you do, Suppressor. But every major news source followed the story. Havelock even did a one-on-one special with Vanessa Wheatley, touring her around the house, showing the world that everything was on the up and up. That kind of media attention turns any story into a national conversation."

Silence flipped through the articles, each headline telling a part of the story, each image capturing a moment in the rising and falling tides of public opinion, each article dominated by a photograph of the same man: Jordan Havelock. Dozens of poses, but the confidence in Havelock's stance was as unwavering as the smirk that often played on his lips. The headlines screamed of his enigma: "Jordan Havelock: Savior or Charlatan?" and "The Charming Prophet: Havelock's Rise to Power."

In every photo, Havelock was impeccably dressed, whether in a relaxed plaid shirt or a more formal vest and tie, an appearance that balanced approachability with authority. He had a chiseled face with contoured angles and a strong jawline. Piercing blue eyes radiated cool confidence, and his hair was a platinum color, flawlessly styled, not a strand out of place. The contrast between his silver locks and his unblemished skin added to his mystery, making it difficult to determine his true age. However, Silence knew Havelock was only forty-five when he died.

"But as time went on, the narrative shifted," Doc Hazel said. "The media, the public, law enforcement all began to see Havelock in a different light—from suspected cult leader to misunderstood spiritual guide. A complete reversal of the initial accusations."

Silence's eyes moved to another article, this one headlined "Havelock's Haven: Sanctuary or Cult?" The accompanying image was a close-up, Havelock's azure gaze piercing through the lens, as if he could charm and challenge all at once. There was a certain smugness to Havelock's grin, a man who knew he had the upper hand and enjoyed it. No doubt, the guy had charisma—it oozed from the glossy pages like ink.

"Then, the tragedy," Doc Hazel continued. "An explosion during one of Havelock's basement meetings. Gasoline barrels, inexplicably stored there, went up in flames. Killed nearly everyone, including Havelock."

Silence stopped at an article toward the bottom of the stack with a photo of a destroyed basement. Debris. Blast marks. Soot. All the newspaper articles and magazine covers at the bottom of Silence's stack were related to the tragedy—as though whoever had prepared the mission materials had ordered them in dramatic fashion—and the photographs here were a stark contrast to the polished images of Jordan Havelock that preceded them.

These photos showed an unfinished basement, its walls gutted, the blackened remains of an upscale home. Support beams stood exposed—most of them broken, all charred. The concrete floor was a mosaic of ash and piping and shards of glass, and among the wreckage, the mangled husks of gasoline tanks lay ruptured.

Silence could practically smell the reek of smoke through the photographs. He felt the heat of the blast. He felt the shockwave, too. And he could hear the screams, echoey and distant, dream-like, a nightmare. He remembered the bang he'd heard—twice—in the VHS tape footage he and Doc Hazel had just reviewed. One of the newspaper articles featured a photo of a firefighter, his posture one of defeat, helmet in hand, as he surveyed the damage—a hero who'd arrived too late, the battle lost before he'd even had the chance to fight.

"Naturally, after the tragedy, the original accusations resurfaced," Doc Hazel said. "People said the event was proof that Havelock had indeed been leading a suicide cult. They thought the explosion was deliberate, the largest example of self-immolation in human history."

Self-immolation—the deliberate choice to set oneself on fire, often in a bold, public manner. It's not about fading away silently; it's about broadcasting a final message. A jarring one.

Doc Hazel leaned in, resting her elbows on the table briefly before quickly pulling back and wiping them clean. She shot a wary glance at the grimy surface before refocusing on Silence.

"All the survivors refuted the claims of self-immolation. All except one..."

She trailed off, and when Silence looked up at her, the coy lift of her lips said she wanted him to put two and two together.

He thought for a moment...

...and then said, "Nathan Fuller."

Doc Hazel nodded. "Right. He was there, one of Havelock's students, one of the few people who weren't in the basement when the gas cans exploded. The other survivors spoke out against the fresh surge of accusations aimed at the deceased Havelock, but Fuller said Havelock *had* led his followers to kill themselves. No one listened to Fuller then, and no one is listening now to his claims against Colin Lennox.

"After Lennox's two-year disappearance, the guy's suddenly back in grand fashion. He's launched his own self-help group, allegedly to continue Havelock's life-saving work. He's gone in the opposite direction of Havelock's showmanship, though. Lennox operates in the shadows, away from public attention, with a tight-knit, secretive membership. No one outside his group knows where he holds his meetings.

"If Nathan Fuller is to be believed, however, both Jordan Havelock *and* Colin Lennox are phonies, and Lennox is finishing Havelock's mission of mass suicide. Fuller thinks Lennox's entire membership will be dead soon."

"And Fuller has..." Silence said and swallowed. "A personal tie to Lennox?"

He was referring to a tantalizing clue Doc Hazel had hinted at when they first sat down with the VHS tape forty-five minutes earlier.

"That's right," Doc Hazel said and handed him the file folder, which held the single remaining item: another photograph. "His sister-in-law, Maya Fuller. She's a member of Lennox's new group."

The photo captured Maya Fuller in soft office light, her Indian American heritage apparent in the elegant lines of her face and high cheekbones. It was some sort of work photo, as she was seated at a desk in a cubicle and the bottom of the image was labeled, *Fuller, Maya, Employee 00087A3*. Dark hair framed her features, which bore the subtle strain lines of the journey into middle age. She wore a buttoned white shirt that spoke of a lifelong existence in the professional realm of office work.

Her large, expressive eyes told a different story than that of a ho-hum corporate minion, one of quiet unrest, as they focused somewhere beyond the then and there. A subtle tension in her forced stance. A slight frown.

"Maya was married to Nathan's older brother, Chuck," Doc Hazel said. A brief pause. "Recently deceased."

Silence glanced up.

"Oh..." he said.

"Car accident. Nine months ago. It turned Maya's world upside down. Her struggle to cope gradually spiraled into suicidal thoughts. She went to the doctor. Got counseling. Medication. And eventually ... went to Colin Lennox."

Silence looked back at the photo, back into the depths of those large, dark eyes, to the consternation he'd noticed earlier. It was elsewhere on her face, too: in the way her lips parted slightly, in the lift of her shoulders.

He put the photo down and pushed the rest of the materials Doc Hazel had given him aside, returning to the initial image: the full-sheet security camera screenshot of Nathan Fuller buying cigarettes in a convenience store.

It was the same image he'd studied moments earlier. But now it had changed.

There was a different story to the wrinkled shirt, the rat's nest hair, the stress wrinkles on the face. This was a man who'd been suicidal two years ago—for reasons unknown—and who then, a year later, lost his brother out of the blue. This was a man who was now trying to save his dead brother's wife from death ... from suicide, the fate he'd self-prescribed to himself so recently, from the grips of a man he viewed to be a charismatic demon.

Silence looked up.

"Fuller has proof for..." He swallowed. "His claims against Lennox?"

"No. None. But *we*, the Watchers, have proof. Of a sort." Doc Hazel then pointed to the television behind them, glowing brightly with the paused snow-pattern static. "Not only does Lennox's suicide tape indicate that Havelock told him to kill himself, but we also have this."

She reached into her case again. This time she pulled out a digital recorder, small and black. She set it on the table between them. Digital audio recorders were a burgeoning technology, one that would be much more common in the upcoming twenty-first century. For now, they were one of the many ahead-of-the-curve gadgetries the Watchers were privy to.

Silence looked at the recorder. Then at Doc Hazel. He raised an eyebrow.

"Lennox's audio log from his undercover investigation two years ago," Doc Hazel said, patting the recorder. "Specialists uncovered it only an hour before you and I met here. They digitized it, sent the file, and I put it on the recorder. Specialists have scanned through the material, but there's been no time for us to listen to it all, and we won't be able to analyze it and get you the summary with Code Red protocols in place. That's why we've digitized it for you; you're going to have to go through the entries on your own."

This was going to be a pain in the ass. Usually, as Doc Hazel had indicated, this sort of leg work would be done for Silence. But during a Code Red, everyone had to chip in, everyone had to suffer a little.

So he just nodded.

He picked up the recorder and thumbed the play button. A crackle filled the room, followed by a voice. Colin Lennox's voice. Youthful. Professional. But also quiet, a little above a whisper, as though he was recording in secret.

Which he undoubtedly was.

November 3rd. Special Agent Colin Lennox. Today marks the start of my undercover investigation into Jordan Havelock and his group. From preliminary reports and intel, there's a troubling picture emerging. Havelock seems to have positioned himself as a savior figure, drawing vulnerable people in with—

Silence pressed the fast-forward button. He held it for a long while. Doc Hazel sat in robotic, unmoving patience. Finally, Silence pushed *PLAY* again.

Lennox's voice filled the room once more. The same. But very different. It was no longer quiet; it was loud. No longer professional, but manic.

November 19th. This will be my last entry as Agent Lennox. I've come to a realization. Jordan Havelock is not just a leader; he's a visionary. His teachings, they're a revelation. The FBI doesn't understand—the stupid assholes.

They can't see the greatness in Havelock's work.

The accusations, the—

Silence pressed *STOP*. He looked at Doc Hazel.

"Shit," he said.

"Well stated, Suppressor. *That's* the proof we have." Doc Hazel pointed to the recorder in Silence's hand. "That's why we believe Fuller's claim that his sister-and-law Maya and all Lennox's other followers are about to die. Fuller knows where Lennox is located because, as a survivor of Havelock's tragedy, he was invited to join Lennox's group. This was before Maya joined, of course. You find Fuller, get his side of the story, and have him take you to Lennox." A pause. She blinked. "And do what you do best."

"Yes, ma'am."

Silence looked at the recorder for a moment, then pocketed it.

It felt heavy.

He took his PenPal notebook from his pocket, flipping back its orange plastic cover and retrieving a mechanical pencil from the spiral binding. After jotting a few notes, he chose two photos out of the mission materials, and placed them on top of everything else, side by side: the convenience store security camera screenshot of Nathan Fuller and the work photo of his sister-in-law, Maya.

Suicide. Nathan Fuller had once flirted with the same dark thoughts now haunting Maya. His brother's death had undoubtedly hit hard, leaving both him and Maya shattered. Nathan, familiar with the ledge, was now doing what he could to keep Maya from slipping over.

Silence gathered the materials into the folder, stood up, nodded at Doc Hazel, and walked away. As he reached the door, Doc Hazel called out to him.

"Hey."

He turned.

"Good luck, Suppressor."

This was the standard farewell given by Watchers higher-ups to an Asset embarking on yet another perilous mission.

Silence lowered his head. "Yes, ma'am."

He left.

7

When Silence left Cincinnati two hours earlier, the sky had been gray and miserable, ready to spit out chilly drizzle but never making good on the threat. During the drive, however, the nasty weather had continued its southeastward progression, so the sky had cleared by the time he arrived at the northwest side of Indianapolis.

A beautiful day had materialized. And warm, too. Bright sunlight. Bold, blue sky.

For Silence, days like this always felt off, like spiritual incongruities. Clear skies and a cheerful sun contrasted with the dark nature of his work. It was a recurring irony—navigating an assassin's grim realities in the backdrop of pleasant weather. Today, as he tracked Nathan Fuller, a man haunted by his brother's death and dreading another impending tragedy in his family, this stark juxtaposition was as pronounced as ever.

Sunlight spilled over marred streets as Silence drove through the run-down neighborhood. His vehicle was another brand-new Infiniti Q45, a near-twin to the one he'd driven during his previous mission three weeks earlier, differing only in color—the one in Montana had been black; this one was blue. In another example of their gleeful duplicity, the Watchers loved swaddling their assassins in luxury.

On the way to Indy, Silence had reviewed the mission materials, synthesized by Specialists using emerging text-to-speech technology and transferred to a CD. The result, a comically robotic computer voice, had emanated from the Infiniti's stereo for the last two hours. With that task completed, Silence now reached for the audio recorder resting on the passenger seat.

No one had entirely reviewed the audio log Colin Lennox kept during his undercover FBI assignment when he infiltrated Jordan Havelock's group two years ago. It would be up to Silence to use his few minutes of free time during the Indianapolis mission to extract whatever insights he could from the recording.

He pressed *PLAY*.

Lennox's voice filled the car, the smooth and gathered tone of a twenty-something professional embarking on a life-threatening yet critical investigation.

> *November 3rd. Special Agent Colin Lennox. Today marks the start of my undercover investigation into Jordan Havelock and his group. From preliminary reports and intel, there's a troubling picture emerging. Havelock seems to have positioned himself as a savior figure, drawing vulnerable people in with his so-called "anti-suicide" teachings. It's got all the hallmarks of manipulation, the kind you'd expect from a charismatic leader preying on the vulnerable.*
>
> *His followers see him as a spiritual guide. I see a cult. The classic signs are all there—isolation, intense devotion, an inner circle surrounding Havelock, who's at the epicenter, wielding his influence like a weapon. The guy's persuasive; I'll give him that. But the extent to which he seems to have convinced people to abandon their old lives for his cause? That's concerning.*
>
> *I've come across similar setups in my career, and they rarely end well. The Bureau's got every reason to be worried. Tomorrow, I'm going to attend one of their meetings. It's time to get a firsthand look at Havelock and this group he's put together.*

There was a shuffle and a beep—the end of the entry.

Silence pressed *STOP*.

After Silence confirmed the address with a glance at the printout resting atop the manila folder on the center console, he brought the Q45 to a gradual stop outside a house that seemed more abandoned than aged. It wore a history of urban neglect: gray paint peeling; sagging porch; windows, a mix of cracked glass and rough boards. The lawn had been recently mowed, a stark difference from the overgrown lots of many of the neighboring houses, but the thick mounds of lengthy clippings—which were beginning to brown—suggested that, until recently, the lawn had been just as neglected as the rest.

It wasn't the house or the neighborhood one expected for a relatively successful accountant. Recent tragedy had plunged Fuller's life into the depths of tragedy, sure, but the mission materials indicated Fuller had bought the place several months before his brother died. Silence wondered if other strife had befallen Fuller before his brother's car accident.

Although Fuller's home was a logical place to start, there was a good chance Silence wouldn't find him. Watchers intel suggested Fuller hadn't been around much lately. The word was he'd been lying low, steering clear of his own place. Fear of Colin Lennox was the likely reason.

Silence killed the engine, stepped out, key-fobbed the Infiniti's alarm—*honk!*—and made his way to the front porch. The boards whined beneath his girth. There was the damp smell of mold. A thin curtain covered a small pane of glass on the door. Through its nearly opaque fabric, one could barely make out the interior of the dark home, with its hardwood floors and outdated furniture.

He rapped on the door. Waited. Nothing. He knocked again, harder this time. Inside, something crashed, followed by the sound of rapid footsteps.

Through the sheer drape, Silence saw a flash of light flood into the gloomy house; it was another door opening in the kitchen at the back, sunlight silhouetting a slight male figure that Silence recognized from his mission materials. Nathan Fuller. He looked rough—eyes wild, hair disheveled, dress clothes rumpled. Alarm flooded his face when he saw Silence.

And the guy was on the run.

Fuller threw a glance over his shoulder toward the front door, and he and Silence locked eyes through the drape for a split second before Fuller bolted out the back and disappeared into the sunlight.

Silence tried the doorknob. Locked. He sprinted down the creaking steps, hopped off onto the lawn. All those piles of too-long grass clippings sprayed over his slacks as his cap-toe double monks burst through them, sprinting.

He pulled around the corner of the house to an alley in the back and saw Fuller scrambling into a battered Ford sedan parked haphazardly by a detached garage. Silence pursued, but Fuller revved the engine and peeled out in a spray of gravel.

Silence slowed to a stop. Exhaled. And put his hands on his hips as he watched the Ford barrel down the path with reckless abandon, throwing up a dust cloud until it reached the first crossroad. The brake lights glowed briefly as the car slowed, then it took off again with another spray of gravel.

Fuller was gone.

Well...

Silence turned. Two concrete steps led to the back door through which Fuller had just fled. A screen door with a loose flap of screen hung ajar, but the main door was shut. Silence took the steps, tried the doorknob. Unlocked. With one hand under his sport coat on his Beretta, he pushed inside, slipping into the kitchen while simultaneously drawing the gun.

The place was a wreck—cabinets hanging open, drawers dumped, trash strewn across the floor. Silence slipped through the doorway, into the living area, and proceeded through the house, clearing each room, finding them all in similar states as the kitchen. Filthy. Unkempt. Full of ancient furnishings and trash. But also finding no one home.

Back to the living room. The couch cushions bore the imprint of a sleeping body. Beer bottles and fast food wrappers littered the coffee table. Silence's gaze snagged on a different table: the console table off a half-bath on the other side of the room. A glossy brochure lay open next to a glass-shaded, banker-style lamp. Silence picked it up.

It was bright blue. Emblazoned across the front: *STEADY PROGRESS SUMMIT*.

He flipped it open.

Steady Progress Summit
May 3-5
Indianapolis Insight Center

Indianapolis, Indiana

Step into a world of personal transformation at the Steady Progress Summit, hosted within the renowned Indianapolis Insight Center. Join us for an enriching experience that encompasses personal growth, healing, and empowerment. Engage with inspiring presentations, delve into interactive workshops, nurture your mind and body with holistic wellness activities, and explore innovative healing approaches. Connect with a welcoming community of like-minded individuals and embark on a journey toward a brighter and more fulfilling future.

Silence looked at the dates: May 3rd to 5th.

Today was May 3rd.

He flicked the brochure with his thumb as his eyes drifted to the side, thinking.

No one knew where Colin Lennox held his meetings except members of his group. Fuller, an automatic invitee to Lennox's group because of his status as a former Jordan Havelock student, was the only person the Watchers knew who could lead them to Lennox. He'd fled moments earlier, undoubtedly thinking Silence was one of Lennox's.

And *this* brochure had been on Fuller's table...

The mission materials indicated Lennox was planning something big tonight.

May 3rd.

Silence's gaze hardened as he put two and two together. Lennox was likely going to be at this Steady Progress Summit, hunting for more vulnerable souls to ensnare into his suicide cult. He could pose as a heroic savior, another guru like Jordan Havelock.

Hell, Lennox might have even rented some space on the convention floor, set up a damn booth where he could hawk his supposed salvation at emotionally crippled passersby.

It made sense.

A cold, logical sense.

Silence folded the brochure, slid it into his back pocket, and left.

8

Beckwith didn't like this sort of skulking. It was broad daylight, yet he felt as if he was operating under the cover of night, like a creature, a bat ... or a snake.

A snake like Lennox...

Shit like this brought up too many memories—and plenty of those memories were recent ones, fresh off the press.

He was parked outside Nathan Fuller's house in an '84 Pontiac Sunbird. It wasn't Beckwith's. Lennox had chosen the vehicle, a perfect fit for the dilapidated neighborhood. The car, like Beckwith, was unremarkable, selected for its ability to blend into the background, another forgettable piece of mundanity. And, just like Beckwith, the car was rattly and rusty.

Beckwith's eyes were locked on the house across the street, Fuller's. It was a worthless piece of shit in a neighborhood crammed with identical pieces of shit. Beckwith's target had been inside the place for the last few minutes.

Lennox had told Beckwith to wait near the house for "a shadow of a man," "a specter." To Beckwith, those words described Lennox himself more than someone else. For hours, Beckwith had waited for Lennox's stranger until, right when Beckwith was beginning to think Lennox had been mistaken, the stranger had arrived.

He'd pulled up in a blue Infiniti Q45. When he stepped out of the car, Beckwith saw that he was "tall" and "broad," just as Lennox described. Easily six-foot-three. Massive shoulders. Dark hair that fell in choppy strands over an angular face that reminded Beckwith a lot of the actor from *21 Jump Street*. What was that guy's name? Johnny ... Deep, or something like that.

The stranger operated with a smooth, confident power, his movements surprisingly agile for his size. He wore a short-sleeved gray button-up shirt and dark slacks over black dress shoes, the kind with strap-style closures.

The man had gone to the door, knocked twice, and stood there waiting. But then, out of nowhere, he spun around. In a sudden burst of movement, he leaped off the porch and bolted around the side of the house.

As inconspicuously as possible, Beckwith had repositioned the Sunbird to get a view down the alley behind Fuller's house, ready to give chase if necessary. But there was no need. By the time he'd gotten the car in position, the stranger had already stopped, hands on his hips, watching Fuller speed away down the alley in the old Ford.

After that, the guy had slipped into Fuller's house through the back door.

Now, Beckwith was back to waiting, eyes fixed on the house.

Beckwith was feeling the pinch, physically and mentally, in the tight space of the Sunbird. Tracking someone didn't sit well with him. Not anymore. In fact, it never had. Doing it again reminded him of a past he'd tried to shake off.

He watched as the front door of Fuller's house opened. The tall figure emerged, more distinct now as he stepped off the porch and into the daylight. This was the clearest view Beckwith had yet. The man's features were sharply defined. His dark eyes looked piercing in the flash Beckwith saw before the man threw on a pair of expensive sunglasses. And there was something else about the guy, an amalgamation of intangibles, that radiated off his aura like the casual power of his steps.

This guy was no mere thug.

Shit, this guy was a killer, the real deal.

Beckwith, of all people, would know.

The man walked with an assurance that caught the eye in L.A. chic attire. His presence was as out of place in this rat's nest neighborhood as the gleaming new Infiniti he'd emerged from. Beckwith, with so many years of experience, noticed it all—the precise cut of the man's tailoring, the calculated sweep of his gaze across the street, a predator assessing unfamiliar territory.

Beckwith sunk back into his seat as the man's eyes swept in his direction, lowering his face.

The stranger approached the Infiniti and slipped in with indifferent ease that spoke of an existence accustomed to such fineries. The car's engine purred to life, a low, resonant sound that cut through the stillness of the ramshackle neighborhood. A crunch of tires on asphalt, and it took off.

Beckwith let a moment pass, then turned the key in the ignition. The rusty Sunbird, so unlike the stranger's vehicle, sputtered to life. He put the gear selector into drive and pulled away, his eyes locked on the Infiniti's rear end.

Beckwith stayed back, allowing a few other cars to come between them, just another vehicle in the lazy traffic of a forgotten part of town. The late morning sun was bright, casting hard shadows across the houses and patchy lawns. The Infiniti sliced through the neighborhood, unaware of the old Sunbird ghosting it, leading Beckwith away from the residential zone and to the ramp for the I-465 interstate.

The Sunbird protested, but Beckwith got it up to speed, drifting into the whooshing traffic and keeping the Infiniti in sight ahead.

As Beckwith merged with the highway flow, his mind fell into a loop, replaying images of a younger man with a scarred face and a dead eye, always with that smug, sinister smile. Taking Colin Lennox's job offer had been Beckwith's only option, but every move he made for Lennox, every task he completed, was another step away from the clean break Beckwith was chasing.

Now, here he was, tailing a stranger on the beltway, a man who had just broken into Nathan Fuller's house. And why? To what end was he stalking this man? Beckwith had no clue. Only Lennox knew.

Yes, Beckwith's life was spiraling further from his goals with every minute he spent under Lennox's grip.

That's when it hit him. The only way out was a game-changer, a bold move to break the cycle, to steer his life off this dark path he'd found himself on.

Tonight was going to be a big night for Colin Lennox; he'd told Beckwith as much, though he wouldn't give the details.

Maybe tonight could be a big one for Grant Beckwith, too, the night he broke free from Lennox and the life he'd always known.

Ahead, the Infiniti's turn signal flashed, and it eased onto the off-ramp, which bore the Indianapolis skyline as a backdrop, towers glistening in the sunlight. Beckwith followed. Taking this specific exit let Beckwith know where the tall stranger must be going: the Indianapolis Insight Center...

...and the Steady Progress Summit.

9

As Silence pulled into the sprawling parking lot of the Indianapolis Insight Center, the audio recorder began the latest of Colin Lennox's two-year-old entries.

> *November 6th. I just came back from one of Havelock's gatherings. I've got to admit, the man's got presence. The way he speaks, it's like he reaches into your soul. I can see why these people follow him. There's a genuine belief in his eyes, a conviction that's hard to fake.*
>
> *I observed the crowd. They're not the lost souls I expected. They're ... normal, everyday people, finding solace in his words. There's something about Havelock that's ... different. He's not just another charismatic leader; there's a depth to him that's hard to ignore.*
>
> *But I must remain detached. My job here is to uncover the truth, not to get swayed by a smooth-talker. Still, it's hard to shake the feeling that there might be more to Havelock than meets the eye.*
>
> *Tomorrow, I'll be meeting some of the group members personally. Let's see if their stories align with Havelock's vision.*

There was a shuffle and a beep as the entry ended.
Silence pressed *STOP*.

He threaded the Infiniti through the crowded parking lot under the late-morning sun. The glare was sharp, but his Maui Jim sunglasses dialed it back. He'd bought the glasses less than a week ago at a new shop back in Pensacola. Metal frames. Polarized lenses. The style differed slightly from his norm, and adjusting had taken him a day or so. Quickly, he'd grown to love them.

The summit's crowd was already thick, a steady stream of attendees funneling into the event. Parking attendants moved between the rows of vehicles, their high-vis vests bright under the sun, fluorescent yellow with reflective silver stripes. One used a few hand gestures in opening-scene-of-*Top-Gun* style to guide Silence into one of the few remaining spaces. Silence put the Infiniti into park and stepped outside.

The Indianapolis Insight Center loomed ahead. Silence took in the building's structure and its bold, contemporary design—clean lines and lofty steel columns. Insight's tinted and reflective glass gave the building a sense of mystery, concealing the activities within while mirroring the blue sky and the surrounding cityscape. Arcs of prismatic light reflected off the surfaces.

In the heart of a metropolis known for its hospitality industry—with conventions being a key economic component—the Insight Center was a newer addition, complementing the popular Indiana Convention Center and sports venues. The Insight Center symbolized Indianapolis's success in the sector; this city had room and ambition for an additional convention center, one funded entirely by private sources.

Insight sat on the outskirts of downtown, offering the luxury of a spacious parking lot, a contrast to its counterpart deep in the city's core, where multi-level garages were the norm. Silence fell in step with the stream of attendees going for the building. The crowd's unhurried pace and the lot's sheer breadth meant a several-minute trek before he reached the front plaza. Here, fountains and trees added serenity to seating areas, while pathways ushered visitors toward the main entrance.

The queue at the doors was progressing quickly, thanks to the efficiency of the organizers. They were all dressed in polo shirts matching the festive blue color featured on the brochure Silence had seen at Fuller's house, each emblazoned with the Steady Progress Summit logo. Silence paid the entry fee, passed through a metal detector, and then merged with the crowd as they moved beyond an oversized partition and into the sprawling convention center floor.

The space opened up before him—a ceiling brimming with trusses way up above and a massive crowd below, an explosion of signs, faces, sounds, and colors, all of it bringing forth an immediate sense of scale and mild vertigo.

The Steady Progress Summit.

Insight's main floor stretched endlessly, filled with thousands of attendees navigating a sea of booths. Above, prodigious banners and digital screens flashed with motivational messages. The air carried a collective buzz—countless conversations blending into a loud, indistinct rumble.

Along the back wall were stages where motivational speakers, visible to hundreds at a time, shared their stories, their voices amplified. In other areas, groups gathered to watch mindfulness and physical well-being demonstrations—yoga, tai chi, and breathing exercises.

C.C. would have loved this shit.

Silence scanned the crowd, taking in the individuals, each face a story of searching—for direction, for a flicker of light in their personal void. Or maybe ... not anyone's *personal* void but a mutual one, that of the collective consciousness. Before C.C.'s death, for all of Silence's adult life as Jake Rowe and even as a child, he'd noticed a shift in the world, a slow degradation starting from the top and working its way down. These souls at the Insight Center could very well—

Focus, love.

It was C.C.

In his mind.

She was, as always, keeping his overactive brain in line. Sometimes, she did this with sage wisdom. Sometimes, with in-depth meditation practices.

And sometimes, all she had to do was tell him to focus.

Thank you, Silence's internal voice replied.

He continued scanning the crowd, searching for that one lost soul among all the other lost souls: Nathan Fuller.

At the same time, he searched for another soul who was *not* lost: Colin Lennox.

If Lennox was enacting the theory Silence had devised for him—establishing a visible role at the summit—then finding the scarred man should, theoretically, be more straightforward than locating Fuller. There were only a handful of vendors and presenters among the thousands of attendees.

Silence's eyes returned to the presenters on the far wall—speaking through microphones, building small crowds within the larger crowd. He looked for a scar-faced version of the young FBI agent he and Doc Hazel had watched on the VHS recording.

Would Lennox be that bold, though? To this point, the man had been secretive, not revealing the location of his meetings, keeping his admissions selective and tight.

It would make better sense for a man like that to meander the convention floor, moving through the masses to poach a particularly distraught soul.

Silence studied the larger crowd again, using one of C.C.'s concentration techniques to allow him to take it all in simultaneously. Faces swam in his field of vision, so many faces. The challenge of picking out either Lennox *or* Fuller from this human jigsaw puzzle was immense, every individual merging into an indistinct sea of features and movements, countless people seeking comfort and relief.

As he looked over the swarm, his mind flashed on the audio log he'd finished as he parked the Infiniti outside. Two years back, Colin Lennox had operated undercover in a scene not unlike this, observing Jordan Havelock's followers, a crowd hungry for answers, solace, an escape. The setting had been more intimate: not this throng of faces, but one of Havelock's more secluded gatherings. Yet there was a clear parallel—Lennox, like Silence now, had been an onlooker among souls adrift.

The audio log had registered Lennox's voice with a grudging respect for some of Havelock's sentiments, even as he hinted at Havelock's dark path for his followers.

This tangled set of thoughts resonated with Silence, and it jolted him into the past, to a time when Silence had similar observations of a man's multifaceted nature.

It took him back in time to an old mission.

His second mission ever.

Richard Keane. A State Department diplomat. A Watcher.

A traitor.

And a father.

It was the heating system that had done it for Silence, that tiny, intimate detail...

...as Silence crouched in the shadows of Keane's home office behind the red leather armchair.

The gentle click followed by a warm breeze from the vent.

Keane's HVAC going to work.

Keane or someone in his family had set the thermostat to a specific temperature; the house's temperature had dropped below the desired setting; and the thermostat had responded as it should, kicking the heater into gear, pumping warmth into the home.

Into the home...

A home.

Silence was crouched in a man's home.

There were photographs on the wall, and Silence understood their significance from the biographical information about Keane that he'd memorized—Keane's college days, a bachelor's degree from Princeton; grad school at Tufts; his first Department of State assignment in Mexico; the next several years at the embassy in Nepal; then the UK; and finally back here, stateside, northern Virginia, where the Octobers were cold enough to kick the heater on at ten o'clock at night.

But it wasn't those photos that had caught Silence's attention when he first bypassed the alarm system's window sensor and broke into the room, settling into the shadows behind the chair.

It had been the photos on the shelf above the desk.

Keane, his wife, and his teenage son.

One of Keane's people was tall and slender, radiant golden hair cascading down her back, piercing blue eyes. A flowing white dress in one photo. Christmas pajamas here. T-shirt and jeans there.

The other wore his hair closely shaved and bore an expression of typical adolescent defiance, wearing graphic Ts in two photos, an oversized hoodie in another.

Keane was an educated man and a diplomat and a Watcher and a treasonous criminal who sold out his country, putting dozens of lives at risk.

He was also a husband and a father.
And...
...he was also a martial arts enthusiast in his spare time.
This meant that the death hadn't been quick.
There had been a struggle. A brief but powerful exchange of blows.

Silence was further hampered in the fight because he'd had to quite literally pull his punches. The mission requirements dictated as much. He couldn't leave any marks on Keane—no contusions, no scratches, no broken bones.

Keane had tried a side kick first, which Silence avoided. Fists flew. Quick, sharp jabs. Silence held back, each strike measured, restrained. A dance of power, brief yet intense.

When it was over, when Keane was dead, Silence looked again at the family photos on the shelf. The wife. The son with the burning teenage angst.

Family *photos.*

The family was now shattered.

C.C.'s voice came to him again. *Focus, love. Detach from the memory. View it objectively. How could the Keane mission be tied to the Code Red?*

She was right. As always. Silence needed to refocus.

He was back in the bustling present moment of the Steady Progress Summit. The crowd. The stifling body heat. The vendors. The presentations at the row of stages in the back.

As C.C. had instructed, he needed to disconnect from the impact of the Keane mission. Certainly, the assignment had flavored his progress into his life as an assassin—as it was so impactful and only his second mission—but what could it have to do with the Code Red? Doc Hazel said that none of the Keane-related materials stolen from the Watchers databases was significant, that all the info was even publicly available through the Freedom of Information Act.

And even if Silence could discern the link between the old mission and the Code Red, was there a link between the Code Red and the Colin Lennox matter, or was the timing insignificant, coincidental? Silence had stopped believing in the fairy tale of coincidences a long time ago.

Mulling these details from the briefing that Doc Hazel had provided made Silence think of something else she'd discussed with him: the Watchers' offer of a one-year sabbatical.

He'd been at this life for years. Richard Keane's family wasn't the only one he'd torn apart.

Maybe one year away from a life of spiritual destitution wasn't such a bad thing.

For a third time, C.C. said, *Focus, love.*

For a third time, she was right.

Thanks, Silence said.

Yes.

Focus.

Prioritize. The mission. Nathan Fuller. A man desperate to save his sister-in-law, Maya, from the grips of the charismatic leader of a suicide cult.

Silence moved once more through the swarm of people, carefully scanning the faces for Fuller. He brought up a mental reference image of the man he'd seen earlier: disheveled and anxious, locking eyes across the length of a dilapidated house's interior before speeding away in that old Ford. Silence strained to find that frantic visage among the sea of people, but doing so was futile; this gathering had countless worried expressions.

Suddenly, his focus was drawn to a strange scene that seemed out of place in the bustling Steady Progress Summit.

The woman stood out. Late twenties, Silence guessed, with parted chestnut hair tinged with auburn that hung in waves, a frame to a contemplative face. Pale complexion with a faint golden hue. She'd chosen casual—a gray sweatshirt paired with jeans—aiming for the everyday look that would blend in at the Steady Progress Summit. But Silence knew a thing or two about clothing. Despite the understated choice, the quality of the fabric and the discreet logos spoke of brands that didn't come cheap.

The man facing her also wore a designer label—a blue suit, no tie, and a white shirt unbuttoned at the collar for a touch of nonchalance. He wasn't yet in his fifties, but was undoubtedly preparing for them. His East Asian heritage was apparent in the lines of his face. Short haircut, styled with purpose, nothing left to chance. Decent physique, the result of gym time, not genetics.

His hands moved as he talked, sharp and precise, a little too deliberate, so much so that the woman was mildly intimidated—arms crossed, nodding her head but never making eye contact for too long. In fact, her overall stance was defensive, a quiet counterpoint to the man's encroachment.

Silence's mind raced back to an earlier thought: the possibility that Lennox or his associates were somewhere in this crowd, laying traps for the unwary. With his mild aggression, the man in the blue suit could easily be one of Lennox's operatives.

And the woman might be the prey.

Before C.C. could tell Silence to focus yet again, his attention jolted back to life, the scene in front of him suddenly more than background noise.

He started moving again, pushing through the crowd, heading straight for the pair.

10

Silence focused on the woman.

Even in her sweatshirt-and-jeans getup, her poise and elegance seemed out of place in the bustling atmosphere of the Steady Progress Summit. Her quiet dignity remained intact, yet she looked browbeaten and meek as the aggressive man in the blue suit verbally assailed her.

Silence drew nearer, shouldering through the crowd, his eyes never straying from the woman and her companion. Yes, the suited man could easily be one of Lennox's operatives trying to get the dignified but vulnerable woman out of the convention center. It made sense. The mission materials noted that tonight was rumored to be a big move on Lennox's part, so—

Silence's approach—and his thought pattern—came to an abrupt halt.

A woman stepped in front of him, blocking his way. Her hair was a blazing shade of red—curly and untamed. Oversized blue eyes. Oversized smile. A denim shirt, worn and soft from countless washes, hung loosely over a simple white tank top, its sleeves rolled up to her elbows.

"Don't even think about it, buddy," the woman said. Neither her smile nor the slightly playful tone of voice matched her sentiment.

Not only was the woman's command at odds with her pleasantly coy expression, but it didn't immediately make sense. So Silence just looked back at her, blinked.

She gestured animatedly toward the woman Silence had been observing.

"I don't care if you're looking for an autograph or a date," the woman said. "It's not gonna happen."

During intel-gathering, it's often wise to stay quiet. It had never been difficult for Silence to remain in silence, what with a ruined throat and all. He sensed that the woman in front of him was a chatterbox, the sort who wouldn't let a conversation go limp for long, and when she mentioned "autograph," the intrigue portion of Silence's senses was activated.

Silence didn't respond.

"Well, that's what you were doing, wasn't it?" the woman said, cocking a hip and planting a fist into it. "Going for Taylor? Come on, bro. I was watching you plow through the crowd toward her."

She gave him a moment to respond.

Silence didn't respond.

"Look, you're tall, well built, well dressed, and hot." With this last word, she let her blue eyes examine Silence, head to toe. "I'm not gonna lie— you're just her type. But I'm her friend. I'm watching over her. And it's too soon. You know this."

Silence didn't respond.

Finally, the dubiously friendly facade changed slightly as the woman raised an eyebrow, narrowed those bright eyes.

"Oh, I get it. You're not from Indy, are you?" She pointed to the woman Silence had been pursuing—Taylor, he now knew her name to be. "And you don't know who that is?"

Silence shook his head.

The woman kept her finger pointing at her friend as she narrowed her eyes a bit more and said, "You don't talk much, do you?"

Silence shook his head.

The woman shrugged. "That's Taylor Perrine. But you probably don't know about the Perrine family as an out-of-towner."

Silence played dumb and shook his head again.

But he *did* know of the Perrine family. As part of his job, he made sure he was knowledgeable about the influential families in the various major cities across the United States.

In the case of Indianapolis, the Perrine family established their fortune through strategic investments in the city's burgeoning railroad and manufacturing industries during the 19th century. As the city thrived, the Perrines not only diversified their business ventures but also significantly influenced the city's cultural and civic sectors, establishing a deep-rooted prominence in its historical and societal fabric. Taylor was of the latest generation or two, placing her somewhere in her thirties.

"Probably the most famous family in the city," the redheaded woman explained. "Old money. Everything they do gets put in the news. But don't you for a second think that Taylor's some tabloid diva! She's good people. And I watch over her."

The woman's smile brightened as she shoved a hand in Silence's direction.

"Kori," she said.

Silence took her hand. It was small and smooth and gave a strong, genuine handshake.

"Chad," Silence said.

Silence adopted a new identity for each mission, always one-syllable names. This helped to lower the number of syllables he ran through his painful throat. Not a significant benefit, but it added up. Every little bit helped.

In Indy, he would be Chad.

At the crackle of his voice, Kori jumped, and for a moment, her mouth gaped, both rows of pearly whites gleaming in the convention center's bright lighting. This was a standard reaction. Silence waited for it to pass.

Quickly, Kori put a polite smile back on her face.

"Look," she said, "you're cute, you look successful, and you're clearly confident just strolling up to Taylor like you were. But you're not from Indy. You haven't read the local gossip columns for the last year. Taylor, she..." Kori's voice trailed off, and her expression clouded for a moment. "Taylor's had a rough time lately. Even more than what the public eye sees."

She leaned in slightly, voice going quieter, just loud enough to be audible over the crowd.

"Taylor's hit a wall," Kori said. "She had a business, a startup, a boutique marketing firm, her shot at doing something without her family's help. It folded about four months ago. For a Perrine, that's not just failure; it's a headline. Then there's her personal life—she found out her douchebag fiancé was cheating. And so, of course, the entire city found out."

Kori's expression hardened slightly.

"On top of everything, she's dealing with health problems, the kind you don't just throw money at, and aside from money, her family isn't helping; the Perrines aren't exactly the touchy-feely types."

Silence looked over at Taylor again. Health problems. That would explain the slight yellowishness in the complexion.

Taylor's arms were still crossed tightly over her chest, and she nodded slightly as the man continued speaking and gesticulating, though her eyes weren't on the guy but on the floor beside his feet.

"I dragged her here, the Steady Progress Summit," Kori said, stating the event's name in a mock lofty tone that she followed with a weak laugh and a wave to the grandeur surrounding them. "She needs help, you know? More than I can offer by taking her to brunch or a chick flick. Definitely more than her family's going to offer And ... I think she might be considering ... worse options."

Kori's voice cracked slightly, emotion bleeding through.

"I've seen the signs, even if she's never outright said the word 'suicide.' But it's there. In her eyes. There's no light left in her."

Suicide...

The word bolstered Silence's theory that the man in the blue suit was Lennox's operative and Taylor was the victim, soon to be led away from the Insight Center to Lennox's upcoming anti-suicide group meeting, one that Silence's would-be contact, Nathan Fuller, believed to be a suicide cult.

"Who's the guy?" Silence said.

Kori glanced over at her friend, back to Silence. Her posture stiffened.

"Tom Radley," she said. "He introduced himself to both of us a few minutes ago, said he's a self-help author and guru. There're a lot of those here." She snickered. "Seemed nice enough, but then he kind of whisked Taylor away for a private chat."

"And you let him?"

Kori snickered again and patted Silence's shoulder playfully. Perhaps a little too playfully.

"You know me that well already, huh? When the guy offered to talk to Taylor alone, I was hesitant. I mean, we'd only just met him. But Taylor insisted, and I didn't want to discourage her in any way from seeking help, you know? That's why I brought her here, after all. But the guy gave me a bad vibe. And the instant they were alone, their conversation shifted to this."

She pointed. Several yards away, Taylor continued to nod and hug herself while Radley continued to do all the talking, gesturing broadly, an inch or two too far into Taylor's space. Radley was smiling, but there was darkness behind the grin. Silence had seen disingenuous smiles countless times. He could spot them from a mile away.

...or from a few yards away across a crowded convention center floor.

Kori glanced at Silence, a playful spark in her eyes.

"Look, I'm keeping an eye on my friend. Maybe you could help me out," she said. "Buy you a juice?"

She gestured toward a nearby booth, a colorful oasis offering mindfulness drinks, proudly announced on neon signage, blends like acai-blueberry, turmeric-ginger, and spirulina-lime. A few tables with tiki-style thatch umbrellas were set up right there in the crowd, people pushing in from all directions.

Kori's blue eyes sparkled, and it nudged at something deep inside Silence, a memory, a shadow of what used to be. C.C. His constant companion. He needed nothing else, not even a cup of spirulina-lime juice. He was about to offer a gentle rejection...

...when he felt something.

A person looking in his direction. Halfway across the convention floor. Silence's gaze locked with that of a familiar face.

Nathan Fuller.

Same frazzled look. Same wrinkled dress clothes. And the same panic, evidenced by the fact that, after a flicker of fear, the guy turned on his heel, taking off into the crowd.

Silence's attention went back to Taylor Perrine, still listening, nodding, avoiding eye contact with the overbearing man in the blue suit.

Immediately, Silence used one of C.C.'s mind techniques.

He slowed his thoughts, and with them, time slowed as well.

The last echo of a bell's chime dwindling away. A bicycle coasting to a stop, no longer pedaled. A pendulum's swing growing shorter and shorter.

An extended moment to think.

Taylor Perrine. Her friend had described her as suicidal, just like Colin Lennox's followers.

Lennox. The mission. The Colin Lennox mission. Silence's point of contact: Nathan Fuller, the man who ran earlier, the man who was running now.

Silence *should* go after Fuller.

But doing so meant he'd be abandoning Taylor Perrine. Silence's gut was screaming at him that this Tom Radley individual confronting Taylor had poor intentions. C.C. had always told Silence to listen to his gut.

Tom Radley was one of Lennox's goons. Had to be.

But...

Fuller was the sole individual known to the Watchers who knew the location of Lennox's meeting that evening.

And Fuller—who was getting away, disappearing into the throngs—was the point of contact.

For the mission.

The mission.

Fuller would lead Silence to Lennox.

From there, at Lennox's meeting, Silence could indeed help Taylor Perrine.

Because if Silence was right, Tom Radley would manipulate Taylor to attend the event later that evening.

He wasn't *really* turning his back on her.

Only temporarily.

Time returned, breezing back into existence with a burst of sound: the crowded convention, numbingly loud.

Silence turned to Kori. She was still looking up at him, still smiling.

"I gotta go," Silence said.

Kori frowned, her effervescence finally subsiding. "What?"

"Sorry."

Silence whipped around.

Fuller was ahead, just visible for a moment, a face among a sea of faces...

...before he vanished into the crowd.

Silence took off after him.

11

Beckwith didn't belong here.

He stood amid the pulsating throng at the Steady Progress Summit. The atmosphere inside the Insight Center was alive with the buzz of motivational conversations. The faces swirling around him were illuminated with hope, eyes sparkling with inspiration, voices blending into a chorus of growth.

No, Beckwith didn't belong here.

Beckwith was a man who killed other humans. Twice now. A junkie yesterday...

...and years ago, a gas station attendant.

He'd meant to disarm the man, to get the shotgun from his grasp. Self-defense.

He'd ended up breaking the man's neck.

Yep, the man had indeed been disarmed. Sure had. The shotgun had landed with a loud clank on the linoleum as the man's eyes went wide and unblinking.

Self-defense, yes...

But Beckwith wouldn't have needed to defend his life had he not been there to rob the place.

Beckwith didn't belong here at the Insight Center among these people looking to make positive changes in their lives. Beckwith wasn't like these folks.

Beckwith was a murderer.

He had been for years.

And this label was solidified the previous evening, killing Lennox's betrayer.

Now, here he was among these good people, doing more of Lennox's bidding, chasing down the tall stranger who'd broken into Nathan Fuller's house.

For the last few minutes, Beckwith's attention had been locked onto a scene he couldn't comprehend: the tall stranger had been approaching Taylor Perrine, the famous socialite, of all people, when another woman of Perrine's age cut him off—a woman with fiery, curly red hair who, after a few minutes, seemed to flirt with the large man.

A few minutes later, Nathan Fuller had materialized in the crowd, making eye contact with the tall stranger before bolting away into the throngs of people. The big guy had taken chase.

Since then, Beckwith had taken chase, too, trying to stay far enough back to not be noticed. This was easy enough, given his quarry's six-foot-three, broad-shouldered, fitness model silhouette—an easy target to follow in the crowd.

Beckwith weaved through the mob of attendees with a singular focus: *do not lose track of the tall man.* This was Beckwith's latest assignment from Lennox, after all, and as worthless as Beckwith now knew himself to be, there was still the primal need for survival. Everyone wanted to survive. With the bargaining chip that Lennox held, Beckwith's only means of survival was appeasing the scar-faced, snake-voiced man.

As he maneuvered through the crowd, he saw someone else joining the chase. It was a security guard—in his forties, black, bald, and clad in a dark uniform. He also pushed through the sea of people, going after the tall stranger and Fuller.

There was something about the guy ... like a familiarity, a sort of camaraderie. He was right at Beckwith's age, and aside from the darker skin and the chrome dome, Beckwith might as well have been looking in a mirror—same height, same muscular yet past-its-prime physique with a bit of a gut hanging over the belt, same lines at the corners of the man's eyes.

But most telling was the man's sense of pathetic desperation. It was so strong that Beckwith could see it at a glance.

Also at a glance, he caught the man's name on the uniform's nametape over his left pec: *MALONE*.

As quickly as this sense of brotherhood developed, it dissipated with a presumption—the bald security guard Malone was undoubtedly not a murderer like Beckwith.

Few people were.

Malone was most likely a good man. There'd be a wife waiting for him at home. A couple of kids, too, if they hadn't already left for college or the workforce. Hell, Malone might be a young grandfather.

He and Beckwith weren't the same.

Beckwith snapped back to the task and narrowed his eyes at the target. The tall guy was closing in on Fuller, cutting through a cluster of people clad in violet T-shirts emblazoned with their company logo, distributing pamphlets.

The crowd's noise was a constant hum, voices merging with those amplified by speaker systems spouting buzzwords: *empowerment, self-realization, transformation*. Beckwith's thoughts raced. He needed to get word to Lennox, not just about this tall stranger's pursuit of Nathan Fuller but also his alarming move toward Taylor Perrine.

Taylor Perrine!

Lennox hadn't mentioned Perrine, but then, there was a lot that Lennox hadn't told Beckwith. Although Lennox had made Beckwith one of only two people who knew the scope of Lennox's deception, Beckwith knew that there was much to which he was being left in the dark.

But targeting someone like Perrine, a high-profile figure who'd dominated headlines for the past year? That was bold. Yet, it made a twisted kind of sense—Perrine was vulnerable, teetering on the brink, exactly the kind of target Lennox would choose.

Beckwith continued forward, weaving through the crowd, eyes locked on the tall, elusive figure ahead. The guy moved with surprising dexterity, his broad shoulders cutting a clear path through the swarm.

For a moment, Beckwith thought he'd lost him. Panic knotted Beckwith's stomach—the fear of failing Lennox, thinking again about the concept of survival and the secret that Lennox was holding.

Then, relief. There was the tall guy, emerging near a display of self-help books. Beckwith's breathing steadied as he picked up his pace, closing the distance. But just as quickly, the man veered right, disappearing again, this time into a side corridor.

Before the heavy metal door shut behind the guy, Beckwith glimpsed someone else in the hallway—Nathan Fuller.

The tall man had caught up with his target.

12

Silence bolted after Fuller, his double monks pounding on the polished concrete floor of the utilitarian hallway—stark fluorescent lights; scuffed, drab walls. This was the backend of the convention center, a place devoid of frills, meant purely for function. As he sprinted, Silence's eyes were locked on Fuller. The distance between them shrank.

Silence closed in just as Fuller neared one of the doorways lining the hall. This was an opportunity. Silence lunged forward, his right hand locking onto Fuller with an iron grip while his left took the door handle. With a swift shove, he propelled Fuller through the doorway.

They crashed into a darkened conference room, the noise echoing off bare walls, sharp and abrupt in the stillness. As Fuller plowed forward, Silence slammed the door shut behind them.

The room was illuminated only by a sliver of light spilling through the glass pane in the door they'd just passed through. This clearly wasn't one of the elaborate public-facing conference rooms; this was for the Insight Center staff, and it hadn't been used for a while. Tables were haphazardly shoved against the walls. Chairs were stacked in piles, creating shadows in the gloom. The air was musty, dusty.

Fuller windmilled back, slapping into a conference table, which brought him to an abrupt halt. He looked at Silence with wide eyes, inching back on the table. His breathing was heavy, labored.

Silence stepped forward, placing himself between Fuller and the door, sealing off the only avenue of escape. The two men faced each other. The only sound in the shadowy stillness was Fuller's ragged breaths.

"Why do you..." Silence said and swallowed. "Keep running from me?"

Fuller eyed Silence with a mixture of fear and uncertainty. "I thought... you were with Lennox," he stammered. His voice matched his wrinkly office attire—the voice of a burnt-out accountant. His eyes darted around as if expecting Lennox's men to emerge at any moment.

Silence reached into his pocket, pulled out his wallet, and retrieved a plastic card. He handed it to Fuller, who took it with trembling hands. Though it was the same size and shape as a swipe card, its frosted translucent plastic showed no magnetic strip on the back. Two blue design elements slashed down the left side, and blue lettering gave a message:

> **MY ORGANIZATION IS AWARE OF YOUR SITUATION.**
>
> **WE UNDERSTAND NORMAL CHANNELS HAVE FAILED YOU.**
>
> **WE HAVE THE MEANS TO ASSIST.**
>
> **PLEASE EXCUSE THIS FORM OF INTRODUCTION.**
>
> **I AM NOT MUTE, BUT SPEAKING IS PAINFUL.**
>
> **I AM HERE TO HELP.**

Still holding the card with both hands, Fuller looked up.

"I ... don't understand," he said. "Who are you?"

"Chad," Silence said.

Fuller jumped, a standard reaction to Silence's ruined voice, much like

Kori had offered a few minutes earlier. Silence said nothing, allowing the moment to pass.

Fuller glanced back down at the card. Another moment passed, and Fuller looked confused as he lowered the card and handed it back to Silence.

"You're with ... an organization? What, are you, like, a fed or something?"

During his investigations, it was common for people to assume Silence was a federal agent. Often, it was in Silence's best interests to let the assumption ride.

Silence didn't respond.

"I contacted the FBI field office after I went to IPD," Fuller said incredulously. "Multiple times. They turned me away, said the Havelock matter was long buried. I don't get it ... Is the FBI investigating, after all?" A pause. "Or are you with some other agency?"

Silence didn't respond.

"*Who* are you?" Fuller insisted, a bit of courage strengthening his words.

"I'm someone who's..." Silence said and swallowed. "Here to help you..." Another swallow. "And your sister-in-law." Another swallow. "The *only* one who will."

Silence figured this would be enough: not only the mentioning of the sister-in-law—proof that Silence knew the situation—but the emphasis on being the only one willing to help Fuller pull his sister-in-law out of Colin Lennox's group, the only person who would listen to Fuller's theory that Lennox was leading his followers to mass suicide.

And he was right. Fuller's face unfurled, and he let out a long breath, shoulders drooping.

"Yeah, I'm trying to find her, my sister-in-law, Maya," he said, his voice a mix of determination and desperation. "She's caught up in Lennox's group ... it's a suicide pact." He paused. "I'm Nate Fuller, by the way. But I guess you already know that."

Silence nodded.

Fuller rubbed the back of his neck. "And you can help me, Chad? You and your organization."

Silence nodded.

Another long inhale and exhale from Fuller.

"Okay. I know where Lennox is holding his meeting tonight. That's our best chance to find Maya." He checked his watch. "Less than an hour till the meeting. And there's something big supposed to happen tonight. Lennox hasn't said what it is, but I'm worried that..."

He trailed off, didn't finish.

Silence's mission materials had noted the rumors of tonight's meeting being significant. Like Fuller, the mission materials didn't know what the significance was.

From Fuller's expression, it was obvious he believed this would be the night Lennox would make his dark wish come true and have his followers take their own lives.

Including Maya.

Silence glanced over his shoulder through the pane of glass in the door and saw a pair of the black-suited security guards entering the hallway.

"Yes, but first..." he said and swallowed. "Let's get the hell out of here."

13

Avery Malone was no hero.

So why the hell was he acting like one?

He was a security guard. That was all. A forty-seven-year-old security guard. Someone who spent most of his days within the walls of the Indianapolis Insight Center. The job was easy, mind-numbingly dull, a waste of life.

He'd had a few encounters, little blips of action. Once, he'd chased off a raccoon that had somehow found its way into the lobby, its scampering paws echoing off the polished floors as it darted between oversized potted plants. Another time, he'd spent an entire afternoon watching a CCTV monitor as a group of teenagers loitered suspiciously near the main entrance, only to eventually wander off without incident.

These were the highlights of his career, if you could even call it that. *Career* was a rather lofty word for someone his age who'd been in this line of work for only seven years.

All the same, less than five minutes ago, something had propelled Avery into action. Now, he was running. Chest heaving. A wreath of sweat rivulets sliding down his bald head, coming from all directions. A sharp stitch had developed in his left ribcage.

He pushed through the hordes of people. The crowd was a living entity, undulating and unpredictable. His gaze was locked on the door at the back where he'd seen the man disappear moments earlier—the tall, mysterious figure he'd witnessed in conversation with the redheaded woman who seemed to be a friend and protector of Taylor Perrine.

The tall guy hadn't been the first man who'd tried to approach Taylor after she'd separated from the redhead, but he'd been the first who seemed to pick up on the situation with Tom Radley. Just before the mysterious man had bolted after the shorter man in the disheveled dress clothes, he'd seemed on the verge of stepping in, of intervening in whatever Radley was orchestrating with Taylor Perrine.

As Avery continued through the crowd, he glanced over and saw Taylor still conversing with Radley. Two minutes earlier, as with the surrounding crowd, the pair had turned to watch as the tall guy chased after the frazzled-looking man. But after the commotion, they'd resumed their conversation, returning to their earlier positions: Radley doing all the talking and Taylor guardedly listening. The redheaded friend watched over them from a few yards away, her bright blue eyes showing concern.

Radley was around Avery's age, Asian American, with short, perfectly styled hair, wearing a sharp blue suit, the shirt beneath tie-less and unbuttoned at the top. Avery knew that Radley was an entrepreneur of sorts, and he only knew this because Montoya had mentioned the man a while back, gloating about the partnership they'd formed.

Had it not been for this earlier conversation, Avery would have thought nothing of the random—albeit awkwardly tense—discussion that Perrine, the local celebrity socialite, was holding with an aggressively forward man in a flashy blue suit. After years of working in a convention center in a city known for hosting conventions, Avery had witnessed innumerable celebrities and seen them engaged in any number of conversations, many of which were tense.

But Montoya had told Avery about his partnership with Tom Radley, hinting at what they were up to, what they'd be doing when the Steady Progress Summit rolled around.

And Montoya was there. Right now.

At the Steady Progress Summit.

Avery checked his peripheral, spotted the guy. Darren Montoya. There.

On the mezzanine, fifty feet away and fifteen feet high, looking down upon Taylor Perrine and his associate, Tom Radley.

Montoya, another security officer at the Insight Center, was dressed differently from Avery. Instead of the standard all-black uniform, he wore a gray short-sleeved dress shirt with jeans. It was supposed to be his night off, yet there he was, back at the Insight Center, likely having planned to take this particular night off for the Steady Progress Summit.

Montoya's posture was relaxed as he leaned over the railing, arms crossed, looking down upon the main floor, but his seemingly wandering eyes always fell back on Taylor and Radley.

Avery's lungs burned. The stitch in his ribs stabbed harder yet. Every one of his forty-seven years made themselves known, laughing at him, taunting.

But he pressed on, around a pod of vendors selling books, past a cluster of people holding an impromptu meditation session, and finally emerged at the far side of the floor. His heart pounded in his ears. The stitch in his ribs gave another sharp jab.

And the scene that greeted him was an anticlimax. A pair of younger security guards, barely out of their teens, stood lounging by the metal door where the tall man had disappeared a few minutes earlier. Jentsch and Wilmet. Assholes, the both of them. Their expressions shifted from boredom to amusement as they took in Avery's disheveled appearance.

One of them, Wilmet, a lanky youth with a smirk that seemed permanently scrawled on his face, stepped forward.

"Too late, Malone," he said, pointing at the door. "Our two mystery men already left the building. Cameras caught them slipping out a side exit."

Jentsch, a stocky blond with a snide grin, chimed in as he gave a theatrical glance to his Timex. "Yeah, and it looks like it's past your bedtime, too, old man. Shouldn't you be clocking out?"

Assholes.

The both of them.

Avery stole a look at the digital readout on Jentsch's Timex. The asshole was right; Avery's shift had officially ended five minutes ago. The dash through the crowd, chasing the tall, mysterious man, had been unpaid work.

Avery looked at Jentsch, then Wilmet. Without replying to either of them, he turned and left.

Behind him, the younger men laughed.

Avery stepped into the cool night air.

A few minutes earlier, he'd retraced his path across the Insight Center floor, this time at a slower pace. As he passed the spot where he had earlier seen Taylor Perrine talking with Tom Radley, he found they were both gone, as was Taylor's redheaded friend/protector.

Avery had arrived too late. He should have approached them first, not chased after the tall guy.

Now, as he stood dwarfed by the vastness of the Insight Center, looking out on the blanket of cars in the parking lot—windshields and paint jobs glistening under the lamp poles—Jentsch and Wilmet's taunts echoed in his mind.

He sighed.

...then shoved his hands in his uniform's pants pockets and started for the employee parking lot.

A few moments later, he was in the Cavalier. It smelled like McDonald's. Yesterday's Big Mac. No ... that was the day *before* yesterday.

He let his head sink into the headrest, his hand sweeping over his shaved scalp, still damp with the sweat of his recent pursuit. Damn out-of-shape old man. His breathing hadn't even fully recovered yet.

But he'd given it his all. He'd been chasing more than just the tall, mysterious man; he'd been chasing the faint, almost absurd hope of joining forces with the stranger to unravel Tom Radley's dealings with Taylor Perrine.

It had been a silly notion.

His mind replayed the scene of Taylor Perrine on the convention floor, ensnared in Radley's charismatic trap. He thought about what Montoya had told him. Montoya's insinuations about his and Radley's intentions were ominous; if there was any truth to them, Miss Perrine could face real danger.

If Avery could have intervened and somehow unraveled Montoya and Radley's plans, perhaps he could have stopped them, not only saving someone from a wicked fate but saving *a famous and influential* someone.

It would have been a chance for Avery to make a real difference.

To be a hero.

But the opportunity had passed. He'd been too late.

He exhaled. Took a sip of flat Coca-Cola from the can that had sat in the drink holder all day. And put his hand on the gear selector.

...and stopped.

There.

A few rows down. Two men in a brand-new Infiniti Q45.

It was the tall mystery man.

And the guy the man had been chasing!

Together. Holding an uncharged conversation. The tall guy was behind the wheel; the other was in the passenger seat.

What the hell?

Avery straightened, leaned toward the windshield, squinted.

As he watched their exchange—which seemed serious but controlled—Avery realized something.

This was a second chance.

Life doesn't toss too many of those in a guy's direction.

So he let his hand drop onto the gear selector, leaving it poised and ready. While he watched.

And waited.

14

Earlier, Silence had chased Nate Fuller, attempting to catch him before the man fled his house. Silence hadn't made it in time, and Fuller escaped in an old Ford, speeding down a gravel alleyway.

Now, Nate Fuller was sitting in Silence's automobile with him.

What a difference an hour can make.

The Q45's engine idled. In the passenger seat, Fuller's profile creased at his forehead and around his eyes. His hands fidgeted.

"It's all a front," Fuller said. "Lennox's group, it's not ... it's not about preventing suicide. It's the opposite; I'm sure of it." He gulped. "He's leading them to death, like a modern-day Jonestown."

His words had come out choppy, rushed. It was clear he had a lot more to say. Silence faced him and said, "Talk," as gently as his ruined voice would allow.

Fuller brought his attention up from his hands, which were running loops over themselves on his lap, and looked out into the brightly lit parking lot, the convention center towering above, the city's skyline sparkling behind that.

"Maya, my sister-in-law," he said, not turning to face Silence but keeping his gaze locked through the windshield, "she's with them. With Lennox's group. And she won't talk to me, not for months. Won't answer my calls, nothing. I'm scared shitless about her, about what he might … what Lennox might be planning."

There was a tremor in Fuller's voice, raw and unmasked. Beneath the surface, a tumult was bubbling, infused with valuable information. But the pot was ready to boil over, so Silence would need to play this carefully to extract all the intel.

For now, no prompting. He remained quiet. Silence's gaze lingered on Fuller, his muteness a well-honed tool, prying without words. It wasn't long before the hush urged Fuller to speak.

"After my brother died," Fuller began. "Maya and I, we … we were grieving. One night, we were crying, hugging, and it just happened. I … I kissed her."

The confession hung heavy between them, floating right there between the seats.

Damn…

Silence frequently worked with people who had suffered recent tragedies. Often, they did unexpected things. And often, they did things they would later regret. It wasn't the first time he'd seen someone torn apart like Fuller was.

Fuller's hands clenched into fists, knuckles white.

"It shouldn't have happened. I betrayed him—my own brother!—even if he was already gone." He sighed. "I played it off. Maya and I *both* waved it off. She accepted my apology. But after that … she changed. She just withdrew from everything." His hands looped faster and faster in his lap. "And then she found Lennox."

"She changed how?" Silence said.

Fuller's gaze drifted. "She became distant, introspective. Before, she was grieving but present. After, it was like she was looking for something, something to fill what we'd … what *I'd* broken." His eyes met Silence's again. "Next thing I knew, she was going to Colin Lennox's meetings. And then she was gone, just … gone."

"Tell me about…" Silence said and swallowed. "Lennox."

"He has a way about him. His voice is all weird and unnatural-sounding, and…" Fuller trailed off, his eyes flashing to Silence's throat in a moment of faux-pas-based regret. After a beat, he continued. "But when he speaks, it's like he's reaching inside you, rearranging things. I went to one meeting, just to see. The things he said, they sounded good, but it was all wrong. Underneath the words, there was something else, like a current, pulling you in."

Fuller shook his head, and Silence could see him replaying the memories, those telltale little twitches of the eyes.

"He talks about transcendence," Fuller continued, "about leaving pain behind. But the more I watched, the more I saw that it's not about overcoming despair; it's about succumbing to it, letting it consume you until there's nothing left to do but end it all."

"You think he has..." Silence said, swallowed. "Something planned?"

"I *know* he does. He's building up to something. Big. Tonight. A grand finale, just like his mentor Jordan Havelock had planned." He turned to Silence. "*They're all gonna die.* Including Maya."

Silence considered this.

And it reminded him of the audio log, of the last two year-old message from the previous version of Colin Lennox. This Lennox—Special Agent Lennox—had said his next move would be to meet with Jordan Havelock's followers to see the man's influence on their psyches.

Given what Fuller had just said about Lennox, the following entry could prove insightful. Silence pressed *PLAY*.

It's November 10th, Lennox reporting. The past few days have been ... eye-opening. I've spoken with several of Havelock's followers, and their stories are compelling. They talk about finding purpose, overcoming their darkest moments. It's hard not to feel moved.

I'm starting to question the Bureau's stance on this. Are we chasing ghosts here? Havelock's methods might be unconventional, but the results ... they're tangible. People are improving, finding hope.

I find myself at a crossroads. My duty as an agent is to protect, but who am I protecting here? From what? Havelock isn't the monster we presumed. There's a sincerity in his approach that's hard to dismiss.

This isn't just another case for me anymore. It's a journey into the complex nature of belief and influence. I need to tread carefully, balance my duty with the truth unfolding before me.

"Who was that?" Fuller said.

"Lennox. Before..." Silence said and swallowed. "The accident."

"Oh ... shit."

"He was undercover..." Silence said, swallowed. "In Havelock's group." Another swallow. "Talk."

Fuller gave a dark smirk of recognition, taking Silence's meaning.

"Talk, huh? Talk about Jordan Havelock." He released a long sigh that whistled through his teeth. "Yeah, I was a part of Havelock's original group two years ago. I was suicidal, like Maya is now, but ... but for different reasons. I was fed up, man. Just with life, you know? This sick existence."

He waved a hand toward the windshield. Whether he was indicating the Insight Center or the skyline beyond or the very air outside, Silence couldn't be sure.

"It's a sick, decrepit world we've inherited, isn't it? But ... when my brother died, I felt what *real* pain is like. I got over my self-pity. I know it's ironic, my trying to stop Maya from doing what I wanted to do only two years earlier, but..."

He trailed off, didn't finish.

"Havelock," Silence prompted, leading the conversation back in his desired direction. He swallowed. "Describe."

Fuller gave a shrug. "I mean, what can I say? The guy was charismatic, charming, just like his protégé, Lennox. And he was going to kill all of his followers, too, just like Lennox has planned. Had those gas cans not exploded that night two years ago, Havelock was going to douse everyone in the gas, have them light themselves on fire—self-immolation."

"Cops, feds, media, academics..." Silence said, swallowed. "All say Havelock was clean."

"Man, I was there!" Fuller's voice surged, almost reaching a shout, the most animated Silence had seen him. He whipped around on Silence, scowled. "What the hell is this? I thought you were here to help. I don't care what those other people said or continue to say. Maybe they're still brainwashed. Maybe Lennox has gotten to them. I don't know. All I know is Jordan Havelock was going to kill everyone that night. And tonight, Lennox is going to finish the job."

Silence pondered this.

"You went to..." he said and swallowed. "One of Lennox's meetings?"

Fuller nodded. "Yeah. The first one. I got an automatic invite since I was a Havelock survivor. But ... Lennox was just too much like Havelock. It was ... trippy." A pause. "I wouldn't have dreamed Maya would have reached out to a man like that. She used my connection to make contact with him."

Fuller pointed at the audio recorder in the center console.

"That's what Havelock did to people," Fuller whispered. "He got inside your head. He got inside *Lennox's* head, and Lennox is finishing the man's work tonight."

Silence put his hand on the gear selector, ready to act immediately. "Where?"

Fuller pointed through the windshield.

Silence looked.

A few blocks away, poking out from a treeline, was the roof of a disheveled warehouse.

Silence took a moment to study the Insight Center, towering over them, then did a quick assessment of the distance separating it from the warehouse—less than half a mile, exceptionally close, especially in a city this size.

"Convenient."

Fuller gave a gloomy chuckle. "Yeah. Convenient is right. The Steady Progress Summit has been planned for a year. Lennox *purposefully* set up close to the Insight Center so he could poach people on his big night, another desperate soul or two to take down with him."

Poaching souls...

Silence's mind flashed back to the convention center floor.

Taylor Perrine.

Suicidal.

Arms folded over herself, avoiding the animated man's gaze, the man in the flashy blue suit.

He turned to Fuller.

"Tom Radley," he said, swallowed. "One of Lennox's?"

Fuller shook his head. "I mean, I've never heard the name, but that doesn't mean he's not one of Lennox's. Why? Who is he?"

Silence didn't respond.

He put the Infiniti into gear, pulled out, and started across the parking lot, keeping the rusty warehouse roof in his line of sight.

Fuller's words echoed in Silence's mind: not recognizing Tom Radley's name didn't rule out Radley's connection to Lennox's crew.

Radley...

As Silence accelerated away, a tight knot formed in his stomach. A quick glance in the rearview mirror presented the brightly lit facade of the Insight Center, and with it, an image of Taylor Perrine flashed through his mind. He was leaving her there, possibly exposed to danger.

He squeezed the steering wheel tighter.

Now, he had one more reason to stop Colin Lennox.

15

Avery's pulse raced as he parked the beat-up Cavalier, placing it two rows away from the sleek Infiniti he had tailed. The Infiniti had already settled into its spot moments before.

Dusk's final rays bathed the parking lot, casting a soft glow on the Infiniti and the other vehicles—a few dozen of them, far more than Avery would have expected in a cracked and weed-infested patch of seemingly deserted urban wasteland. The people exiting the vehicles were all converging on a warehouse complex, its pair of buildings marked by flaking paint and sealed-off windows.

But it wasn't the dilapidated buildings alone that set Avery's nerves on edge; it was the lone figure standing guard at the warehouse's sole entrance. Clad in a maroon henley and black jeans, the man was motionless, exuding the watchful aura of a seasoned bouncer.

Avery shifted his attention from the guard back to the Infiniti while his own car emitted a quiet tick as the engine cooled down. The Infiniti had been stationary for a short while now, its lights extinguished, everything still.

Inside that car was Avery's reason for being here—the tall stranger, the man Avery had observed at the Insight Center, who had almost stepped in between Taylor Perrine and Tom Radley before being distracted, chasing after the frazzled man who was now with him in the Infiniti.

The tall man had the air of a professional—a city detective or maybe even a fed. Avery saw in him a potential ally. Once Avery made contact, he planned to share everything he knew about Tom Radley and Darren Montoya. This was Avery's chance to become a key player in a team—a team *he* would form to save someone in trouble.

Then, Avery would be a hero.

A hero like his brothers, Calvin and Flynn.

"Calvin the Cop" and "Flynn the Fireman," that's what Avery called them. How perfect that their names started with the appropriate letters, C and F.

What would that make Avery, then?

"Avery the Amateur"?

"Avery the Avoider"?

Avery wasn't cut from the same heroic cloth as his brothers—Calvin, with his unwavering commitment to justice and bravery on the streets, and Flynn, who unflinchingly dashed into blazing buildings to save others. They were embodiments of courage and selflessness. Messiahs.

Avery had long harbored dreams of heroism and had no good reason for delaying for so many years. Call it subconscious cowardice.

Perhaps even conscious.

It wasn't until his late thirties that Avery mustered up the courage to chase his dream, applying to join the police force. But his aspirations were swiftly derailed during training; his physical conditioning wasn't up to snuff. By the time he got into shape, he was past the upper age limit, forty years old.

Shortly after this setback, he found work at the Insight Center. The job came with a uniform and a badge, but to Avery, they felt unearned, lacking the authenticity and honor of the uniforms and badges his brothers, Cal and Flynn, wore.

Now, Avery's one chance to achieve heroism was in an unconventional way, outside the traditional paths of organized heroics. His opportunity to be a hero would have to come through a singular, brave act.

An act like saving someone from Tom Radley and Darren Montoya.

Avery shifted in his seat, his hand resting on the keys still dangling from the ignition. Across the lot, the Infiniti's doors swung open. The tall man emerged from the driver's side, his companion from the passenger's side. They started across the parking lot toward the warehouse and the guard at the door.

Avery's gut knotted as he watched them.

He's getting away, Avery told himself. *Move! He knows about Radley. You followed the guy here; now, go talk to him!*

Avery didn't move.

He would, though. In just a second.

Just one more second.

Dammit, Montoya! If the guy hadn't been so boastful, Avery wouldn't even be aware of the threat Tom Radley posed to Taylor Perrine—and he wouldn't be sitting here, wrestling with indecision.

Two weeks prior, during a mortgage brokers symposium, while Avery and Montoya patrolled the Insight Center's perimeter, Montoya had let slip to Avery about a new alliance with someone named Tom Radley. Montoya had divulged far more than he should have.

That's the trouble with pride. It talks too much.

And Montoya was nothing if not prideful.

Outside, the tall man and his companion continued across the lot, disappearing into the shadows.

And Avery remained rooted to his seat.

He wanted to leap into action, to explode out of his car and head straight for the warehouse. But as the seconds ticked by, he remained seated.

16

Silence and Fuller navigated the crumbling asphalt of the parking lot, heading toward the compound.

The warehouse loomed ahead, a once sturdy construction now succumbing to the ravages of time, its façade marred by peeling paint and oversized tear stains of iron oxide. Attached to its western side was a low, one-story building. This structure, which Silence presumed was a former factory or office space or combination thereof, mirrored the warehouse's derelict state. Its flat roof and plain walls hinted at a practical past, now overshadowed by the relentless decay that had also befallen its taller companion.

Despite the place's forsaken appearance, there were signs of life. Silence counted fifty-six cars in the lot, many parked at odd angles to avoid the potholes. There was also a guard—who wore black jeans and a maroon henley shirt—standing by the warehouse's sole door, a windowless slab of steel on the otherwise blank front side.

Additionally, the low drone of machinery filled the air, a sound that might have been mistaken for engines at work. But Silence recognized it for what it was—the thrum of gas-powered generators. Lennox was breathing electrical life back into the deceased structures.

As they walked, Fuller fished a pack of cigarettes from his pocket, tapped one out. Toyed with it. Brought it to his lips. Toyed with his lighter. And finally lit the damn cigarette.

A long drag. A long hold. And a long release, using the corner of his mouth to direct the smoke away from Silence. A small, thoughtful gesture.

The nicotine seemed to calm his nerves a bit, but he still looked like he had something to say, despite keeping his eyes forward, never looking over at Silence. Finally, the words came.

"If we do find her, I'm not sure what I'll say. It's been..." He had to think for a moment. "Jeez, two weeks now since she stopped taking my calls. Things were never the same between Maya and me since she kissed me. Wait! I mean, I mean since *I* kissed her... Ah, shit."

His head dropped. He exhaled. Another drag from the cigarette, another cloud of smoke.

Finally, he turned to face Silence. "Okay, I lied about one thing earlier. I'm sorry. It's something I've had to lie about for a while. The kiss, it happened. But Maya initiated it. After Chuck passed, everything was chaos in the Fuller family. And Maya had always worked so hard to be accepted by them, my family—when she and Chuck were dating and even after they got married. I mean, she's a good person, but she can be a bit standoffish. And there's the whole interracial couple thing. Not everyone in the family approved of it. I know, I know. There are some real jackasses among the Fullers.

"The kiss would have been one of those awkward life things had Kaley not walked in on us after Maya's ... lips were on mine. Kaley's a younger cousin, thirteen, gossipy. Of course, then the entire family knew. So..." He took another drag. "I told everyone I instigated it. Now I'm the black sheep, not Maya. I'm the awful pervert who took advantage of the emotionally distraught widow of his recently-departed brother."

Damn.

Suddenly, Silence had a new respect for Fuller. On the surface, he could seem like just a frazzled office drone with a bad smoking habit and a filthy house. But this was a man of quiet, unassuming honor, ready to shoulder blame for the sake of another.

Fuller flicked the cigarette away, shoved his hands in his pockets, and looked ahead at the warehouse.

"I don't know if I can get you in," Fuller said. "Lennox has a set list of attendees for his meetings. I'm a Havelock survivor, so I'll be cleared, but I'm not sure if I'm permitted a guest since—"

Silence cut him off.

"Don't worry about it," he said.

Fuller opened his mouth to object, but Silence didn't wait for the words. He slipped into the shadows, skirting the warehouse's decaying wall, going for the adjoining building, leaving Fuller standing there, his intended protest dying on his lips.

Alone now, at the edge of the poorly lit parking lot, Silence reached into his pocket and pulled out the audio player. From the start of the mission, he'd known there would be scant opportunities to work his way through all the log entries. Once inside Lennox's stronghold, his free time would be even scarcer. He had to take advantage of every free moment.

So he fitted the earbuds, and with a press of a button, he was back inside the mind of two-years-earlier Colin Lennox.

Lennox here, November 14th. Things have changed. The more time I spend around Havelock and his followers, the more I understand their perspective. Havelock isn't just helping people; he's transforming them. The Bureau doesn't see it. They're blinded by prejudice and fear.

Silence slipped through the shadows of the northern side of the building, noting that the doors and windows were all sealed tight in a hodgepodge mix of steel bars, sheet metal, chains, latches, bolts, barbed wire, and particleboard. There were copious PRIVATE PROPERTY and NO TRESPASSING signs, dry-rotted and sun-damaged, the formerly red proclamations faded to benign pink, their white backgrounds now tinted yellow.

He moved around the corner and surveyed the western side of the building, taking in the layout, pinpointing spots where security cameras might be hidden, and scanning for any hint of guard movement or canine patrols. He searched for a potential entry point, calculating the risks, mapping out a strategy.

The audio continued, Lennox's voice growing more impassioned.

We're interfering in something we don't understand. Havelock's work, it's … it's remarkable. The secrecy, the exclusivity—it's not a sign of something sinister. It's a necessary part of their journey, a safeguard against judgment and misunderstanding.

Silence's gaze settled on a section of the wall particularly ravaged by the years—a potential entry point. At the same time, he mulled over the intel filtering through his earpiece. Lennox's shifting perspective was a familiar tale of blind faith, a dangerous road many had walked before, usually to their downfall.

He thought of the silver-haired man in the photos he'd studied with Doc Hazel. That smug grin. Confident stance. Piercing blue eyes.

Jordan Havelock.

Deceased. Gone for two years.

But the rot of his influence had lingered. It had infected Lennox, who was now finishing the deadly agenda Havelock had left behind.

Silence felt a slight wobble as he ran his hand along the rusted metal wall. He looked down. There was a warped panel near the ground, its curved edge revealing a gap. A slice of light beckoned through this fissure, an invitation into the building's hidden depths.

Perfect.

As Silence crouched near the gap, FBI Special Agent Colin Lennox's words echoed in his head. Each subsequent audio log unraveled the story of a man's spiraling descent, pulled deeper and deeper into Jordan Havelock's manipulative grasp. A narrative had formed: a young person's identity being systematically dismantled and replaced against his will, reshaped by forces beyond his control.

In a sick way, it reminded Silence of his own situation with the Watchers. They had obliterated his original identity, Jake Rowe, and in its place forged Silence Jones. But the transformation was never finished, always subject to the Watchers' whims and adjustments. It was a constant meddling, a game of manipulation that left him perpetually unsettled, deprived of any true sense of peace.

Of course, they'd recently offered him *momentary* peace.

The one-year sabbatical.

The thought of a sabbatical, a pause from his life of vigilantism, struck him as fundamentally wrong. If he wasn't an Asset, then what the hell was he?

The thinking. The investigation. The hunt. The kill. These were now embedded in his core.

A righteous assassin. An Asset. This was what he'd become. This was his semblance of an existence.

Silence zeroed in on the warped section of paneling, a nondescript point along the warehouse's perimeter. He reached his hand into the gap, pulled.

In his ears, Lennox's voice was now imbued with a fervent tone that carried a distinct hint of reverence.

I'm finding it harder to justify this investigation. We're not just watching a group; we're intruding on a profound transformational process. Havelock's intentions are pure, and we're standing in the way of something extraordinary.

Silence applied steady pressure to the warped paneling, feeling the rusted metal give way under his firm grip. It gave a reverberant moan. Silence widened the gap.

Lennox's voice continued, impassioned and unyielding.

I never thought I'd say this, but maybe we're the ones in the wrong here. Havelock deserves a chance to continue his work, free from our interference.

A shuffle, and the entry came to an end.

Silence pressed *STOP*.

He stared at the audio recorder. Bounced it a couple of times in his palm, feeling its weight, considering the message it had just relayed. Then he stowed it away.

Easing his body through the narrow gap in the metal siding, contorting slightly to fit, Silence stepped through the space and emerged in an empty hallway. He stood.

Immediately, a musty odor of disuse assailed him—a blend of old paper, rotten wood, and the acrid bite of rust. Debris was strewn across the floor. Above, exposed pipes and ductwork ran the length of the ceiling, intersecting with the wiring that had once powered the building. In the corner was a security camera with a glowing red light; Silence lowered his face.

The original light fixtures hung lifelessly, offering nothing. Instead, Lennox had improvised a ramshackle illumination system. Bare bulbs dangled from wires stapled along the wall in a haphazard non-pattern. The lights flickered, revealing dancing flecks of dust.

A different, brighter light source glowed from beyond the turn at the hallway's terminus. Silence moved in that direction, dodging puddles and rotten pallets.

Approaching the corner, he slowed and cautiously peered around. At the end of another hallway, a row of opaque, industrial-style windows lined the wall, lit up from the inside. The space opened dramatically upward, showcasing the warehouse's lofty height. Through an open sliding door, Silence saw the main warehouse floor, now an impromptu assembly room with rows of folding chairs facing a makeshift stage—a jerry-rigged affair of particleboard that bore a battered podium, likely salvaged from a dumpster or landfill.

The space was abuzz with activity. About fifty people were scattered in quiet conversation outside the open doorway and throughout the warehouse's expansive floor.

Silence had found Lennox's followers.

Among them were several men clad in maroon henley shirts and black jeans, mirroring the attire of the guard Silence had seen outside; these were Lennox's enforcers.

His eyes roved over the people, searching for any signs of membership identification—nametags, lanyards, wristbands. Nothing. No overt markers of allegiance. Other than the possibility of ID cards—which Silence assumed they would have presented to the guard outside—these individuals bore no distinguishable branding. The group wasn't large; it was conceivable that Silence could be spotted as an interloper. However, according to Fuller, Lennox's group was known for its high membership turnover.

Silence would risk it.

He rounded the corner, heading toward the meeting, sticking to the shadows to evade the scrutiny of the guys in maroon shirts and another security camera.

As he moved, he continued visually searching Lennox's followers, this time for a specific face. A mental image of her resurfaced, drawn from the photograph and textual information included in Silence's mission materials.

Five-foot-four. One hundred ten pounds. Shoulder-length hair. Indian American.

He couldn't find Maya Fuller.

Silence scanned the faces once more, this time for Maya's brother-in-law.

He couldn't find Nathan Fuller either.

There was a smell, and it grew stronger the closer he drew to the crowd. It took Silence only a moment to recognize it: incense. The earthy scent was not at all unfamiliar to him. Many of the stores C.C. enjoyed, when she was indulging her more hippie-oriented side, had burnt incense—crystal shops, traditional yoga supply stores, and the like.

As Silence drew closer, the collective murmur intensified, and the crowd, as if responding to a silent cue, began to shuffle through the doorway. Tilting his head to avoid the gaze of Lennox's men, who were now flanking the entrance, Silence flowed with the group onto the warehouse floor—the makeshift auditorium. Everyone settled into the metal folding chairs. Silence followed suit, taking a seat in the back.

His eyes adapted to the brighter environment. Overhead, the light fixtures were, once again, non-functioning, their use supplanted by Lennox's makeshift solution—rows of bare bulbs strung along the walls, the same as the setup in the hallway.

But it wasn't the wall-dangling bulbs that heightened the illumination in this space relative to the hallways; rather, it was the harsh light from tripod-mounted construction lamps dotting the perimeter, their orange extension cords snaking to the back of the space, feeding off the generators that Silence could hear humming just on the other side of the wall.

Also posted in the back, on either side of the stage, were a dozen five-gallon red metal gasoline cans.

...just like the ones that had supposedly exploded accidentally in Jordan Havelock's basement two years earlier.

It was conceivable the gas cans were a fuel source for the generators outside, but the coincidence of the similarity to Havelock's setup would be astronomical.

And Silence's disbelief in coincidences bordered on hatred.

The stage was stark, unadorned save for a lonely microphone waiting on the podium. The chairs facing it were arranged in a subtle arch, adding to the sense of unearned grandiosity.

Sitting there, Silence felt the weight of the charged air, which smelled of the incense, its source hidden somewhere. This was the epicenter of Lennox's domain. Every folding chair was a pew for the converted, the desperate, those clawing for a promise of something greater.

Silence surveyed the crowd. These were faces sculpted by harsh realities, eyes that betrayed sleep-deprived nights and minds besieged with anxieties. Some were emaciated, their pallid complexions stark under the unforgiving artificial light. Others carried their burdens visibly, carved in the deep lines across their foreheads and the downturn of their lips.

His eyes landed on Nate Fuller, seated on the far side of the area. Fuller looked in his direction. Their eyes met. Fuller's expression registered surprise. For only a moment. Then he quickly composed himself. He gave a tiny nod. Silence returned it and looked away.

That was one Fuller accounted for.

But where was the other?

Silence did a visual sweep of the group, searching for any signs of a petite Indian American woman, finding no matches.

The hum in the crowd intensified. The woman beside Silence was visibly agitated, her hands rubbing her knees in a rhythm of growing anxiety. Both the mission materials and Nathan Fuller had alluded that Lennox was planing something momentous for tonight's gathering.

Fuller believed it was going to be mass suicide. Self-immolation.

Silence glanced at the gas cans.

Then back to the woman beside him. Her hands worked her knees faster and faster as she stared forward at the stage, bug-eyed. The crowd's murmuring swelled around them.

At that moment, the lights began to dim.

17

Beckwith's new employer had names for the rooms in his overtaken factory complex.

Lennox called this space the "ready room."

Beckwith stepped out of the dank hallway and into an unexpected haven. Red velvet curtains, thick and heavy, hung against the stark metal walls. Armchairs, their plush leather worn and soft, were positioned here and there, several facing tables loaded with magazines and paperbacks—islands of comfort on the concrete floor. The centerpiece of this bizarre domain was an oversized mirror ringed with bright bulbs, like something straight out of a Broadway dressing room.

Beckwith closed the distance, stopping a few yards short, and waited.

Under the harsh glare of the mirror lights, Lennox's scars became a piece of modern art, the details thrown into sharp contrast, sparkling the peaks, shadowing the valleys. Nowhere was this effect more pronounced than on the trio of deep fissures that slashed across his neck.

The scars were a brutal biography of survival. Beckwith often had to remind himself of that. Lennox was cunning, manipulative, and ruthless but also undeniably gritty.

The man had survived a *freaking gunshot*. And an explosion. And the subsequent fires that ravaged his face, ruined one of his eyes.

No matter how much of a snake the man had turned into, Beckwith had to give him some credit. Colin Lennox was a survivor through and through.

There was an undeniable vibrancy about Lennox, a spirit at odds with the battered exterior; it radiated from his very being. He shook hands vigorously, laughed regularly, smiled constantly. He moved. He glided. He bounced. He even danced.

When Colin Lennox entered a room, when he first opened his mouth to hiss out a few of his serpentine words through his perpetual showman's grin, the room seemed to bend around him, his charisma altering the very atmosphere of the space.

Beckwith watched the man now from his supplicant-appropriate distance. The dynamic was clear: Beckwith was the muscle, the enforcer, and one of a pair of confidants. Lennox had needed at least a couple of people to understand the true depths of what he was doing, where the charade began and ended ... and where it melded with reality.

The trust Lennox had given him was an honor of sorts. But it didn't change the essentials. In this intricate dance of power and control, Lennox led every step. Beckwith remained simply the muscle, the enforcer.

Beckwith waited, but Lennox showed no sign of turning around. Unable to restrain himself any longer, Beckwith let the urgency take over.

"Lennox," Beckwith said, his voice steady despite the tension. "The tall guy you're interested in, the one I've been following, he's—"

"The operator," Lennox hissed, not bothering to turn away from the mirror as he made more adjustments to his hair.

That was all Lennox ever called him: "the operator."

"Yes, the operator," Beckwith said. "Um, he's ... he's here. Right now, blending in with the crowd."

Beckwith's words hung in the air. He awaited something momentous.

Instead, there was a non-reaction.

Lennox, still lost in his reflection, kept on primping. The brush in his hand continued its steady motion, tracing the contours of his scarred face. He didn't turn around.

Finally, he said, "Good."

Feeling a surge of boldness, Beckwith inched closer and gestured toward the monitor on a small table by the mirror. The screen, split into quadrants, displayed black-and-white footage from four of the facility's many video feeds. While the "control room," another of Lennox's strategically named areas, displayed the full array of video feeds, this setup focused on just a select few.

One quadrant showed the meeting space on the warehouse floor. At that moment, it captured Lennox's followers seated in the rows of folding chairs, the lights having just dimmed for Lennox's impending appearance, all eyes fixed on the stage in eager anticipation. Among them, in a back row, sat the tall man Beckwith had been doggedly pursuing.

The man on the monitor, seated among the others, staring at the stage like the rest of them, seemed to be a still point in a turning world. Dark eyes, dark hair, broad shoulders. He sat motionless, yet there was an undeniable sense of readiness about him, a coiled energy. Dangerous.

"He's here!" Beckwith repeated, stabbing his finger toward the monitor. "In the crowd!"

Finally, Lennox stopped primping and faced him, grinning.

"I said," he began, stretching the S in that snakelike way of his—*sssssaid*, "good."

In that moment, facing Lennox, Beckwith felt the full force of the man's presence. An intangible force. Wicked charisma. A power that had drawn the fifty-odd souls on the monitor into his orbit.

...and kept them there.

Even for someone like Beckwith, who had navigated his way through life's darkest corners, this power of Lennox's was overwhelming. Faced with it, Beckwith felt an unsettling helplessness, a biting reminder of his own comparative insignificance.

"Come on," Lennox said, turning for the door. "Follow me."

For a moment, Beckwith remained rooted to the spot, bathed in the harsh light of the mirror.

The relentless shadow in Beckwith's mind surged to the forefront: his forced loyalty to Lennox, a bond forged from the necessity of survival that collided brutally with his deep-seated desire for change.

Lennox embodied everything Beckwith had grown to loathe in his life. The revulsion he felt toward his new employer, toward himself for being a part of this twisted narrative, was a constant, increasingly unbearable burden.

But Beckwith had no choice but to follow his new leader. Lennox knew Beckwith's secret, and the snake man kept this secret stowed away like ammunition, one special bullet he could release if the need arose.

Lennox had said, *Follow me.*

So Beckwith followed Lennox out the door into the dim hallway.

18

It had been several minutes since the lights had dimmed.

Colin Lennox truly was a showman.

As he waited, Silence kept the two massive sliding doors—one on each side of the warehouse floor, one closed, one partially open—in his peripheral vision, waiting for movement, waiting for Maya Fuller to appear.

But the doors hadn't opened. Maya Fuller hadn't appeared.

He did another scan of the surrounding crowd, now buzzing with edgy anticipation, on the verge of erupting. He considered the chance that Maya had ducked down earlier, unintentionally evading his notice, or had been obscured from view. It was a long shot, but it merited a double-check.

Silence looked for Maya's features in the faint lighting—the mocha skin, shoulder-length hair, and petite frame.

She wasn't there.

For a moment, he feared the worst, that Maya, unable to endure the wait for the event, might have taken a drastic step, perhaps ending her own life before Lennox's meeting had even commenced.

Shaking off these thoughts, he redirected his attention to the opposite side of the seating area. There, he spotted Nate Fuller and wondered if Fuller's mind was being tormented by the same possibilities.

But when he spotted Fuller—who was staring forward at the stage like the others, albeit with zero fervor—the man's face was expressionless. Undoubtedly, he'd registered Maya's absence and likely entertained a dreadful notion similar to Silence's. But evidently, he'd remained stoic.

Feeling Silence's gaze, Fuller turned, and their eyes met.

Still nothing.

Still that blank stare.

He gave Silence another discreet, barely noticeable nod, mirroring the one he'd given earlier. Silence returned the nod and turned away.

Another dark thought materialized. What if Maya was indeed here but not among the crowd? Fuller had mentioned losing contact with Maya. Maybe she'd attended one of Lennox's gatherings and never left.

Maybe she was somewhere in the rear of the building.

Maybe she wasn't the only one...

Silence filed the theory in the back of his mind.

As his eyes swept across the group again, he did another search, this time for a new person.

He looked for Taylor Perrine.

But she, too, was absent from the crowd.

He'd now searched for two people among Lennox's followers, coming up empty both times. The first absence was a disappointment; the second, a relief.

He considered Taylor again. Her presence at the convention center had been memorable, marked by a blend of grace and underlying distress, an aura of quiet turmoil. He recalled the image of her in conversation with a man whose presence was starkly contrasting—sharp, predatory, exuding a dangerous air.

Tom Radley.

Silence was sure this man was one of Colin Lennox's associates, though his attire—a designer blue suit—set him apart from Lennox's usual maroon-henley-and-black-jeans-clad henchmen.

He remembered Taylor Perrine's protective friend. The redhead. Kori.

Kori's words about Taylor resurfaced in Silence's mind, sketching a portrait of vulnerability. He envisioned a woman beleaguered by life's harshness, teetering on the brink of despair. Such vulnerability was exactly what predators like Lennox exploited. The ultimate target would be someone like Taylor Perrine, who was not only damaged but *prominent*.

His thoughts then drifted to a different Colin Lennox—the younger one, who had once served as an FBI special agent. Silence mentally replayed a fragment of the latest audio log he had listened to, letting it echo in his mind.

Havelock's intentions are pure, and we're standing in the way of something extraordinary, younger Lennox had said. *I never thought I'd say this, but maybe we're the ones in the wrong here. Havelock deserves a chance to continue his work, free from our interference.*

Silence had never met the man, never even seen him, never heard the infamous, snake-like voice. That would change soon when Lennox appeared on stage. Still, the younger voice in the recording was a far cry from the modern-day Lennox Silence knew from reports and briefings—a different person.

In the dimness of the warehouse-turned-exhibition-hall setting, Silence sensed the overpowering effect of Lennox's influence surrounding him, the seductive pull of his promise in the crowd's energy. He looked at them now and watched anticipation shiver through the crowd, a taut string waiting to be plucked.

In the eager faces surrounding him, he caught the same intensity he'd heard in Special Agent Lennox's voice when he talked about Jordan Havelock—a kind of unwavering focus, almost an obsession. Lennox, once under Havelock's spell, was now casting the same magic himself.

C.C.'s voice cut through his thoughts. *You're in a loop, love.*

She had a point.

Silence's thoughts often raced in circles, especially when he was in high-stress situations—like now, waiting with a crowd of Lennox's devotees for the man to take the stage and start a meeting that could very well end in attempted mass suicide.

To snap out of it, his mind drifted to something he hadn't considered in a while, at least an hour.

The Watchers' Code Red.

Again, this mission presented him with a coincidence: the Code Red coincided with his Colin Lennox assignment, with Silence directly linked to the Code Red situation.

Silence didn't need to remind himself that coincidences were as make-believe as the Easter Bunny.

There was a link he was missing, some sort of connection.

A suicide cult led by the scarred survivor of a separate suicide cult that dissolved—calamitously—two years earlier.

And...

A Code Red—an alarm signaling the Watchers' confidential data being digitally extracted from their secure networks.

The only discernible pattern in this Code Red was the collection of meaningless intel related to an old operation: Silence's second-ever assignment, the elimination of a State Department official.

So, what the hell was the connection?

Silence's thoughts were a dark tide, pulling him back to the old mission.

A different year.

A different lifetime...

There'd been the red leather office chair.

The click and the hum and the warm breeze as the house's heating system sprang to life.

There'd been the wait.

The photos on the wall. The more important photos—the family photos—on the shelf.

More waiting.

And then Keane entered.

Dressed in a suit, jacket removed and slung over his shoulder. Sleeves rolled up. Top button undone. Tie loosened.

With a shit-what-a-day sigh, Keane approached the desk.

Then, from just a yard's distance, Silence burst from his cover behind the armchair.

Had Silence been authorized to shoot or stab or slice or snap a neck, it all could have been over in a flash.

But such methods were off the table.

Luckily, Keane's passion for martial arts would provide a believable cover for any contusions or scratches. But it also meant that Keane wouldn't go down easily.

Keane came at Silence with a side kick. Silence dodged it, getting in position for a left jab, which Keane parried.

Keane threw a series of swift jabs, which Silence deflected with equal agility. He countered with a sharp uppercut, clipping Keane under the chin. Keane landed a kick, but then a swift right hook from Silence grazed Keane's cheek, signaling a shift in the momentum.

Seizing the opportunity, Silence darted behind the other man. He locked his arms around Keane's neck, applying a chokehold.

Keane clawed at Silence's forearms.

Wet gasps. Desperate swipes.

But Silence's grip was unyielding, slowly squeezing the life out of Keane's throat.

It had been the only permitted method.

Not Silence's preferred method.

It took a while.

Longer than it should have.

When it was over, Silence stood, panting. He'd broken a sweat. He used his forearm to wipe it away, and as he pulled his arm to the side, his eyes caught the family pictures.

The wife. The son. The happy couple. The whole family.

At the end of the row of frames was a photo of the son, solo, sitting in front of a computer.

Oh, shit...

Silence looked down, confirmed. The computer in the photo was the same one sitting on the desk in front of Silence.

Shit...

Brendan Keane, seventeen. Silence had read up on him. A kid with his dad's knack for computers. In the picture, his hair was cut short. A black T-shirt with a red anarchy sign on it. He wasn't smiling; he was scowling.

Typical teenage angst.

Teenage. Nearing adulthood.

But still a kid.

Silence looked away from the pubescent glower, back to the body.

Keane's pants were wet at the crotch. Silence smelled piss.

Another long sigh.

Then, Silence hooked Keane beneath the armpits and lifted the body off the floor, moving it to the chair and beginning the preparations.

The crowd erupted into a frenzy. Silence's attention snapped forward as a door at the back of the space swung open. Two of Lennox's men—decked in those maroon henleys—flanked it.

This was it. Lennox was about to make his entrance.

The doorway remained tantalizingly still and dark. The guards were motionless.

Lennox was stretching this out for all it was worth.

He really was a showman.

Then it happened.

Colin Lennox breezed onto the stage.

The shift in the room hit like a sudden jolt, electric and raw. Faces that had been strained with the shadows of their personal hells now shone with something that might pass for hope, all thanks to the man making his way to the podium. Lennox's followers erupted in a chorus of fanatical devotion.

Silence sized him up. About five-foot-ten. Lean, the kind of build you'd expect from an ex-FBI agent. His face's twenty-something confident handsomeness couldn't be bothered by the scars on the left side. Medium blond hair. Eyes mismatched—one brown, the other an eerie pale blue, almost white.

But his vibe was what truly captured Silence's attention. The guy was all over the place, buzzing with energy, like one of those corporate motivational speakers or a too-enthusiastic JV basketball coach. Not the sort of aura you'd peg on an anti-suicide advocate.

His slick style aligned with that energy of his. The blond hair was perfectly cut, perfectly styled, combed just so. He sported a dark, stylish, slim-tailored suit, worn sans tie, collar laying casually open...

...not so very different from the blue suit worn by Tom Radley back at the Insight Center.

Lennox took his place at the podium. He raised his hands, grinning broader. His followers hushed.

He adjusted the microphone. Looked into the crowd. Grinned some more.

Lennox's voice, when it came, was so strange that Silence had to keep himself from jumping in his seat. In a bizarre moment of existentialism, he recognized that this must be the shock others felt upon hearing *his* voice for the first time.

The guy's voice was eerily serpentine, just as Fuller had described. It slithered, a blend of hisses and breathy tones, with each word undulating out of his mouth sinuously.

"We are gathered here," Lennox began, his mic-amplified hisses resonating against the warehouse's walls, "not as lost souls, but as seekers of truth."

The crowd swayed with his words. A few overly enthusiastic individuals barely contained their premature cheers.

Silence reeled with silent revulsion. He could see the threads of Lennox's influence, how they wrapped around the wills of his listeners, threads woven from despair and longing.

"And so we rise," Lennox said, "not just to face our fears, but to step beyond them, into a new existence!"

With a sweeping gesture, Lennox changed his stance, causing the construction lights to cast shifting shadows across his face. Silence noticed the trio of deep gashes in the scars on Lennox's neck, musing whether they were remnants of shrapnel from the explosion.

He felt a prickling sensation at the nape of his neck—the unmistakable signal that he was being watched. His eyes shifted to the periphery, seeking the source.

In the shadowy fringes behind the stage, a man lurked. He was dressed simply in jeans and a white T-shirt, an ensemble out of place among Lennox's forces, seemingly chosen to blend in. His attention was focused firmly on Silence. Like his employer, this man's face was scarred, though much less pronounced than Lennox's—a prominent scar slashed across his chin.

For a split second, Silence's mind flashed back to Montana, the Bowie knife slicing through his prosthetic chin.

He and this man shared a bizarre brotherhood.

They were chin brothers.

Nestled near the man was a door, partially ajar—the one through which Lennox had entered. It revealed a sliver of darkness that teased access into Lennox's inner sanctum. The two maroon-shirted bruisers had moved to other parts of the warehouse floor, leaving only this new man behind at the door.

Squinting through the dim light, Silence discerned more details of the man's appearance—the rugged lines of his face, the stubble that shadowed his jaw, the intensity of his stare. He was built like a brawler and had a hard-won sharpness, the kind crafted by years of living on a knife-edge. This was no ordinary member of Lennox's staff; this was one of the top guys, hence the position of prominence at the doorway.

If Maya Fuller was hidden anywhere, it would be beyond that doorway, past the threshold, in the guts of Lennox's operation. A plan crystallized in Silence's mind as he watched Chin Brother melt back into the shadows.

Silence rose.

While Lennox's amplified serpent voice spoke sweet nothings to his followers, Silence stepped to the back of the seating area, pivoting to head for the door at the far end of the space.

19

Silence closed the gap between himself and the rugged figure guarding the door, Chin Brother. As he neared, the other man's body tensed at the bold, unexpected approach.

Now standing just an arm's length away, Silence scrutinized the details that had escaped him from across the room. Up close, the man's rough exterior revealed not only a hardened resilience but also traces of sorrow and defeat, particularly in his eyes. He was middle-aged, with a receding hairline of slightly thinning brown hair, his features plain but not disagreeable.

"What do you want?" the man said.

"Looking for..." Silence said and swallowed. "The bathroom."

The man tilted his face slightly at the sound of Silence's voice. His reaction was less intense than most first-timers, suggesting a familiarity with life's harsher realities.

Or maybe Chin Brother was just desensitized to strange voices after being employed by the snake-voiced Colin Lennox.

Silence could see the calculations running behind the man's guarded eyes, weighing the intentions behind Silence's seemingly innocuous but overtly smartass bathroom request.

After a moment, the man waved a hand toward one of the massive sliding doors on the other side of the space, the one that was slightly open.

When the lights had dimmed earlier, the door had been left partially ajar, creating just enough space for someone to slip through.

"Bathroom's out there," he said, his voice carrying a note of impatience.

Undaunted, Silence gestured beyond the man toward the cracked-open door and the dim hallway it led to.

"I'm sure there's one..." he said and swallowed. "Back there." Another swallow. "That's the one I want."

A fleeting expression of confusion crossed the man's face—a hint of doubt in response to Silence's unanticipated defiance.

Silence capitalized on the moment of hesitation, combining techniques from his two principal teachers, C.C. and his Watchers trainer, Nakiri.

First, he employed C.C.'s method of slowing down his perception of time. Simultaneously, he tapped into the stealth training from his initial days with the Watchers, his onboarding period. Stealth was a particular strength of Silence's, a curiosity given his proportions.

Merging these two approaches, Silence glided past the man with effortless precision. He entered the hallway, his sizable frame moving soundlessly.

Once past the threshold, Silence immediately pivoted, turning to face the direction he came from, knowing the other man—a seemingly formidable tactician in his own right—would be right behind him.

His assumption was correct.

No sooner had Silence positioned himself for a counterattack than the other man lunged forward with a burst of brute force. His movements carried the weight and power of a seasoned brawler. The first swing, a broad arc aimed at Silence's head, cut through the air hard and fast.

Silence ducked under the swipe. He countered with a swift jab to the man's midsection. But the other man barely flinched, absorbing the hit with a grunt and continuing his assault.

Chin Brother's style was raw and unfiltered, each blow thrown with the goal of a knockout. Silence countered that by allowing the man to wear himself out, moving with surgical precision, his strikes methodical.

He deflected a powerful right hook, pivoting to deliver an elbow strike to the other man's ribcage. As the man doubled over, Silence spun, delivering a roundhouse kick that connected with the side of his opponent's head.

This proved to be the definitive blow.

The other man's movements suddenly began to slow, the initial ferocity waning. Seizing the opportunity, Silence sidestepped a sloppy punch and positioned himself behind the man, where he applied a guillotine choke, encircling the man's neck and clamping down on the carotid arteries.

The man's struggle was fierce but brief before his body went limp. Silence lowered him to the concrete floor.

Standing over Chin Brother, his chest heaving slightly from the exertion, Silence paused to collect himself before he turned his attention to the path ahead: the hallway that led into the mysteries of Lennox's operation. He took off.

The hallways resembled the earlier ones—equipped with Lennox's rudimentary lighting and strewn with refuse—but these were narrower, their ceilings sealed with drywall, not open with exposed plumbing and electrical elements like the ones he'd seen earlier. Clearly, this section had once housed office spaces.

He came upon a partially open door, spilling artificial light into the hallway. A quiet hum of electronic activity emanated from within. Pushing the door open, Silence stepped into what was evidently Lennox's command center.

The room was outfitted with an array of monitors, computers, and file cabinets. The screens, set in a half-moon formation, displayed a dozen or so live black-and-white surveillance feeds.

Silence stepped forward. One particular screen caught his eye—it displayed the ongoing meeting on the warehouse floor. Lennox was at the center of the image, gesticulating away in silent zeal, a figure of charismatic command even in grainy monochrome.

A file folder lying open on one of the desks drew Silence's attention. It was overstuffed with business papers—letters, invoices, and other documents poked out the side. He grabbed it, flipped it open. The prevalence of Chinese characters and addresses struck him immediately.

China?

He rifled through its contents with growing confusion, separating the

Chinese documents from the rest. Though Silence couldn't read Chinese, the papers seemed mundane at first glance—routine business correspondence—yet their presence in this context was anything but ordinary.

...especially since they all appeared to be sales-related.

Silence lowered the folder to the desk as his eyes slowly turned back to the monitors, and he refocused on the screen displaying Lennox, still putting on one hell of a show for his audience.

What sort of business was Colin Lennox doing with China?

20

Avery was still in the damn car.

Sitting there, rigid, behind the wheel. Parked in a crumbling lot outside a tired old factory complex. Eyes locked on the single entrance at the front of the building, where a beefy guard was standing watch.

The Cavalier's engine had been shut off for some time now. With each of its dying clicks, the weight of hesitation grew heavier.

Inside the building, Avery knew, was the tall, mysterious stranger he'd seen at the Insight Center. Avery's mind kept replaying the brief encounter, the stranger's imposing figure burned into his memory.

But Avery remained in the Cavalier, frozen, his hands clamped on the steering wheel.

His inner voice was a relentless critic echoing in the confines of the car.

Coward, it taunted.

That word cut deep.

That word was the opposite of *hero*.

He reminded himself of this pursuit he'd inexplicably embarked upon, an opportunity to be the hero he had always dreamed of being. He held on to his theory that the man from the Insight Center was the key to deciphering what Montoya and Tom Radley were up to.

Taylor Perrine was out there somewhere, very likely with Tom Radley, and needing help. Avery Malone could be the one to offer it. Avery could be more than a bystander in this world for once.

He took a deep, steadying breath.

Then he released the steering wheel, each finger uncurling individually, breaking free.

All right.

Let's do this.

He looked down at his all-black security uniform. That wouldn't cut it. The people he'd watched exiting their vehicles and heading toward the warehouse were in plain streetwear, no uniforms in sight. Avery glanced to the back of the Cavalier, spotting his jean jacket strewn across the rear seat.

Maybe...

He grabbed the jacket, threw it on, and gave himself a once-over in the rearview mirror. It wasn't a flawless disguise, but it was close enough. Clad in the jean jacket, the lower part of his uniform could be mistaken for regular black pants, not unlike the black jeans worn by the bouncer at the door.

Avery's eyes lifted slightly, taking his attention off the reflection of his modified outfit and meeting his own eyes in the mirror. A moment passed. Then he swung open the car door.

Broken asphalt crunched under his boots. His heart thundered.

As he approached the entrance, the figure of the bouncer grew more apparent, more real. The young man was over six feet tall and built like a fortress, muscles rippling under his maroon shirt, which was skin-tight. His stance was wide, arms crossed. His gaze locked on Avery as he neared.

"This is an invitation-only event," the man uttered.

Avery nearly turned around and left. Instantly. Instinctively. The comforting anonymity of his Cavalier was just a few steps away.

Hell, he'd almost apologized, his lips parting, the words nearly slipping out.

...but he stopped himself.

He reached for his wallet and opened it to reveal his badge, using his thumb to obscure the *SECURITY* text at the top. That was all the badge displayed: *SECURITY OFFICER,* with *security* written at the top and *officer* at the bottom. No badge number. No name. Not even a mention of the Indianapolis Insight Center. It was a cheap, generic job.

His heart pounded as he presented the badge to the bouncer.

"I just need to look around," he said, feigning authority.

The bouncer scrutinized the badge, then Avery, his eyes narrowing. "You got a warrant for this?"

"No. No warrant. Just wanna have a look around," Avery repeated, his voice steadier than he felt. "Nothing serious."

The bouncer's skepticism lingered.

Avery swallowed, tried to hide it.

Finally, the bouncer stepped aside. "Make it quick."

Avery nodded and stepped past the man, crossing through the threshold...

...and exhaled.

He hadn't realized it a moment ago, but he'd gone lightheaded.

Entering the warehouse, the buzz of a crowd and a wall of glowing industrial-style windows guided Avery toward what must have been some sort of gathering, evidenced by the open sliding door revealing a setup of folding chairs facing a slapdash particleboard dais. A group of people milled about, conversing. The event must have been holding a scheduled break.

He moved toward the activity. The hallway was lit by a makeshift arrangement of bare bulbs strung up and stapled haphazardly along the walls, a strange juxtaposition to the unused overhead fixtures. The floor was littered with various debris.

Guilt ate at Avery for the deceit he had just committed back at the door. He'd never actually said he was a cop—so he hadn't committed the crime of impersonating a police officer—but he'd certainly implied as much. Criminal or not, he'd committed an act of stolen valor.

Yet, intermingled with the remorse was a surge of excitement, a thrill that came from stepping into the unknown, from taking action after years of resignation.

As Avery drew closer, the hum of the crowd intensified. Somewhere among these people was the tall, mysterious figure he was searching for. Avery would find the man and ask him what he knew about Tom Radley, and together, they'd get to the bottom of what Radley and Montoya were up to with Taylor Perrine.

...and possibly many other victims.

Avery was on the brink of something that could redefine his life. The prospect of exposing the truth, of truly making an impact, was both daunting and exhilarating.

As he approached the crowd, the cacophony of voices enveloped him.

21

Silence held the Chinese documents, his mind struggling to avoid a mental loop.

It simply made no sense...

But as he looked away from the papers and into the starkly lit control room, a more pressing matter surged to the forefront: the search for Maya Fuller.

He set the papers back on the desktop and refocused.

Swiveling in his seat, Silence directed his attention to the banks of monitors. Each screen displayed a different view, offering snapshots of the various sections of Lennox's gathering. He leaned forward, squinting his eyes as he systematically scanned each feed, searching for Maya's distinct features, for any trace of her among the faces in the crowd.

But she remained elusive.

Like a ghost.

As he double-checked, a memory tugged at the edges of Silence's concentration—the image of Taylor Perrine standing among the Steady Progress Summit crowd, arms crossed in a self-hug, avoiding Tom Radley's stare. Her elegant poise was marred by an undercurrent of personal tragedies. He remembered Radley's sly grin, aggressive posturing, the California-chic suit.

The thoughts made Silence's gaze harden with renewed intent, searching the faces on the screen not just for Maya Fuller but for Taylor Perrine as well.

...because Tom Radley could have brought Taylor over here, the prize victim plucked from the Indianapolis Insight Center a quarter mile away.

Silence shifted swiftly from one screen to the next, seeking any trace of Taylor or Maya among those gathered at the meeting.

Nothing.

Shit!

Silence's teeth ground together.

He closed his eyes.

Breathed.

He felt for his contact points ... where his feet touched the insoles of his double monks ... where the shoes touched the floor ... the folds of his clothing brushing his skin.

Eyes open.

A five-second meditation. Another one of C.C.'s techniques.

He'd needed it.

Centered now, he considered that maybe—*just* maybe—he was wrong about Radley's connection with Lennox. It seemed a long shot, coincidences being the bullshit that they were, what with the men wearing the same style of slick suits, having the same cocky arrogance, and approaching the same sort of confused souls.

But...

If Radley wasn't connected to Lennox, Silence was certain the man was still up to no good with Taylor Perrine, and he felt the urge to help regardless of whether Radley's antics were tied to Silence's current mission against Colin Lennox. He would seek the truth of Taylor Perrine's circumstances either way. It was a compulsion of his that went beyond orders, beyond protocol.

Silence thought of the stringent directives of his superior, Falcon, who always chastised Silence for using his Watchers-gifted skill set to help people in non-Watchers-sanctioned circumstances. *No involvement in local matters* was Falcon's admonishment.

Silence frequently disobeyed this directive.

He would disobey it again if need be to find out what Tom Radley had been doing with Taylor Perrine.

He could almost hear Falcon's voice.

No involvement in local matters.

When Silence defied the directive, he always did so with the skills, funding, tech, and logistics afforded him by the Watchers. So many times, he'd gone rogue, helping out souls who needed it but had not been cleared by the Watchers' brass.

This notion made Silence think again about the one-year sabbatical Falcon had offered.

A year away from the bloodshed, the covert operations, the relentless dance with death. The thought of it hung in the air like a specter, both alluring and disquieting. To step away from the life of a Watcher was to step away from the identity he had forged in the shadows. This forging had been hard-earned.

Yet, it also meant stepping away from the ability to use the resources at his disposal to make a difference on a more human scale, to engage in the "local matters" that his heart pulled him toward.

The sabbatical offer was a choice between the life Silence knew, woven from threads of violence and necessity, and a one-year glimpse of the life that might be. Peace. Relaxation. Recuperation. Maybe he could spend some time at the beach and get a taste of what life would be like should he live out the post-Watchers beach retirement fantasy that Doc Hazel had made him concoct.

A life without violence.

Violence...

Strangling a man to death.

In his own home.

The smell of piss.

He'd hoisted Richard Keane's lifeless, urine-soaked body off the floor and deposited it unceremoniously into the leather chair in the man's home office.

Then Silence had begun arranging the body the way the Watchers had instructed.

Staging a man's corpse...

In his own home. Beneath smiling photographs of his wife and son.

Regardless of the man's misdeeds—and Keane's had been particularly grievous—the deed carried a nauseating weight.

In the stillness of the command center, surrounded by the gentle hum of machines and the dim light from monitors, Silence found his thoughts drifting back to the Keane mission. This time, however, he didn't dissect the memories for connections to the Code Red situation.

Instead, his mind lingered on the photographs.

The frames lining the shelf—mundane objects like that are often heavy with unspoken stories. Silence's mind wandered back to earlier in the day, to the toy car on the keychain, accidentally activated by Doc Hazel in her attaché case. Its playful *Vroom!* echoed in his memory. He'd wondered then if the car held a deeper meaning for her or perhaps someone close to her. Why else would it have been nestled among her Watchers' gear?

There was no doubt that Keane's framed photos bore that sort of significance, however. They were right there. On the recessed shelf in his home office. Images of family members.

Images of a family now broken. A wife, Claire, now a widow. A teenager, Brendan, now a fractured youth. Their lives would be irrevocably altered when they found their husband and father dead in the family office, an overdose suicide...

...never knowing that the man had been part of a secret organization known as the Watchers; never knowing that he'd been a traitor to the organization and to the United States; never knowing that the man *hadn't* overdosed on heroin, that he'd been murdered.

Silence had killed him.

And he'd staged the body and props perfectly.

For a moment, Silence allowed himself to consider the merits of a life without killing, without tying off a dead man's arm with a length of rubber cord and injecting him with a ludicrous amount of opioids, without placing a *Goodbye, cruel world* note beside the body in a carefully crafted rendition of the man's handwriting.

He considered a life without the weight of such memories.

He considered the beach fantasy.

Doc Hazel always told him to *live* in the fantasy, not to simply see it, a sentiment that echoed C.C.'s teachings of years past. Right now, Silence touched the sun-bleached boards, tracing his fingers along the house's siding as he stepped through the sand—warm between his toes—toward the shadowy foliage and the crashing waves beyond.

The smell of the sea.

The caw of the gulls.

Focus, love.

C.C.

Of course.

She was right.

As the fantasy unfurled in his mind, Silence felt the pull of the present. The beach and its promise of peace would have to wait. Duty called him back to the urgency of now.

With a shake of his head, he banished the images and rose from the chair, approaching the filing cabinets at the side of the room.

Tugging open the top drawer, Silence scanned the tabs, the names typewritten. He flipped through them to the Fs and found the file he wanted: *FULLER, MAYA.*

He pulled the folder out.

Next, he closed the drawer, opened the one below it, and searched the Ps.

There was no *PERRINE, TAYLOR.*

He checked again in hopes of a misfiling.

Nothing.

He flipped Maya's folder open, rifled through the contents. The pages were a meticulous compilation of her physical attributes, with measurements and statistics that one might expect in a medical dossier rather than a file from a self-help group—height, weight, body mass index, body fat percentage, blood type.

But no psychological profile. No notes about her suicidal tendencies. Not even a mention of her husband's car accident death.

Just a physical write-up.

Strange...

Silence's eyes flicked to the desk, to the first folder he'd seen sitting alone on the desktop when he first entered the office.

China.

Chinese paperwork. Business-related. Sales documents.

Hmm...

Silence jumped.

An unsettling noise had snapped him out of his mental conundrum—a distant banging that was out of place amidst the quiet hum of the surveillance equipment.

He stilled, listening intently.

It was coming from the hallway. Muffled by distance. Somewhere deeper in the building.

The banging was rhythmic, insistent, as if someone were trying to break through a barrier. It was quickly joined by a woman's voice, high and laced with panic, cutting through the stillness of the room.

"Help me! *Please*, help me!"

Silence's skin prickled.

His mind flashed on an image, a name.

Maya Fuller.

The woman's folder was in his hand, confirmation that she was one of Lennox's followers...

Her brother-in-law hadn't been able to make contact with her for weeks...

And Silence hadn't found her at the meeting that night despite searching multiple times, thoroughly, in person and via security camera feeds...

Another scream.

"*Help me!*"

With a rush of adrenaline, Silence snapped into action.

The file dropped from his fingers, contents fluttering to the floor.

He sprinted out the door.

22

Avery moved through the open doorway, set in a wall made up of industrial-style windows, and into a space that was vast and alive. However, the din wasn't the usual warehouse hum of machinery and labor; this was different. The place had been repurposed, transformed.

He took in the scene—an assembly room thrown together on the fly. Rows of metal folding chairs, about fifty in total, were lined up in a slight arch facing a makeshift stage. The stage was simple, made of particleboard, and held a worn podium.

The atmosphere was thick with expectation. It was like stepping into a stadium during a timeout or a theater at intermission. People drifted from their chairs, forming small groups, buzzing with the kind of tension that comes from anticipation, talking in low voices about what was to come.

Avery scanned the crowd. At the center stood a man in a suit as loud as his smile, with a grid of scar tissue claiming one side of his face. He was the focal point, effortlessly commanding attention. The scars spoke of something terrible in his past, but his booming laugh and lively actions painted a portrait of an enthusiastic leader. He must have been the event's presenter.

Even amidst the ambient noise, snippets of the man's voice reached Avery. It was a breathy, sibilant voice. Very distinctive.

Avery found it hard to pull his eyes from the man, but he reminded himself of his reason for being there, his singular focus: to find the tall stranger from the Insight Center. Avery felt deep down that this stranger was the missing piece, the one who would unravel the puzzle of what Montoya was doing with Tom Radley and how it related to Taylor Perrine.

His gaze moved from one face to another, searching.

No towering man with dark hair, dark eyes, and razor-sharp cheekbones.

Avery would need to take a more direct approach. Spotting a woman who was momentarily alone after a friend exited, he approached.

"Excuse me," he said. "Have you seen a tall man, dark hair, dressed all in dark?"

The woman's eyes flicked to the side, searching her memory bank, but offered just a soft shake of her head, no other reply.

Avery pushed farther into the crowd. A few steps away was another lone soul. This one was a man, standing apart, lost in his own world, his eyes unfocused, maybe deep in thought, or just not interested.

Avery made his way toward the man.

As he crossed the space, Avery's eyes kept flicking back to the guy with the scarred face, clearly the big star of this get-together. He even had bodyguards—two muscly guys standing on either side of him, silently making sure the man's hangers-on didn't hang on too aggressively. Both men wore maroon henley T-shirts and dark jeans.

The scarred man was the epicenter of the whole scene, moving among his group with a smooth, practiced ease. The guy had a pull, an undeniable charisma. His people were hooked, hanging on every word he said, their faces lighting up every time he hissed a few words in their direction.

The man's scarred face shone in the light, and it was only then that Avery pieced together a detail that had been nagging at him subconsciously. He now recognized that the scarring, rather than detracting, oddly enhanced the man's youthful good looks. It skillfully skirted around his dark blond hair, traced the line of his cheek, and edged over his jaw down to his neck, terminating with a pleasing taper.

Avery brought his attention back to the solitary figure he was approaching.

"Looking for someone," Avery said. "Dark clothes, dark hair, about six-foot-three. You seen him around here?"

The guy nodded slowly, detached.

"Yeah," he said in a smoker's voice, "saw a guy like that. Headed that way."

He pointed toward the shadowy rear end of the warehouse, the area behind the stage.

"He was talking to some dude in jeans, white shirt," the man continued. "Looked pretty serious. Then he just slipped through that door back there. It was like he broke into the place, because immediately the guy in the T-shirt bolted after him."

Yes!

The tall stranger was back there somewhere.

Avery felt a jolt of adrenaline, his heart kicking up a notch. He nodded his thanks, his eyes already locked on the door the man had pointed out.

But he didn't move.

He just stood there. Doubt had crept in again—subtle, insidious.

Yet a louder, bolder voice drowned out the fear. The idea of being a part of something bigger than himself was a strong push, aligning with a choice his gut had already made.

He took a deep breath, straightened up, and started for the back of the warehouse floor.

23

Beckwith blinked back into consciousness.

The darkness of the hallway closed in on him, thick and suffocating. He felt the chill of the concrete seeping through his clothes, numbing his skin.

Struggling to regain his bearings, he pushed himself up on his elbows, the world tilting dangerously for a moment before stabilizing. His eyes, still blurry, squinted into the darkness, trying to make sense of his surroundings.

That's when Beckwith saw the silhouette a few yards away—a figure moving stealthily through the faint illumination coming from the cracked door at the back of Lennox's warehouse auditorium.

The man was of a solid build, black, shaved head, in his early forties, clad in a jean jacket over dark pants. His movements were cautious, yet his stride had an unmistakable sense of purpose. Beckwith didn't recognize him.

Or, wait...

No, he did!

He *did* recognize the man. It was the middle-aged security guard from a couple of hours earlier at the Insight Center, the one Beckwith had spotted chasing the operator through the crowd.

It was then that Beckwith saw that the man wasn't wearing just any dark pants; he'd thrown a jean jacket on over his security guard outfit.

The man seemed oblivious to Beckwith's presence, lumped on the shadowy floor. He continued moving, his pace steady but unhurried. He stepped past Beckwith.

Grimacing silently, Beckwith planted his fists on the concrete and pushed himself up. He teetered to the side, caught himself on the wall, and looked ahead to see the other man turning a corner, disappearing in the darkness.

Beckwith gathered his bearings and started after the man. Within a few yards, his balance had returned. His footsteps were careful, measured, blending into the ambient sounds of the warehouse. He turned the corner and saw the security guard midway down the next hallway, half his figure illuminated by Lennox's stringed-up lights.

Bearings restored. Balance restored. Now was the time.

Beckwith bolted.

The security guard turned back and spotted Beckwith, eyes going wide, before he sprinted off. He moved with a surprising agility that belied his middle-aged dumpiness. After a few long strides, he darted into a room filled with stacks of cubicle components, remnants of the building's past life.

Beckwith spun around the doorway and lunged after the man. Suddenly, a crate toppled, missing Beckwith by inches, a deliberate distraction. The security guard had pushed it over, probably thinking it was a clever move. Actually, it was a rookie mistake; Beckwith dodged to the side, shouldering one of the crates away effortlessly.

The man was within yards. Beckwith leaped forward, his arms outstretched, ready to bring the stranger down. But at the last moment, the man veered sharply, narrowly avoiding Beckwith's grasp. This sudden movement threw Beckwith off balance, sending him crashing into a stack of crates.

Okay, that wasn't nearly as rookie-ish as his last move.

In fact, it was damn impressive.

The impact was jarring.

Undeterred, Beckwith pushed himself up, throwing the battered crates to the side. His eyes fixed on the fleeting figure of the stranger. Beckwith jumped, tackling the security guard in a move that was part desperation, part calculated risk, taking him down before the man could pull another clever trick.

They hit the floor with a force that shook the shelves. Then there was a mess of fists and elbows and knees, each man scrambling for control. The security guard was surprisingly tough, scrappy even, fighting with a raw, unpolished ferocity.

But Beckwith was the true brawler here, and he quickly gained the upper hand. The security guard kept clawing, but Beckwith tangled the man's arms behind him and smacked his face into the concrete.

Entirely pinned and fully aware of it, the guard stopped squirming. Beckwith relaxed, too, only slightly. His opponent had already proven himself unpredictable.

Now that Beckwith had the man subdued, only two tasks remained.

Finding out who the hell the guy was.

And breaking the news to Colin Lennox.

24

Silence charged down the hallway.

With the situation's urgency, the building transformed into a concrete labyrinth, echoing with distant, desperate screams punctuated by an occasional heavy thud of a body whacking against a metal door.

"Help me!" Maya screamed. "*Please!*"

Thud!

Silence's breath was even and controlled, but his heart was a different story. It pounded in his chest. But there was no room for hesitation, no second thoughts. Every scream, every bang wound up the knot in his gut.

The corridor stretched before him, deceptively long, seeming to grow, each turn leading to another endless expanse of hallway.

The cries grew louder, more insistent. The fear in those cries was raw.

Thud! Thud!

"Help!"

Finally, the screams intensified to such a volume that they had to be close. When Silence turned a corner, he encountered a closed door. It was unmistakably clear that the source of the noises was behind it.

Approaching the door, Silence's hand moved instinctively to his shoulder holster and drew the Beretta. Every sense heightened. Every nerve ending buzzing. Experience had taught him that any situation could spiral into chaos in a heartbeat.

Silence plastered himself to the wall just beyond the doorframe and paused for a fraction of a second, listening for any hint of movement, any hint of a threat buried in the auditory storm of Maya's screams.

"Someone, please!" she screamed. "Please!"

Thud!

"Maya!" he yelled, sending a jolt of pain down his throat. "I'm here to help." He swallowed. "Are you alone?"

"Help me! Please help!"

A panicked non-response.

Mania...

Or perhaps she *wasn't* alone.

Silence readied himself.

With a swift movement, he burst through the door, Beretta leading the way, clearing the space.

The scene that greeted him drastically differed from the mayhem he'd prepared for.

Instead of Maya and an assailant, he found a room dominated by a high-quality sound system, its speakers blaring recorded screams.

A computer screen glowed ominously in the semi-darkness, displaying a cartoon woman, her mouth opening and closing in an extreme scream that wasn't synchronized with the sounds.

An oversized ceiling fan turned languidly. From one of the blades dangled a pink rubber-coated three-pound dumbbell, the type used for low-intensity workouts. Standing in the doorway, Silence stepped out of the way as the weight spun at him, trying to whack the door yet again.

Silence's initial rush of urgency gave way to a cold, sinking realization.

The distress calls, the banging—all of it had been a ruse.

Confusion enveloped him, a rarity.

The cold steel of the Beretta in his hand was a grounding reminder of the danger that still lurked, unseen and unknown.

C.C., too, served as a reminder.

Love! she shouted.

Silence snapped to.

He spun on his heel, exiting the room with the same speed he'd entered. The hallway, once a path to a potential rescue of Maya Fuller, now felt like a constricting snake, the walls closing in with each step.

He made a beeline for the control room, turning the corner, finding a closed door blocking his path, grabbing the handle—

Whack!

He collided with it, his shoulder and temple whacking into the steel.

Locked.

He spun around, taking the corner again, sprinting back past the open door and the screams, getting a flash of the cartoon woman and the dumbbell floating through the air.

He turned the next corner.

Found another door that shouldn't be closed.

Tried it.

Locked.

Silence stood there. And noticed something. The air was thick with the scent of Lennox's incense, different here, stronger than anywhere else in the building.

But there was something wrong with it.

It wasn't just incense. There was something else mixed in. Silence could smell it, picking up on the pungent cue over the musky base of the incense.

It was then that he noticed...

...his head felt light.

Whatever the hell was in the air, lacing the incense, it was a weapon.

The incense, the locked doors, the layers of lies—it was all part of a plan, a well-oiled machine.

He felt exposed, vulnerable.

Because, for once, he was trapped.

25

Colin Lennox couldn't be happier with how tonight's performance was turning out.

That is, he *had been* entirely satisfied until his right-hand man, Beckwith, broke the news: there was *another* intruder, beyond the one they were expecting.

Lennox strode into what he had dubbed "general-purpose room 2" within his commandeered warehouse. The room bore traces from its past —crusty mops, boxes, and tools.

A figure on a folding chair sat in the center of the room, which was dimly lit by a solitary bulb. The man was black, middle-aged, and anxious as all hell. He wore a security officer uniform. A jean jacket—the man's, presumably—lay in a ball on the floor. Lennox's gaze lingered on the stranger before shifting to the watchful Beckwith at the periphery.

As Lennox's eyes met Beckwith's, he offered a brief nod of approval.

"Good job," he said, though the words were more a statement of expectation than praise. Beckwith was a big, ugly son of a bitch, but Lennox still had to be mindful of the guy's stupid feelings. Like the captive on the chair, Beckwith had an air of middle-aged pitifulness, so Lennox offered positive reinforcements now and then.

Beckwith nodded in response, but Lennox caught a flicker of something unusual in his right-hand man's expression, something like veiled apprehension. It was a troubling sign. Lennox filed the observation away.

Turning away from Beckwith and the captive, Lennox's attention was drawn to the surveillance monitor in the corner of the room. The screen, divided into quadrants, displayed various angles of the warehouse. He kept the same set of four top-level feeds on a matching monitor in the "ready room," the four angles that Lennox most wanted to monitor. Elsewhere, in the "control room," the entire collection of his surveillance feeds was displayed on a collection of monitors.

His eyes narrowed as they found the image of the operator. There he was, staggering in the hallway where Lennox had trapped him, clearly succumbing to the effects of the tainted incense Lennox had strategically placed.

The operator planted his back against the wall. Then put his hands on his thighs. Then slid down, ass hitting the floor, allowing his head to drop between his knees. His chest heaved. He looked ready to pass out.

A smirk spread across Lennox's face. Yes, tonight's performance was going great, with all the players doing their part, including the looping audio file of a woman screaming for help. The plan was working just as Lennox had intended. Because there was the operator, captured.

Lennox savored the moment, watching the operator struggle against the invisible foe he'd unwittingly inhaled. The operator tried to stand up. Couldn't. Remained sitting with his hands between his knees.

Lennox grinned.

With a final glance at the defeated figure on the screen, Lennox returned to the task at hand, ready to address the unexpected guest in his sanctuary. He turned back to the captive and moved closer, his steps echoing in the silent room. He stopped, leaned down.

The man looked up, trying to be tough, trying to be impassive, but there was no hiding the fear. It was smeared all over his sweaty, bald head, which was so wet that it glistened in the faint light.

Bringing his face a foot within the other man's, Lennox said, "Name."

The other man swallowed, shrinking under the scrutiny. "Avery Malone."

"Malone, are you with the operator?" Lennox said, pointing to the monitor.

Malone squinted at the screen, and his expression quickly shifted from fear to ... something like hope. The guy was practically smiling now!

Perplexing.

And annoying.

"I'm not *with* him, but I followed him here," Malone said, his brow furrowing. "You bet I did. I'm here because of Tom Radley. Whatever Radley's doing with Taylor Perrine, I'm going to stop him, and that man can help." He pointed at the operator's image on the screen just as Lennox had a moment earlier. "He was ready to interfere at the Insight Center when your man confronted Taylor."

Lennox's smirk faded as he processed Malone's words. Tom Radley's name was entirely unfamiliar, but the mention of Taylor Perrine caught Lennox off guard. Perrine was a young member of Indianapolis royalty who'd been in the news the last year or so for all the wrong reasons—personal tragedies. His interest was piqued. This was a fresh development in the storyline he was concocting.

"And how exactly is Taylor Perrine involved in this?" Lennox said.

Malone's demeanor changed at the mention of Taylor's name. His spine straightened, and a look of resolve hardened his features. "Whatever you're doing with Miss Perrine," he said, his voice firmer now, "I'm not going to let it happen."

This show of defiance from Malone was unexpected, and it intrigued Lennox. First, Malone seemed utterly convinced that this Tom Radley person was one of Lennox's—a fascinating notion.

More notably, here was a man, captured and at Lennox's mercy, yet displaying a protectiveness and a resolve that spoke of deeper motivations. Lennox leaned back slightly, observing Malone with a newfound interest. And even respect. This was no ordinary captive; Avery Malone was a wild card, an element Lennox could not have foreseen in his original plan.

The revelation of the operator's interest in Taylor Perrine—and her tie to this Tom Radley individual—was a puzzle piece that Lennox couldn't place. His mind raced.

...and he verbalized his conclusion to his lieutenant, turning to Beckwith with a smirk. "Looks like we got us a case of wrong place at the wrong time, Mr. Beckwith."

Beckwith didn't respond, just kept looking back at Lennox with that stupid, pathetic expression—a beaten dog.

Lennox's attention suddenly pulled to the monitor just past Beckwith's shoulder. He saw a patch of of empty hallway...

...where the operator had been sitting on the floor, nearly incapacitated, only moments earlier!

Lennox rushed to the monitor, shoving Beckwith out of his way.

Empty.

The goddamn hallway was empty!

The operator was *just there* only moments earlier.

"*Shit!*" Lennox hissed.

He grabbed the control pad, connected to the monitor via a coiled cable from the nearby shelf, and frantically stabbed a button.

Hallway 1.

Hallway 2.

3, 4, 5, 6, 7!

Assembly hall.

Control room.

Ready room.

General-purpose rooms 1, 2, and 3.

Exterior feeds 1 through 9.

Nowhere!

The operator was gone!

Lennox whipped on Beckwith, who looked even more pathetic, almost frightened, the big galoot, the brawny idiot. Lennox raised the control pad, nearly threw it at him ... and controlled himself.

A deep breath.

And another.

Lennox closed his eyes.

After a final breath, Lennox shifted his attention back to Malone. The man's moments earlier shift from nervousness to determination had been notable, this pathetic sense of heroism to save some Indianapolis high-society whore. It was clear that Avery Malone was a new threat, one that could potentially disrupt Lennox's carefully laid plans.

Or the guy could serve as an opportune and strategic convenience...

Malone could be the perfect bait.

Lennox's lips curled into a half-smirk at the thought. The operator had a penchant for playing the hero. What better way to draw him out than using someone in apparent need of rescue?

He stepped closer to Malone. "You're an unplanned-for part of the story I'm crafting, Malone. An unexpected plot twist. But all the best storytellers know to seize upon moments of serendipity when they occur. You're going to help me draw out the operator. You seem to want to be a hero. Well, let me tell you, the operator just looooves to play the hero. Like you, he loves saving people." Lennox paused here for dramatic effect. "He especially likes saving the injured ones."

The tools lined against the wall of the room—one of them would be useful. But which one?

Hmm...

Ah.

There it was.

Lennox casually strolled over and picked up a sledgehammer. The weight of it was nice. Hefty. Substantial.

Turning back to Malone, Lennox's action was immediate and decisive. With a sudden swipe, he brought the sledgehammer crashing into Malone's ankle. The crack of shattering bone was sickeningly clear in the quiet room, reporting like a small rifle. This noise was followed immediately by Malone's agonized scream.

Beside him, Beckwith recoiled, his face contorted in shock and horror. Lennox observed this, his suspicions about his right-hand man's loyalty deepening. Two weeks ago, Beckwith had seemed like the perfect potential lackey—big, strong, stupid, and an easy mark for manipulation, especially with Lennox holding that one damning secret over his head.

This change, this seed of doubt in Beckwith, was a dangerous variable that Lennox could not ignore.

"Malone shouldn't be going anywhere now," Lennox said, "but I'm not taking any chances. Secure him to the chair."

He tossed the sledgehammer aside and went to the rusty metal shelving. He slapped a spool of twine, showing Beckwith the means with which to tie down Malone, then grabbed one of the gas masks and shoved it in Beckwith's direction.

"Then put the mask on and go find the operator."

Beckwith, still visibly shaken by the act of violence, hesitated. His eyes flicked between Lennox, the howling Malone, and the gas mask in Lennox's outstretched hand.

Lennox observed Beckwith's hesitation. Absolute control and loyalty were crucial. Beckwith's momentary faltering threatened Lennox's meticulous plans.

The room pulsed with tension, the aftermath of violence. Lennox's gaze locked onto Beckwith. When Beckwith spoke, Lennox realized it was the first time the pussy had done so since Lennox entered the room to confront the captive.

"I can't do this anymore, Lennox," Beckwith said, gaze shifting to the screeching Malone, zeroing in with glazed-over eyes on the man's broken ankle. "I'm out." A pause. "And I'm exposing you."

Lennox snorted.

"Exposing me? I see. What about your secret, Beckwith?"

Lennox strode over to the screaming man, placed a hand on his shoulder, then swiftly withdrew it. Malone's pain was so intense it had soaked his shirt with sweat. Lennox wiped his hand on the back of the chair. *Disgusting,*

He leaned close to Malone's thrashing head, its bald dome shining with perspiration. He angled his lips toward the man's ear and hiss-whispered, "You can be the first to know the secret, Avery Malone. Beckwith, here, and his cousin pulled off a heist back in the '80s. They were desperate to pay a hospital bill for Beckwith's aunt—his cousin's mother. She was close to dying, see. They thought they'd hit a convenience store after hours, easy in, easy out.

"But they didn't know the shopkeeper was still there, in the back, counting his day's earnings. When he came out, shotgun in hand, Beckwith tackled him. It was clumsy, a real mess. The shopkeeper crashed into the counter, neck snapping. It was supposed to be a simple job, no one getting hurt. Just two guys trying to save a life. Ended up taking one instead.

"How do I know all of this? Well, I'm pretty damn good at uncovering encrypted records and reanalyzing them. For years, no one knew who killed the shopkeeper. A cold case. But I was able to use advanced technology—what we in the field call artificial intelligence—to clarify the grainy security footage. I cross-referenced that with police databases and got a hit with a mugshot of this ugly son of a bitch here." He paused for dramatic effect once more. "Now I own him."

Lennox stood up, left the thrashing Malone behind, and stopped in front of Beckwith.

"Do I make my point?" Lennox hissed.

The threat hit its mark. Beckwith's defiance wavered, his eyes flashing with fear and anger. The unspoken secret hung heavily in the air.

Lennox pushed the gas mask forcefully toward Beckwith once more, this time striking him in the chest with it.

"Do your job!"

Beckwith took the mask but couldn't look Lennox in the eye.

Of course he couldn't.

Lennox pointed at the spool of twine, then to Malone, and said to Beckwith, "Secure him to the chair, then find the operator."

Beckwith stood there with a stupid browbeaten look on his face, shoulders drooping, gas mask hanging limply in his hand, and nodded like the subservient piece of shit Lennox knew him to be.

With a final, contemptuous sneer, Lennox glanced at his watch.

"I have a flock awaiting their shepherd," he said with a wink.

He turned on his heel and strode out of the room.

26

Silence edged forward in the oversized vent, the metal groaning under his weight. He was a big guy, not built for the confines of industrial ductwork.

At the T-junction, his progress halted. His limbs struggled to push against the walls, each pop of the metal amplified in the confined area. He grunted, the sound echoing harshly.

The sweat on his brow wasn't just from exertion; something else was at play. The incense he'd inhaled back in the hallway was making him feel lightheaded and sick to his stomach.

Two minutes earlier, he'd spotted a grate on a wall directly beneath one of Lennox's cameras, out of sight. Two hard tugs, and the grate came off. Then, a few moments ago, in a brief flash, he could have sworn he saw a hallucination...

Panting, he paused to collect himself. The air in the vent was thick, tainted. He'd thought that ducking into this metal maze would serve two purposes: escaping Lennox's cameras and escaping Lennox's tainted incense. The primary power was out in the building. No power means no HVAC, and that means the vents would be full of clean air—this had been the thought process.

But no such luck.

Another whiff of the tainted incense made Silence's nose scrunch. The poison was noxious...

...and there was that hint of a hallucination he'd seen a few minutes earlier.

He searched the mental files from his Watchers training, ticking off the names of drugs that could cause hallucinations: LSD, psilocybin, perhaps even a synthetic like 2C-B. If aerosolized, all of them would be likely culprits in Lennox's incense.

He tugged at his sport coat, pressing it against his mouth in a futile attempt to filter the air. It was a small comfort against the creeping disorientation. But it did nothing.

Silence realized then that not only was he feeling the beginning effects of hallucinations, but whatever the hell was in the air had also worn him out. He didn't have the strength to fight his way around the T-junction, yet he couldn't back out of the vent either, leaving from where he entered—not yet, not with all of Lennox's cameras.

He needed a momentary distraction, something to ground him.

But he couldn't lose focus on the mission.

There was one more audio log to listen to. That would be productive.

Fumbling in his pocket, he pulled out the digital audio recorder and pressed *PLAY*.

Special Agent Colin Lennox's voice filled the small space.

November 19th. This will be my last entry as Agent Lennox. I've come to a realization. Jordan Havelock is not just a leader; he's a visionary. His teachings, they're a revelation. The FBI doesn't understand—the stupid assholes.

They can't see the greatness in Havelock's work.

The accusations, the suspicions—they're baseless. Havelock is offering a lifeline to those in despair, and we're trying to cut it. I can't be a part of that anymore. I can see clearly now. The truth is, we need more people like Havelock, not less.

I'm leaving the Bureau. My place isn't there, shackled by ignorance and fear. It's with Havelock, helping him spread his message, his vision. This is where I belong, where I can truly make a difference.

Jordan Havelock is changing the world, one soul at a time. And I'm going to be a part of that change.

As the audio log played, the effects of the poisoned air had grown stronger. By the time the message was over, Silence's head was spinning, his stomach churning.

He felt himself slipping, the toxins wrapping around his mind, pulling him under. The world tilted, his senses betraying him as he fought to stay conscious in the vent, this damn metal tube.

A vent was a lousy place for a large man.

Silence felt every inch of his size as he squeezed through, the metal cold and unyielding against his skin.

Things felt weird.

And though Silence had a chaotic mind space, he was also trained well enough to know reality from fiction, to know when he was unfocused and when he was truly hallucinating.

Right now, he was hallucinating.

Because C.C. was there with him.

Except not *there* in the vent but on the hardwood floor. The Farone mansion. Lying in a puddle of her blood. Hair splayed. Arms and legs twisted.

Silence gasped.

He was back in the vent. C.C. had looked real enough to touch. But it was a trick of the mind, nothing more—a painful reminder of what he'd lost, courtesy of Lennox's poisoned air.

Silence started a deep-breathing exercise, one of C.C.'s techniques...

And stopped himself.

It would be pretty stupid to purposefully breathe more of the shit in.

He brought his sport coat back to his mouth. Frustrated again, he threw it down after one breath.

Better to focus on the task at hand: the T-junction in front of him. He began to pull himself around the bend, grunting. His hips caught on the corner, the metal edge digging through his pants.

Shit, what if he got *stuck* here?

Another pull, another grunt, and he was three more inches to the side. Now, if he could—

He saw Lennox.

Not the scarred man with the snake voice.

The younger one from the audio logs. In an unfinished basement. With a gun.

The scene played out with brutal clarity.

Sweaty dress clothes. Tousled hair. Manic eyes.

Lennox put the Smith & Wesson 459 under his chin.

He pulled the trigger.

Crack!

Blood and tissue and teeth erupted from the side of Lennox's face.

Silence gasped again, this time jerking hard enough that the metal popped loudly beneath him, rattling the entire vent.

This is bad, Silence thought. *Oh, shit. This is bad.*

He shook his head, trying to clear the visions.

This wasn't just some mild disorientation; it was a full-blown poisoning.

Turning his focus back to the vent, Silence pushed himself backward. To hell with making it around the T-junction. To hell with Lennox's cameras, too. He could deal with them or anything else Lennox had out there in his creepy hallways.

Right now, Silence just had to get out of the cramped, drug-infested confines of the vent.

He pushed backward.

But didn't move.

A split second of denial before he could concede…

Then chilling acceptance.

Silence was stuck.

27

Avery's existence had condensed into a singular, all-consuming sensation: pain.

Nothing else mattered. Not the instinct to survive. Not the undercurrents of mystery. Not even those ridiculous delusions of playing the hero.

Only the pain.

Sitting on a metal folding chair in the utility room, his shattered ankle howled. Rising above this howling, the memory of the scarred man's voice slithered through his thoughts: *Secure him to the chair.*

Avery's eyes, heavy with the suffering, drifted toward the other man in the room with him—the rough guy with the receded hairline and sad-looking eyes, the man who'd been given the command to tie Avery to the chair.

The man was approaching. Beckwith. Avery had learned both his name and that of the serpent-voiced Lennox in the earlier conversation...

...moments before Lennox shattered his ankle.

Avery's heart thundered as Beckwith moved closer, and his eyes instinctively stole a foolish glance at the twine on the shelf. *Secure him to the chair.*

His ankle screamed. Sweat ran down his face into his eyes.

Beckwith had the edge in every way that mattered. Large. Tough-looking. Muscular. But Avery Malone wasn't the kind to back down, not when everything was on the line.

Then, driven by a sudden surge of desperate bravery, Avery lunged

His ankle flared in agony.

The room blurred into a chaotic whirl of motion as Avery threw himself at Beckwith. The fight was a mismatch from the start. Avery, with his injured ankle, was at a distinct disadvantage.

...as if he wasn't already disadvantaged compared to this brute.

But desperation lent him a frenzied strength, an unpredictable edge that caught Beckwith off guard. In this moment of confusion, Avery managed to take Beckwith down at the knees.

He used this split-second opportunity to scan the room, searching for anything that could serve as a weapon.

A rusty toolbox.

Grappling with the pain, he reached for the toolbox and swung it. Hard. The heavy metal case connected with Beckwith's jaw right as the man returned to his feet, a solid, satisfying thud that reverberated through Avery's arm.

Beckwith staggered back. Avery didn't pause to savor the moment. He swung the toolbox again, this time driving it into Beckwith's chest, right where the abdomen meets the ribcage.

He'd flipped the script, but only for a blink. Then it all came roaring back—the pain, the overwhelming fatigue. Avery's punches became slow and heavy. He could feel his juice running out, and in desperation, he began swinging wildly.

Beckwith anticipated Avery's sloppy moves and capitalized on his weakened state. With a turn of the elbow, he disarmed Avery, the toolbox clattering to the floor. Beckwith was like a machine, all business, knocking back Avery's desperate swipes.

Avery felt his momentary advantage vanish.

And he felt something else...

...Beckwith's leg slipping behind him in some sort of takedown maneuver.

Whack!

Avery hit the floor, his back slapping the concrete, a wave of pain rocketing down to his ankle, where it exploded Fourth-of-July style.

White pain flashed across his vision.

Cornered and defenseless, Avery braced for the final blow. His body was a solid mass of hurt. He looked up at Beckwith, expecting to see a cold, unforgiving gaze.

But what came next was unexpected.

Beckwith's grip, which had been machine-like a moment ago, suddenly loosened.

"Don't worry. I'm a friend," he said.

Avery blinked in disbelief. He crawled backward, putting a cautious distance between himself and Beckwith. His ankle bellowed at him, pulsing all the way up his leg and into his temples.

Beckwith didn't follow. Instead, he showed his palms in a gesture concurrent with his offer of friendship.

"The operator," Beckwith said, "you think he's here to help? To take down Lennox?"

Avery breathed hard. Studied Beckwith for a long moment. Then nodded.

"I do," Avery said.

Beckwith ran a hand along his jaw. "Then I need to find him." He paused to look at Avery's ankle. "And we gotta get you out of here."

He grabbed a second gas mask from the shelf.

"I'll be right back. I promise," Beckwith said. And then, after another quick glance at Avery's ankle, he smirked and said, "Don't go anywhere."

Avery gave a nod.

And managed a grin of his own.

It was a gesture of acceptance, not just of the broken ankle predicament, but of this new partnership.

Beckwith fitted the mask on his head, pulled it down.

And he slipped out the door.

28

For a few moments, Silence had thought his head was clearing.

It didn't take long to realize he was mistaken.

Trapped in the unforgiving confines of the industrial air duct, Silence found himself immobile, his hips wedged into the T-junction.

He kept pushing, though, repeatedly ramming his bulk against the unyielding metal. His breaths, ragged and heavy, echoed off the tight walls.

His body was jammed hard into the corner, the sharp edge biting into him. He twisted and shoved, muscles straining. The cold metal pressed unyieldingly back against him.

Then, the voices began.

C.C.'s came first.

Look at you, she said. *The world-renowned assassin. The Watchers' top Asset. The Suppressor. Stuck like a rat in a trap.*

She laughed, and it echoed around him, ghostly and warped in the metallic tunnel.

Her voice had come from his mind, as always, but it wasn't the C.C. he knew. The real one wouldn't have mocked him like that.

Then, it was Lennox's turn to speak. *Young* Lennox. FBI Special Agent Colin Lennox. He echoed his words from one of the audio logs.

Jordan Havelock is not just a leader; he's a visionary. His teachings, they're a revelation. The FBI doesn't understand—the stupid assholes.

Lennox again. But a different voice. A snake's voice. The current Colin Lennox.

Looking for Maya Fuller, are you? Taylor Perrine, too? They're not hiding in my air ducts.

Will you make it out in time? Or will you rot up there while I send fifty people to their graves?

Silence's body jolted.

For a moment, he was back in the real world—trapped in that metallic prison. Cold, painful, cramped. His muscles burned as he pushed against the stubborn metal, struggling to back out of the T-junction.

But the line between reality and illusion blurred once again.

No voices this time.

Visions.

C.C.'s face appeared, overlaying the drab gray of the air duct. She smiled. Dark, curly hair. Olive complexion. Ageless Italian beauty.

Destroyed.

Half of her face was ruined flesh. Blood and tissue. Dead. The way he found her on the mansion's hardwood floor.

Laughter.

The scornful laughter of Colin Lennox blended with the metallic creaks and moans.

C.C.'s face was replaced with Lennox's. Where C.C.'s ruined flesh had been, Lennox's scars appeared. He sneered.

And then there was Doc Hazel. Clinical. Cold. Looking at Silence, assessing him.

She held something up, pinching one end of it between her fingers, something that dangled like a miniature pendulum—a tiny red car on a keychain.

She blinked.

And she was gone.

Silence grunted. For a fleeting moment, he glimpsed the metallic tunnel encasing him, the air duct. He was wrestling to distinguish fact from fiction, to stay anchored in the brutal reality of his metallic tomb while his mind threatened to spiral into delirium.

Lennox's face reappeared, flickering in and out of existence, morphing into a sinister shadow. The man's descent into extremism churned violently in Silence's already stormy consciousness, like a spectral documentary playing before his eyes.

Passionate oration. An audience erupting in cheers.

A sinister plan taking shape. The eyes of his followers, wide with blind belief.

The sounds of Lennox's radical rhetoric, that thunderous applause, reverberated against the metal walls of the air duct, creating a jarring cacophony.

Silence unleashed a primal roar, his voice slicing through the cramped space, a desperate attempt to dispel the hallucinations.

And then, reality snapped back into focus.

He was staring down a T-junction, a real-life dead-end mirroring the impasses in his mind. He heaved his body against the metal, muscles tensing, the framework creaking in protest. For a brief moment, he inched backward, progress measured in agonizingly small increments.

But then, progress halted. He was well and truly stuck.

Panic started to claw at his determination.

So he reminded himself...

The mission.

Silence's mind snapped into focus. He latched onto his mission, the very reason he had crawled into this air duct.

Rescue Maya, Nathan Fuller's sister-in-law.

Investigate Taylor Perrine.

Stop Lennox and his deadly plan.

This clarity was a lifeline, yanking him from the brink of delusional chaos...

...and back to the grim reality of his situation.

Regaining focus, Silence ignored his screaming muscles, focusing solely on the task at hand. Each movement, every exertion, was a contest—a duel with the air duct and a struggle against the mental fog looming on the edge of his consciousness.

He shoved with his arms, thrusted with his legs and his back.

And moved an inch backward.

Then another.

One more.

With a pop of metal, his hips cleared the corner.

He exhaled, a tiny smile of triumph playing on his lips. He began shuffling backward through the tunnel...

...when someone grabbed his ankle.

29

Beckwith's muscles tensed. His breathing came in short, heavy gasps through the mask. He gripped the operator's ankle and pulled hard.

The operator was a dead weight in the ventilation shaft. Beckwith hauled him backward with a firm grip, dragging him out of the steel tube.

Once out of the vent, the operator's large body crumpled onto the floor, sprawling in an ungainly heap in the confined space. Motionless.

Beckwith stood over the man, a surge of pity flooding through him as he took in the operator's bedraggled appearance. The air in the ventilation shaft, contaminated with a powerful drug, had evidently overwhelmed the guy.

Beckwith's role in Lennox's scheme had numbed him to many things, but the sight of this man, so clearly incapacitated yet still imposing, stirred a sense of empathy within him.

However, this moment of compassion was short-lived.

Because as Beckwith bent down to assess the man's condition, the tall man's hand shot up with a speed and strength that belied his drugged state. His fingers wrapped around Beckwith's throat in a vice-like grip, the suddenness of the attack catching Beckwith entirely off guard.

The strength of the grip was shocking. This guy was half-dead only a moment earlier!

The man's eyes, clouded with the effects of the drug, bore into him. Primal. Raw. It was a look that Beckwith had seen on many faces in alleys and dive bars and shadowy back rooms—the look of a man pushed to his limits, fighting for survival.

Beckwith grappled with the operator's hand, trying to pry the fingers from his throat. Shit! It was as though they were mechanical—five pneumatic rods boring into his flesh. He gasped for air.

That this man, even in his drugged and confused condition, could pose such a challenge spoke of an elite level of training and physical conditioning. This guy really *was* an operator, just like Lennox called him. The grip on Beckwith's throat was proof.

He grabbed the operator's arm, pulling with everything he had, and finally heaved the massive adversary aside, freeing himself from the grasp. The piston-like fingers slid off, lubricated by Beckwith's perspiration.

Pop, pop, pop, pop, pop.

Beckwith coughed and gasped for air, rubbing his throat. He stumbled back.

The room spun for a moment as he regained his footing. He looked at the operator, still dazed from the drugs but now sitting up, shaking off the lingering fog.

Cautiously, Beckwith extended the extra gas mask in the operator's direction.

Equally cautiously, the operator scrutinized the mask without taking it. A long moment passed.

Finally, the operator yielded, fitting the mask over his face in a manner that seemed to acknowledge Beckwith's gesture as an olive branch.

Next, Beckwith extended his hand toward the operator. Beckwith watched the gears of caution turning behind the operator's inebriated eyes, visible through the mask's transparent shield.

A moment of this, then the operator's hand reached up.

Beckwith took it and pulled the man to his feet.

They took off.

A moment later, they stopped to get Malone. Beckwith dipped his shoulder to offer support. As Malone draped his arm over it, he let out a sigh of relief.

Beckwith navigated the trio through the gloomy hallways, past all of Lennox's strung-up lightbulbs. He kept checking for anyone in a maroon shirt and dark jeans.

The weight of his decision pressed heavily on him...

He'd already defied Lennox once. Now he'd done so *twice more* ... in grand fashion. He was breaking out Lennox's prized target and the mystery security officer who'd breached Lennox's stronghold on the night of Lennox's big event.

The consequences if Beckwith were to get caught would be dire.

The image of Malone's broken ankle—a reminder of Lennox's mercilessness—spurred him on.

Reaching a locked door, Beckwith pulled out a keycard and swiped it in the box. A green light illuminated. The lock clicked. And Beckwith led them into another hallway. The air was fresher here, free of the drug that had clouded the operator's mind.

And with the fresh air, Beckwith's whole being snapped into focus, a laser-sharp clarity cutting through the fog. He was no longer a puppet dancing on Lennox's strings. This was his path now, dangerous, sure, but the only path that made sense.

Another swipe of the card. Another green light. Another doorway cleared.

Beckwith led the way down the final hallway. Malone leaned heavily on him. The tall operator, still disoriented but quickly regaining his senses, followed closely.

An exit door was ahead.

Beckwith pushed through it.

And the three of them stepped out into the cool night.

A few minutes later, they were in the darkness of a wooded area on the edge of the rotted parking lot, outside the glow of the neighboring property's exterior lighting and the reach of Lennox's copious cameras.

It was as far as they could go with a man with a broken ankle.

Malone looked bad. Really bad. He was sitting on the ground, back against an oak, sucking in big gulps of air, drenched in sweat.

The operator, though clearly on the mend, was still grappling with lingering aftereffects of the drug. It manifested in sudden, uncontrollable gestures—his hands rushing to his face, his eyes squeezing shut.

A few moments earlier, he'd introduced himself—in a terrible gravelly voice, as distinctive as Lennox's, but completely different—as Chad. He was with an "organization." That's all he would give them. Beckwith pegged the man as a fed.

And since Lennox had labeled Chad "the operator," Beckwith assumed the man was a very special type of fed—CIA Special Activities Division.

This begged the question: who the *hell* was Colin Lennox to pull in this kind of heat?

Beckwith shot another wary glance at the injured man on the ground, then turned his attention to Chad.

"Listen," Beckwith said, "everything here is a setup. It's all fake. Staged. Lennox doesn't have followers. They're all paid actors, extras, you might call them. Lennox is no guru. There is no anti-suicide group ... it's all theatre, all one big performance staged to lure you in. A trap."

For a moment, Beckwith wondered if he had bombarded Chad with too much, too fast. The drug's lingering effects were surely bothering the guy more than he was letting on, and the more Beckwith had said, the more Chad's face furrowed with concentration.

However, it was Beckwith's final revelation that really jolted Chad: the suggestion that Lennox's entire ruse was a trap set expressly for Chad himself. That piece of information seemed to rock the man to his core.

"*Me?*" Chad said.

Beckwith gave a slow nod. "He's always been cryptic about the details. Never even given me your name; he just calls you 'the operator.'"

Chad's brow furrowed some more. He looked away into the darkness of the trees.

Beckwith sighed. "I can't be a part of what Lennox is doing anymore. He's got me cornered, threatening to expose a secret that could destroy me ... and my mother. He knows about my past, that I ... I killed someone, got away with it."

Admitting this aloud was strangely liberating. Like a cleanse.

Chad brought his attention back from the trees. He wasn't as affected by the confession as Beckwith would have thought. In fact, he didn't seem affected at all. No shock, no judgment on his face, just the same unreadable, blank expression.

Malone was unaffected as well. He didn't look like he'd heard a word Beckwith had said. Eyes pinched shut. Grimacing. Drenched in sweat. Pain was the only thing registering to him.

"But now I know," Beckwith continued, "that it doesn't matter what Lennox has on me. A person can always do the right thing, even if they're branded with a permanent negative label."

He glanced across the parking lot to the warehouse, then faced Chad again.

Beckwith looked at them both in turn.

"I'm sorry, this is all I can offer," he said. "I gotta get back before Lennox realizes I'm gone."

Chad nodded his understanding, and in that wild voice of his, he said, "Go."

30

Lennox raised his arm in a sweeping gesture designed to punctuate his words.

This was a performance. A well-crafted tale, nothing more.

One big ol' story.

Yet, in this narrative, Lennox was the main character, so he had to be the best actor out of them all. He went big with his movements, made them expansive, filled his voice with fire. Though the "followers" facing him were there for purposes not entirely as they seemed, Lennox still needed to stay in top form, in character.

So, knowing gurus thrived on showmanship, he let his hands slice through the air, every word he threw out punctuated with a dramatic flair.

He dominated the makeshift stage set upon the warehouse floor, commanding the seemingly undivided attention of his crowd. The dim lighting cast dramatic shadows across his face as he addressed them; this was by design, perfect positioning of the stringed bulbs and the construction lamps.

"This is a pivotal moment," Lennox said. "A chance to rewrite the rulebook." He paused a beat as he surveyed the crowd. "Death? It's not the final curtain. It's a crossroads. A decision we make."

Whispers rippled through the room. They were playing their roles perfectly.

"Tonight's about personal power, about taking the reins of destiny into our own hands," Lennox continued, his gaze unwavering, drilling into each person. "We're not just ceasing to be. We're transcending. Tonight, we're more than mere mortals. We're trailblazers."

The crowd's reaction was electric, a wave of fervor and readiness.

Lennox grinned as he looked out upon them.

The grin suddenly dropped.

He spotted a discrepancy that set off an alarm in his meticulously ordered mind—Beckwith wasn't in his usual spot.

Beckwith was not there at all.

A sense of disquiet swept over Lennox, an irksome notion that something was off, that his missing henchman was a harbinger. Lennox's plan was a masterpiece of precision, and it hinged on everyone playing their part. A single loose thread threatened to unravel his entire scheme.

Sure, Beckwith's no-show could be happenstance. Maybe the guy had to piss real bad. Middle-aged guys have prostate problems and kidney stones.

Maybe he'd lost track of time. Unlikely.

Or maybe his absence had something to do with the operator...

Forcing a smile, Lennox gave a slight bow, signaling the commencement of the next break. As the crowd rose from their seats, buzzing with excitement for the final act, Lennox's thoughts were elsewhere. He wasn't mulling over his performance or the narrative's progress; he was fixated on the nagging concern that his carefully orchestrated plan was starting to fray at the edges.

And at the crux of this anxiety was the operator.

Descending from the stage, Lennox wove through his followers. He offered nods and reassuring words, but his attention was elsewhere, searching the crowd for one individual.

He spotted him.

The man stood alone on the far side of the meeting space, past the chairs, out of the light. Disheveled hair, crumpled dress shirt, haven't-shaved-in-two-days scruff, smoker's twitch.

Politely excusing himself from a conversation, Lennox made his way through the crowd. A few more nods and smiles and hissing words of faux encouragement offered to faux admiration—*Yes, we're all brave here, aren't we?* and *You have strength; I can see that in your eyes*—then he stepped into the shadows.

Approaching the other man, the surrounding hubbub seemed to recede, turning into a faint hum.

"It's time to drop the 'Nathan Fuller' charade, Mike," Lennox said.

Mike's response was minimal, yet telling—a slight clench of the jaw and an almost imperceptible shift in posture. He masked his shock well. He was a talented actor.

Leaning in, Lennox whispered, "I think we have a traitor among us."

31

Beckwith's return to the warehouse was like stepping back into a nightmare he thought he'd escaped

His boots echoed against the hallway's concrete floor. Lennox's stringed bulbs glowed on the walls, casting elongated shadows that twisted along with Beckwith's every step. As he moved toward the main floor, his mind was torn between the relief of freeing Chad and Avery and the dread of facing Lennox's wrath.

For two weeks, Beckwith had been Lennox's shadow, his silent enforcer. He'd carried out orders without question, his conscience numbed by the steady flow of blood and violence.

He'd even killed for the man.

He'd become a murderer twice over for Colin Lennox.

But in freeing Chad and Avery, Beckwith had stepped out of that shadow, defying the man who had been both an employer and a tormentor. If this betrayal was discovered, it would not go unpunished.

But even with the fear gripping him, there was an unfamiliar sense of pride. For the first time in his wretched life, Beckwith had done something good, *something right*. A rare, almost forgotten action took place then.

A brief grin cracked his cold facade.

But as Beckwith neared the entrance to the warehouse floor, his moment of self-reflection was shattered. The grin vanished.

The sight before him was unexpected—the crowd, usually seated and subdued, was out of their seats, mingling and chattering. The gathering was on its second break already, the final interlude before Lennox's grand event.

Beckwith checked his watch.

Shit!

He'd entirely lost track of time. Of course he had. That'll happen when you're freeing two people from a madman's funhouse, one of them a federal hitman and the other a rogue security guard.

In doing so, he'd been absent for an entire portion of Lennox's presentation.

Beckwith quickened his pace. Every second he was late, every moment he was absent, raised the likelihood that Lennox would suspect something amiss.

An image flashed through his mind: Lennox's sudden swing of the sledgehammer, annihilating Malone's ankle.

It had been so easy for Lennox.

Almost mundane.

The fear of what might happen if Beckwith's betrayal was discovered sent a wave of panic surging through him.

He rounded the corner, and the warehouse floor—Lennox's "assembly hall"—was before him, all those industrial-style windows aglow. Yes, the presentation's second interlude had already commenced, people milling about.

Beckwith's gaze swept over the crowd. Small groups formed and reformed, their conversations a low hum in the vast space. Beckwith searched for Lennox, couldn't find him.

Somehow, that was both a relief and not a relief at all.

If it happened to be that—

Oh…

Oh, shit!

Beckwith's heart pounded even harder at an unexpected sight. There, off to the side in the shadows, away from the throngs of followers, stood Lennox, deeply engaged in a conversation with Mike Pushard.

Pushard ... Lennox's *other* right-hand man. The one who'd been tasked with portraying Nate Fuller, the character who was written to draw the operator into Lennox's twisted theatre performance.

Beckwith and Pushard were the only two people Lennox had divulged his plans to; they were the only people aside from Lennox himself who understood this was all a charade.

The fact that Lennox and Pushard were conversing alone—and doing so after they'd surely noticed Beckwith's absence—was a terrible harbinger.

Because according to the script, Lennox was never supposed to speak personally with "Nate Fuller."

This was bad.

Really bad.

They could only be discussing one thing: *Beckwith*.

Panic tore at Beckwith. He couldn't afford to be seen by Lennox, not now, not ever again.

He thought of the sledgehammer once more...

Lennox's perpetual ringmaster smile had never left his face—not when he grabbed the hammer, not when he swung it, not when he looked down at Malone's mangled foot with screams ringing in his ears.

His expression never changed.

Beckwith backpedaled, fast. He turned, his boots barely making a sound as he dashed down the hallway.

32

In the wooded thicket skirting the parking lot, the drugs in Silence's system began to relent, grudgingly releasing their hold on his faculties. He leaned against a tree. Below him, Malone remained seated, clinging to consciousness, muttering.

"Montoya told me..." Malone said and grimaced. He'd moments earlier explained that Montoya was a coworker at the Insight Center. "He gave me the gist of his plan with Tom Radley. It's about getting people to spill their secrets on camera, pretending it's for some kind of self-help video diary. Then..." Another grimace. "They turn around and use it for blackmail."

That bit of intel changed Silence's belief that Radley was collaborating with Lennox. Two separate scumbags, unrelated. It was one of those sheer coincidences Silence normally refused to believe in.

He filed the notion in the back of his mental cache, right next to a reminder of Falcon's frequent admonishment: *No involvement in local matters.*

Silence's vision, which had been a jumble of drug-induced mirages, was sharpening, snapping back into a clarity that was almost painful in its intensity. His gaze fixed on the warehouse looming across the neglected expanse of asphalt, a dark silhouette against the night. The sense of purpose that had been smeared by the drug's haze was clawing its way back to the forefront of Silence's mind.

He turned to Malone. "I'm going back in."

Malone looked up at him with a mix of concern and disbelief. "Chad, you can't do that!"

Silence didn't respond.

His attention shifted to Malone's ankle, grotesquely swollen. The skin was stretched taut, discolored. Silence reached into his pocket, pulled out his keys, and reached them down to Malone, who accepted them with a weak, shaky hand and a dubious look despite the pain.

"Hospital a mile down the road," Silence said, his mind recalling the modern structure with its gleaming six-story tower he'd noted during his earlier drive to the Insight Center.

Silence always made a mental note when he spotted a hospital. A precautionary measure. Watchers Assets sustain more than a few injuries.

He swallowed. "Can you make it there?"

The question was as much about practicality as it was about compassion. He was acutely aware that even a journey of less than a mile would be an ordeal for Malone, given his current state. But there was no choice in the matter. Silence couldn't take him himself. There were lives at stake, dozens of them, including Maya Fuller, all on the brink of being snuffed out in Lennox's grand spectacle.

Malone's gaze dropped to the keys clasped in his shaking hands. The enormity of his injury was plainly evident on his face. Yet, in his eyes, where the pain was most pronounced, there was something else—a different kind of pain, one that transcended the physical. He raised his eyes to Silence.

"I tried to be a hero tonight," he said, voice small, "but I guess some things are better left to real heroes like you, Chad." A pause. "Or to my brothers, 'Calvin the Cop' and 'Flynn the Fireman.'" He smirked. "There are labels you can't shake once they're attached to you, no matter much you resist, and others that you can't claim, no matter how bad you want them. And me, I'm no hero."

Malone threw that word around a lot—*hero*—as though it were a credential, something worn by some and not by others, something definitive and absolute, black and white.

Silence didn't think it was that simple.

He thought of what Doc Hazel had said in her moment of kindness that morning in Cincinnati. She spoke of life as a journey of self-discovery, of shedding old skins to embrace new identities.

Maybe Avery Malone just hadn't realized how heroic he'd been that night.

Silence gave his throat a preemptive swallow. "Tonight, you've done a great—"

But his words halted abruptly, and it wasn't the usual interference from the scar tissue in his larynx.

This time, it was something in his head.

Hallucinations were setting in again.

...this time in the form of a nightmare of his past.

Richard Keane's house.

The Watchers Specialist. The State Department diplomat. The traitor.

A red leather office chair.

The click and the hum and the warm breeze as the house's heating system sprang to life.

Waiting.

Photos on the wall.

Other, more important photos on the shelf, Keane's family photos.

More waiting.

Attacking. Death. Piss.

The family photos.

The wife. The son. The happy couple. The whole family.

Claire, the wife. Blonde hair and smiles.

Brendan. A son. A teenager ... a kid. Shaved head. Brooding glower.

Giving his head a shake, Silence fought to regain control, to return to the present. The images of Keane and his family slowly faded. He was back in the forest.

Not a forest.

A wooded area.

In a city. A large city. Indianapolis.

He was in a copse on the edge of the parking lot of an abandoned business usurped by Colin Lennox, the man who was about to lead dozens of people to their deaths.

The man with Silence in the trees was Avery Malone. Security guard. Injured. Broken ankle, courtesy of Colin Lennox.

Silence was back.

He glanced at the warehouse, reminded himself of the urgency, then turned his attention to Malone.

"Go to hospital…" he said and swallowed. "Before you pass out."

The tone of voice he imparted through his ruined throat left no room for argument.

Malone just nodded. He clutched the keys Silence had given him.

Silence offered a hand. Malone took it and immediately howled as Silence yanked him to his feet.

Unfortunately, there was no time to be gentler.

A few minutes later, after helping Malone out of the trees and into the Q45, Silence trekked across the parking lot.

His legs were unsteady—the unrelenting hold of the damn drugs in his system—but he reminded himself of the reasons for returning to the warehouse, for walking back into the laced incense.

Maya Fuller.

Nate Fuller.

Taylor Perrine.

…and the need to confront Colin Lennox.

These thoughts coalesced into a singular drive, a fortified resolve as he continued his trek back to Lennox's domain.

33

In the control room, Colin Lennox stood alongside Michael Pushard, who'd been playing the role of Nate Fuller, their attention riveted to the wall of black-and-white monitors before them.

The screens flickered with living images of the warehouse's hidden corners and corridors, the world Lennox had engineered, a world that was now falling apart right in front of him.

As Lennox watched the screens, he unconsciously scratched at the scars on his neck. Realized what he was doing. And stopped.

Lennox's suspicion, the dark fear he'd given birth to moments earlier in the assembly hall, was confirmed. The surveillance footage, a patchwork of different angles and views, told a story *he hadn't scripted*, each scene playing out before him.

Infuriating.

The narrative unfolded with Beckwith—who should have been one of Lennox's trusted allies alongside Mike, now a traitor—in a hallway. He was with two others: Avery Malone and the operator.

All three wore the gas masks from general-purpose room 2. Beckwith supported the others as they walked—Malone hopping on one foot and the operator wobbling under the effects of the special incense. Malone leaned heavily on Beckwith's shoulder, while Beckwith's hand was firmly placed on the operator, keeping the man balanced.

The trio hobbled off.

Seeing the three together, a hastily formed band of allies, was like a silent sign of Lennox's slipping control. His well-crafted drama, the complex webs of lies and power, were being undone, piece by piece.

But Lennox had ways of pulling the story back to his script...

The outside camera caught the group's last moments on site. They made their way across the decrepit parking lot, navigating the vehicles, and soon slipped off the edge of the screen, disappearing into the world outside Lennox's domain.

Lennox smacked the control panel hard enough to make Mike jump beside him. In his rage, Lennox still managed to hit his target: the pause button. The screen he and Mike were watching froze, now marked by a pair of static lines running horizontally across it.

His thoughts raged, a whirlwind of wrath, the classic response of a man backstabbed by his own.

Beckwith...

The fact that it was *that* stupid buffoon who'd started the unraveling of Lennox's narrative was almost too much to bear.

But, really, it hadn't been Beckwith.

It was the operator.

Lennox's hands balled into fists. His mind was already a few steps ahead, writing the next beat in his amended outline. The operator wouldn't evade him for long.

He checked the timestamp on the frozen screen. Beckwith's breakout was recent. A glance at his watch to confirm. Yes, less than ten minutes ago.

Turning to Mike, he said, "They couldn't have gotten far, not with one drugged-up guy and another with a busted ankle." He jabbed his finger at the monitor that displayed the now-empty parking lot. "Check it."

Mike gave a curt nod and left the control room without wasting a moment.

Michael Pushard. Once a user, now a dutiful lackey. And a damned fine actor, too, as it turned out. That's why Lennox had chosen him for the most crucial of all the roles in his production.

Lennox was alone now with his screens and his thoughts. The room was quiet, just the soft hum of electronic equipment. The images flickered.

He didn't move, staring at the monitor that had shown the last glimpse of his betrayer, Grant Beckwith.

34

He could smell the damn incense the moment he stepped back into the building.

Silence had just re-entered Lennox's compound a few minutes earlier. He used the same entry point—where he'd earlier broken in through the flap of bent metal siding—but eschewed the stealth with which he'd entered the first time when he'd carefully avoided the cameras. Lennox was already aware of Silence's presence and possibly his departure; he'd be stunned to know Silence *wanted* to return.

Silence's movements faltered under the lingering influence of the drugs. Each step was a fight against disorientation, his body swaying unsteadily as he navigated the now-familiar yet hostile environment.

Delving farther into the building, Silence's hand instinctively reached for the Beretta tucked beneath his sport coat. The familiar weight was a comforting presence amid chaos. He needed that comfort now.

But as he grasped the handle, his trembling fingers betrayed him. Straining to focus, he glanced at the weapon in his hand, saw that it was wobbling violently, and had to concede—in his current state, he had no business with a firearm. Reluctantly, Silence shoved the Beretta back in its holster.

The quiet of the warehouse was punctuated by the distant hum of conversation. As he cautiously advanced toward the assembly hall, a sudden flash of movement caught the corner of his eye.

Instantly, his hand darted toward the Beretta again. But in the split second it took to react, he remembered and adjusted with a different approach.

He lunged toward the figure emerging from the shadows with a swift, fluid motion. His hands found their target, and he slammed the figure against the wall. The sound reverberated in the empty space.

Silence's face was inches from the person he'd pinned. His eyes, still struggling to focus, slowly registered the other man's identity.

He released his grip.

It was Beckwith.

"Chad, what are you doing back here?" Beckwith gasped. "You should be getting medical help, not ... not this."

After the brief scuffle, Silence's symptoms flared, and he barely registered Beckwith's words.

The mission.

Focus.

Focus on the mission.

"You said everything..." Silence said and swallowed. "Is staged. Talk."

Beckwith nodded, his expression turning grave. "Yes, it's all a ruse. Everyone here, the so-called suicidal guests, the staff ... they're all part of Lennox's performance. This is theatre, nothing more."

He paused, looked up and down the hall.

"All of Lennox's 'followers,' they *are* suicidal, but they never came to Lennox for help. Lennox found them through some sort of electronic database. They're all homeless people, many of them drug-addicted, many of them military veterans, all of them suicidal, all of them dirt-poor. He's paying them each a hundred bucks to follow tonight's script, to act like they're members of a group that doesn't exist."

Silence's eyes narrowed, processing the information. The reality of Lennox's manipulation was more extensive than he had imagined.

"*Tonight's* script?" Silence said, swallowed. "What about..." Another swallow. "Earlier meetings?"

Beckwith shook his head. "Man, there never were any other meetings.

That's all part of the story, too. The backstory. None of this is real! Lennox hired me only two weeks ago, but he's been building up to this for years, evidently."

Silence's head was spinning. The drugs in his system weren't helping matters.

"And tonight's big event?" Silence said.

"I don't know. Lennox told me most of it, but he wouldn't tell me what's actually happening at the end of the night. I'm one of only two people Lennox trusted with the background information. The other inside man is—"

"Me," a voice echoed from the end of the hall.

The scrape of shoes against concrete echoed down the hallway. Both men pivoted toward the sound.

It was Nate Fuller.

Fuller emerged from the shadows. And not by himself. He was propping up Avery Malone, who hopped on one foot, grimacing painfully every time he landed. Fuller had a knife pressed threateningly against Malone's side.

Behind Fuller, Lennox's other personnel materialized—all those maroon henley shirts, black jeans, and brawny figures—and the goons formed a tight circle around Silence and Beckwith. Their faces were masks of stoic indifference, hardened expressions of men accustomed to violence.

And then, striding forward with a demeanor that exuded power and control, came Colin Lennox himself. Flashy suit. Scarred face. Broad smile. Hands shoved in his pockets.

His eyes locked onto Beckwith with a cold, calculating gaze.

"Was it worth it, Beckwith?" Lennox asked, his snake voice devoid of emotion. It was more a statement than a question, an acknowledgment of the betrayal.

Beckwith stood defiant yet resigned. He met Lennox's gaze.

"To do the right thing? You bet it was," he said.

In Beckwith's eyes, there was a flicker of something akin to peace, a man who had come to terms with his fate.

Lennox shrugged. "Fair enough." His eyes swept over his muscle men. "You know which one to grab and which one to bring down."

Before Silence could react, chaos erupted.

As Lennox's goons surged forward, Silence moved with a blend of instinct and skill, but the drugs smeared the edges of his precision.

He launched a vicious palm strike—a krav maga technique—to the first attacker, feeling the satisfying crunch of nose cartilage. But as he pivoted, a second goon's fist grazed his jaw.

Silence stumbled back, then retaliated with a swift Muay Thai elbow strike to the man's temple, a move as efficient as it was brutal. This was a routine strike for Silence. Typically. But this time, his equilibrium warbled, making his footing falter.

He stumbled forward a few paces, regained his balance.

And stopped.

Because Lennox's goons were backing away.

Lennox was to the side, laughing.

And Silence spun just in time to witness Beckwith's fall.

The body crumpled to the concrete. A dark red halo spread instantly.

Fuller stood over Beckwith. He wore a macabre grin. The blade in his hand glistened wet. Blood dripped from the tip.

Beckwith's leg spasmed. Then, he was entirely still.

Silence's unexpected ally, the one person who could navigate him through Lennox's physical and psychological maze, was dead.

To the side, Malone was in the grasp of a pair of maroon-shirted men standing beside Lennox.

And in the middle of it all was Silence.

Panting.

Wobbling from the drugs in his system.

Completely encircled.

Lennox took a couple of steps forward, hands going behind his back.

"Let's chat for a moment, shall we?" Lennox said. With a snarky grin, he pointed at Silence's throat and added, "Don't worry. I'll do all the talking."

35

The air was heavier now, charged with a sense of death.

Silence fought to clear his head, but the drugs in his body were relentless, turning each breath into a laborious task.

Lennox seemed almost energized. He stood there, looking James Dean-casual as he leaned against the wall, his eyes shining with a harsh, predatory intelligence. The room felt smaller with him in it, as if his very presence sucked the space into himself.

"You see, Chad," Lennox began, his voice steady and sure, "the guy you've been chasing, Nathan Fuller, he's not who you think. His real name's Michael Pushard." He moved around the room, a serpentine predator slithering through its cage. "Pushard's a hard case, a real piece of work. Armed robbery, extortion, he's even a suspect in a bunch of missing persons cases. But his real gift, his true talent, was being a chameleon. Becoming whoever he needed to be. That's what made him so valuable to me."

Silence looked over at Pushard, standing over Beckwith's body. The knife had stopped dripping. Pushard winked.

Silence's mind reeled. Nate Fuller, the guy he'd been tracking, the guy who dodged Silence's every attempt to help, the guy who took him to Lennox's meeting location...

Nothing. It was all a sham. A role played so flawlessly that Silence never once doubted its truth.

And why should he have? The intel from the Watchers had been crystal clear—photos, a full biography, everything...

...right down to the guy's address.

Silence remembered Fuller's house. Run-down. A jungle of weeds for a yard. Old furniture.

If he hadn't known better at the time, the Silence of earlier that day might have sworn the house was abandoned.

It probably was. A derelict house that Lennox had repurposed for his charade.

Just like this forsaken factory and warehouse...

"And Maya," Lennox went on, lips curling into a sick grin, "the poor, suicidal sister-in-law, was nothing but a fictional character. A tool to toy with you, to draw you deeper into the web. She was the perfect emotional bait, wasn't she?"

The room seemed to close in on Silence. His legs buckled again. A wave of dizziness swept through him. Every truth he'd clung to during this mission was unraveling.

A gleam of perverse excitement shone in Lennox's eyes as he leaned in, ready to unveil something delicious.

"So, here's the grand finale of our little drama," he said. "Those people over there in the assembly hall, they think they're just extras in a staged mass suicide. A bit of grim theatre, nothing more, right?"

He paused, letting the suspense hang in the air.

"Here's the twist. When they start acting out their 'deaths,' thinking it's all just for show, that's when I make my move. I've got a little surprise in store tonight that's going to turn their pretending into something very real."

He stopped again, long enough to pin Silence with a sharp gaze.

"Remember the rumor about Jordan Havelock? That he intended for the gas cans to explode and kill all his followers?" Lennox gave a dismissive shake of his head. "Wrong. Havelock was genuinely trying to help suicidal people, and that blast was an accident. Just like the official story says. Just like everyone believes. But me and this guy," he gestured toward Fuller, or

Michael Pushard, as it turned out, "we had you convinced that Havelock, an entirely decent human being, was a monster."

Lennox laughed heartily.

"Tonight, just for kicks, I'm going to bring to life the fiction I fed you. The gas cans in the assembly hall? The actors think they're just props. But they're not. They're filled to the brim with gasoline. And I've rigged a reaaaaaally long fuse." He paused for effect, then added, "*Boom!* These people have been loyal, keeping my secrets for a miserable hundred bucks a piece. But after tonight?" He shrugged. "Who can say? Loose ends aren't something I can afford."

A bunch of unsuspecting souls, duped into playing a part in a mock mass suicide, unknowingly marching toward a meticulously planned mass slaughter—all just to ensure there were no survivors, no one to expose Lennox's acts.

The full weight of Lennox's plot crashed over Silence. The looming tragedy, the lives hanging in the balance. Confusion twisted inside him, a knot of unanswered questions.

"Why me? Why these innocents?" Silence said and swallowed. "What's your endgame?"

Lennox just smirked in response.

"You still don't get it, do you?" he said, seeming to savor the torment he was inflicting. "You'll have to piece it together on your own. For now, just know this—you'll be here, powerless, as they perish. Their blood will be on your hands."

Time was slipping away. Silence needed to act. A wave of resistance surged within him. He refused to be just another player in Lennox's script. He couldn't let this tragedy unfold.

Silence sprang into action. He hurtled toward Lennox, intent on taking him down.

But he didn't make it far.

Instantly, Lennox's maroon-shirted men swarmed him. One assailant lunged, aiming a clumsy blow at Silence's head. With a swift sidestep, Silence dodged, his arm shooting out to deliver a sharp jab to the man's throat. The attacker staggered back, gasping for air.

Silence staggered, too, the momentum of his swing pulling him forward through his inebriated balance.

Another guy came at him from the side, but Silence was already turning, his leg sweeping out in a low arc, knocking the second man off his feet. The man dropped, hit the concrete hard, and gasped for air.

More of Lennox's men closed in, their faces twisted in aggression.

Silence shifted his weight, readying himself for the next wave, stumbled, and realized this was futile; the drugs had dug in too damn deep. He needed to escape, to buy time for the chemicals to work their way out of his system.

A smaller guy lunged at him. Silence sidestepped, seized the man's arm, spun him around full circle, and released. The man crashed into his approaching comrades, creating a brief window of opportunity.

It was all the time Silence needed.

He dashed around the corner, and his eyes caught the potential hideaway he'd noted earlier—a crawl space entry at floor level, lined up with the cracks in the wall, almost unnoticeable. It was a gamble, but his only chance.

Diving into the crawl space, Silence narrowly escaped the men thundering up behind him as they peeled around the corner. He crammed himself into the tight, dusty spot. His heart pounded, the sounds of his chasers dulled by the confining walls.

Huddled in this makeshift shelter, Silence tried to focus, to plot his next move. He had to intervene, to stop the impending mass murder. But as he strained to strategize, a fresh wave of dizziness overwhelmed him, the drugs reminding him of their dominance.

Nausea churned in his stomach. His limbs grew heavy and unresponsive.

His body was betraying him.

Trapped in the crawl space, Silence was hit by a dark realization: he might be too late to prevent Lennox's plot.

36

Nothing but a bunch of losers.

Lennox smirked as he surveyed them from his elevated vantage point on the stage.

In the expanse of the main warehouse floor, his assembly hall, an air of anticipation hung heavy. The rows of metal folding chairs, arranged with military precision, faced the stage, and seated in those chairs, Lennox's so-called disciples, his so-called loyalists.

Actors, all of them.

But not *paid* actors. Not yet, anyway.

It's astounding the lengths a junkie will go for a few bucks. The homeless are born performers, feigning ailments and sob stories to wring a few coins from passersby. It had been an easy way for Lennox to fill his cast.

Cokeheads, ex-cons, alcoholics, drifters—it was a motley crew occupying those metal folding chairs, each one plucked from the neglected corners of Indianapolis society.

Outside these walls, their faces were bedraggled, sun-stained, wrinkled, sunken. But here, transformed, they wore expressions of hope, of unwavering faith, all eyes fixed on the stage.

Lennox surveyed the gathering, pausing to appraise individual faces among the throng. Every person had been handpicked for their perceived theatrical talent, their innate ability to play a role in Lennox's master plan.

The crowd returned his gaze, their eyes shining with admiration and wonder. They were primed to hang on his every word, to follow his commands unquestioningly. They were believers, converts to his vision of a world reshaped in his image.

But, really, none of it was real.

Because they were all just actors.

Damn good actors.

Rather than addressing them, Lennox reached for a remote control on the podium. The crowd leaned in, their collective breath caught in anticipation. They expected a speech, a rallying cry to stir their souls.

But Lennox pivoted, his gaze fixing on a camera nestled unobtrusively in the corner of the room. The camera's red light glowed. With a press of the button, the light winked out. The camera, the unblinking eye that had captured every moment of the evening, was now dark.

Murmurs rippled through the crowd.

What is this? someone whispered.

We were told we wouldn't break character, another voice added.

Lennox raised his hand, the gesture commanding immediate quiet. His face broke into a sly grin. The crowd, still puzzled, watched him with bated breath. They were the players in his play, and the script was about to take an unexpected turn.

"There's been a small change of plans," Lennox said. "We're not going to continue with the third portion of the performance." He paused, letting his words sink in, relishing the tide of reactions that flowed through the room.

His eyes swept over the crowd, taking in their expressions of confusion and curiosity. "Instead, we're going straight to the big event: the faked suicide."

The words hung in the air, bold and unapologetic.

"It's time," he continued, pointing to the now-dark camera. "When I turn that camera on and give my spiel, you wait until I leave, then give it a couple of minutes before you drop to the floor and start spasming. Got it?"

The actors in the crowd exchanged perplexed glances. The change in the order of events was unexpected, but they were Lennox's pawns, and his word was taken as dogma.

Throwing away all vestiges of pride for a few measly bucks...

Yes, nothing but a bunch of losers.

Slowly, they nodded.

The stage was set, the actors ready.

The next act of Lennox's twisted play was about to begin.

"Good," Lennox said. "Then resume your roles." When he continued, he spoke in an over-the-top rendition of a movie director. "Places, people. Annnnd ... action."

He aimed the remote control at the camera and pressed a button.

The red light glowed.

Recording.

37

Silence was coiled tight in the confined space, a spring under tension.

His thoughts were swimming, as turbulent as his stomach. The air was stale and heavy.

And the drugs wouldn't let up.

In this claustrophobic hideaway, reality lost form, twisting into grotesque shapes. Time fractured and warped.

Then her voice, soft and hauntingly familiar, cut through the haze.

Chad, C.C. said. *You need to leave this place.*

Silence jerked back, suspicion igniting in his fogged mind.

This wasn't right. C.C. had never used the name "Chad" when she was alive; "Chad" was a cover he'd cooked up just that day for the Indianapolis job.

His mind flashed back to the last time he'd heard C.C.'s voice echoing in the air ducts. That had been a cruel distortion of his fiancée, a wicked phantom voice.

This time, however, she was speaking sweetly.

Yet she had called him "Chad"...

This was just another wicked hallucination, far from the C.C. he held in his thoughts.

This isn't you, Silence's internal voice replied. *You're just another lie this poison is telling me.*

Still, she persisted. He sensed, rather than saw, her drawing nearer.

Love, listen to me. You're tougher than you know. You can beat this poison. Avery Malone needs you. You're the only one to help him.

Avery Malone. The name cut through the mental murk like a beacon. Avery was real, a solid anchor to the world beyond this fevered dreamscape.

But how would C.C. know about him?

Listen to me, Chad, C.C. said. *Get out. You have to get out. You've got to help Malone, and—*

Don't call me Chad!

Silence was about to add something else when another voice broke in, also saying "Chad."

But the voice was different.

It was a man's.

"Chad!" The call cut through the mirage, an urgent plea from the reality beyond the haze.

It was Avery Malone, out there somewhere in the building, his voice fearful.

He was in trouble.

C.C. was right.

Silence's heart raced. His mind's version of C.C. must have merged with the drug-induced hallucinations and the actual voice echoing from somewhere in the building.

Reality and mania blurring into one.

Love, go to him, C.C. urged, her voice fading away.

She was right.

Whether it was the usual spectral form of her that he harbored in his mind or an illusion crafted by the drugs, she was right.

She always was.

"Chad!" Malone's voice echoed from somewhere in the distance, in the real world. "Chad, you've got to get out!"

Summoning a burst of determination that overpowered the narcotics coursing through his veins, Silence forced himself up. His actions were sluggish and uncoordinated yet fueled by a resurgent purpose.

But the body has its limits...

A surge of nausea and a tidal wave of hallucinatory chaos swept over Silence. He collapsed back down, his head thudding against the wall.

From outside, Malone's voice rang out again.

"*Chad!*"

38

Avery felt the guy's breath, hot and uneven, against his ear.

"Say it again!" Pushard barked.

The knife pressed hard against Avery's side. He could feel the deadly sharp edge even through the thick cloth of his uniform.

Avery followed the command and shouted into the hallway once more. "Chad!"

His voice, though forced, carried real pain and fear. And he hated himself for it.

"Chad, he'll kill me if you don't come out!"

Pushard shoved Avery forward another yard down the hallway. With his arm slung over Pushard's shoulder—much like it had been over Beckwith's earlier—Avery staggered...

...and all his weight fell right onto his shattered ankle.

He stumbled, but Pushard caught him.

Avery screamed as pain erupted from his leg, sweeping through him. The agony had been relentless to this point, a fierce tide threatening to pull him under, but now that he'd taken a full-weight step on his bad foot, the tide was just about to pull him into its dark depths.

Avery gritted his teeth, fighting back.

White spots danced at the edge of his vision.

He was drifting into delirium. His head felt light, and he couldn't tell if it was the pain or if he'd breathed in the same toxic incense that had floored Chad. Either way, his body was a paradox of cold and warmth, tingling and drenched in sweat and, conveniently, somewhat numb to the world.

Losing consciousness seemed almost inviting.

But every time he came close to escaping some of the pain, it surged back—because Pushard kept shoving him forward. Every step was a battle against the searing protest from his ankle.

The tidepool grew stronger. Avery felt its undertow. He welcomed it, a tumble into nothingness, something to escape this agony.

Avery staggered.

Vaguely, he was aware of Pushard's grip, an iron vice around his shoulder—part support, part forced march through the twisted passageways of Lennox's stronghold. The makeshift lighting cast unnerving shadows on the walls, the surrounding darkness pulsating.

And the knife.

Always the knife—the blade's presence unwavering, prodding into Avery's side whenever he dared slow down.

Just as Avery's consciousness threatened to slip away, Pushard's voice cut through the fog.

"Again!"

Suddenly, the blade jabbed into Avery's side, the tip piercing fabric and flesh, a white-hot flash burning through the haze clouding Avery's mind.

Avery's scream bounced off the walls, harsh and jarring.

And he obeyed. "Chad, come out!"

The words tasted poisonous.

Because they were both a surrender and a betrayal—surrendering to Pushard's will and betraying Chad, drawing the man out while he was drugged, defenseless, unable to protect himself or Avery.

But there was the knife.

And the pulsing agony from Avery's lower leg.

Avery had no choice but to submit.

Or did he?

Those earlier dreams of heroism, Avery's burning ambitions to be something more, something greater, flashed through his mind.

So did a single word he'd repeated to Chad in the trees: *hero*.

Would a hero be in this position? A prisoner supplicating at knifepoint? A man willing to draw a friend out of safety to save his own hide?

This isn't me, Avery thought.

No. Not at all. Avery knew he was more than this.

The forced march continued, but inside Avery, something changed. His thoughts crystallized into a sharp, unyielding focus: this was his moment.

Yes, Avery was ready to break free from the chains of fear and doubt. He realized then that heroism wasn't about grand gestures or dramatic confrontations; it was about making a stand, no matter how modest, in the face of growing darkness.

With newfound determination fueling him, Avery pulled together every shred of strength and clarity he had left.

Then he made his move.

He lunged at Pushard.

39

Lennox glanced up at the camera in the corner. The red light flashed.

Returning his attention to the seated "followers," Lennox's voice filled the space, adopting a dramatic, theatrical tone.

"Ladies and gentlemen," he began, his words echoing off the walls, "we stand at the precipice of something extraordinary."

His voice rose and fell with the cadence of a practiced performer—which, of course, he was.

"Life," he continued, "is just a fleeting moment, a brief dance in the light before we return to the darkness from whence we came."

The actors assembled before him listened with faux-rapt attention, their faces a mix of fascination and solemnity. Accordingly, Lennox put forth a commanding image, his aura that of a prophet delivering a final, undeniable truth.

All of it for the camera.

He paced slowly, his steps measured.

"Death is not an enemy to be feared," he said, adopting a more philosophical tone. "It's a natural part of our journey, an inevitable destination that gives meaning to our existence."

The actors were totally convincing in their pretend captivation. Lennox couldn't have been prouder.

He was a bit disappointed in himself at that moment, however. For all his planning, he'd still not put enough time into writing the final speech. He'd gone through four drafts, but it really could have used a fifth. It was just a bit too lofty, a bit too melodramatic.

Oh well.

Such were the eternal frustrations of a perfectionist.

"Many fear death because they do not understand it," Lennox continued, letting his gaze sweep over the crowd. "But tonight, we embrace it as the ultimate liberation, a freeing of the soul from the shackles of this earthly realm."

The crowd nodded in agreement, their faces showing a mixture of awe and relief.

Lennox's voice, still rich with dramatic inflection, took on a more somber note as he prepared for the big moment.

"And now," he said and paused for effect, "we come to the culmination of our journey together."

The actors, their attention unwavering, waited for his next words with a hushed expectancy.

"The time's come for us to embrace our destiny. You've all agreed to this fate, to end your lives in a demonstration of our ultimate freedom from the bonds of this world." He took a moment to let the gravity of his statement sink in, then added, "After I leave this room, it'll fill with a pleasant gas, infusing the incense you're already breathing. For those of you who want to make a more poignant exit, I would suggest *that* gas."

He pointed to the gasoline cans on the opposite side of the room.

"I want to offer that as an option, but I feel that's the one way—the *one way*—Jordan Havelock was mistaken. Self-immolation, it's too violent. I would suggest you simply breathe in my special incense. It will be quick, painless, and you will pass into the next realm with dignity."

The actors, fully immersed in the reality Lennox had crafted, nodded in agreement. Their faces, illuminated by the dim lighting of the warehouse, showed for the camera a solemn acceptance of their fate.

Lennox acknowledged the display of acquiescence by offering a final message.

"I wish you peace," he said quietly. "And know that I will see you all on the other side."

With that, he turned slowly and went for the door. As he walked, the actors kept doing their thing—they *really* wanted their hundred bucks a piece—feigning mass anticipation, a gentle but fervent murmur.

As Lennox neared the door, his eyes involuntarily traced the line of the detonation fuse—a thin, unassuming cord. The fuse snaked its way around the warehouse's perimeter, right where the floor met the wall, barely perceptible, starting beyond the doorway Lennox was approaching, going past the stage, around the rear of the space, and to the gasoline cans.

He looked at the cans sitting back there in the darkness. Five-gallon drums. Red. Just like Havelock's had been.

He smirked.

But almost as soon as it appeared, Lennox undid the grin, smoothing his features back into the composed, impassive mask he usually wore. He couldn't afford even the slightest crack in his facade, not when he was so close to achieving his goals, not when the camera was still rolling.

Lennox reached the door and used both arms to pull its substantial weight along its track.

The door shut with a resonant thud.

40

Wedged into the narrow confines of the crawl space, Silence wrestled with the mind-bending hallucinations the drugs were throwing his way.

Shadows twisted and pulsed around him, warping into grotesque forms that danced on the fringes of reality.

C.C.

Doc Hazel.

Younger Colin Lennox—the FBI agent.

Modern-day Colin Lennox—the lunatic.

Silence's fingers scoured the rough concrete, searching for something solid in a world slipping away. Whispers danced around him. *C.C. Doc Hazel. Lennox.* His heart hammered in rhythm with the procession of unsettling sensations.

Digging deep, he sharpened his focus, forcing it to cut through the fog. Because he'd heard it again. Malone's urgent call. *Chad!* Sharp and clear. It hadn't been another hallucination. He knew it. Malone needed him. It was time to move.

Silence heaved himself out of the crawl space.

And back into the real world.

He took off, wobbling down the hallway. The stringed-up bulbs along the walls danced in his vision, creating streaks of light.

As he rounded the corner, he saw something that helped his mind to recenter, bringing his mission to the forefront.

It was Avery Malone.

And the guy was in trouble.

Malone and Michael Pushard, the man Silence had known as Nate Fuller, were locked in a desperate struggle. Malone, battered but unyielding, fought with a raw ferocity.

In an instant, Silence sized up the scene. There was Malone, hopping on one foot, drenched in sweat. Silence's gut screamed at him to jump in, to pull Malone out of the fray and take down Pushard. But just as he tensed to move, the fight took a sudden turn.

Malone got an impressive grip on Pushard's wrist, yanked the man's arm behind his back, and put Pushard into a sleeper hold, his forearm clamping around Pushard's throat with unexpected expertise.

Pushard's resistance turned frenzied, then hopeless, as the hold took its toll. His swipes slowed, turned sluggish, and then stopped. He collapsed.

Silence stood there, dumbstruck for a moment by the swift reversal.

Malone, whom he had pegged as a sitting duck because of his broken ankle, had just flipped the script on a formidable opponent. Silence had severely underestimated Malone's determination and grit.

Staggering on shaky legs, Silence lumbered toward Malone and Pushard. Each step was a struggle. The momentary clarity he'd grasped was slipping away, replaced by a disorienting fog that blurred his vision and scrambled his thoughts.

Ahead, Malone's knees gave way, and he crumpled against the wall, sinking to the floor in a heap. His breathing came in gasps, the aftermath of the fight and the torment of his shattered ankle clearly overwhelming him.

As Silence reached the pair, he suddenly leaned a hand against the wall for support. The world around him swayed and dipped, but he fought to stay upright, to stay conscious. He glanced down at Pushard, noting the steady rise and fall of the man's chest—knocked out, but breathing.

His attention then shifted to Malone. Despite the agony on the man's perspiration-drenched face, Malone had taken down Pushard, a remarkable feat under the circumstances. Silence understood the torment of broken bones all too well, making Malone's accomplishment even more notable.

In the haze of his disorientation and amidst the unfolding chaos, Silence's eyes went to the wall of industrial-style windows at the end of the hallway, its cracked-open sliding door offering a view into the main floor of the warehouse, Lennox's so-called "assembly hall." Through the crack, he saw Lennox's actors, the men and women who were portraying his hangers-on, gathered together in anticipation of what they believed to be a staged mass suicide.

Recalling what Lennox had said, Silence understood the reality of the scene ahead. These people, duped and deluded, were teetering on the brink of disaster. Lennox had twisted their theatrical ruse into a lethal snare.

Despite the haze shrouding his thoughts in that critical moment, Silence pieced together a plan. Time was ticking away; he needed to act swiftly to avert a tragedy. The finer details of his strategy were blurred, his mind wrestling with the lingering effects of the drug, but a rudimentary blueprint was emerging amidst the turmoil in his head.

With the plan forming, Silence shifted his focus to Pushard's prone figure on the floor. He moved cautiously, mindful of his wobbly stance, as he rifled through Pushard's pockets.

His fingers closed around something small and metallic. He pulled it out. Pushard's lighter.

As he pocketed the lighter, Malone's eyes met his. Malone, still propped against the wall, now regarded Silence with a blend of bewilderment and interest.

Silence responded to Malone's unspoken question with a simple, "Be right back."

There was no time for explanations.

Turning away from Malone, Silence started toward the assembly hall.

41

This was it. They were about to go out with a literal bang.

All of them.

The dumb shits.

Tucked away in a shadowy corner of the dim hallway, Lennox held the detonation fuse in one hand, a lighter in the other. A wicked grin played on his lips, and the electric buzz of imminent triumph electrified his senses. This was it—the culmination of a plan so meticulously laid out, it had taken years to reach this crescendo.

Only moments away.

Lennox's mind churned with exultant thoughts. This moment would be a crushing defeat for the operator. Each life that was about to be extinguished in the warehouse, every scream that would echo in the halls, would be a manifestation of Lennox's genius and the operator's failure. The weight of this catastrophe would crush the operator, a burden too heavy, too dark.

Lennox reflected on the web he'd spun, the deceit, the manipulation. Every move was a carefully placed piece of a complex puzzle, now aligning flawlessly.

The bitterness of past slights, the injustices he'd swallowed, the losses he'd suffered—they all burned within him, fueling this moment. This wasn't just mass murder; it was a reckoning, a settling of scores against those who'd wronged him.

And the operator was the centerpiece, the targeted embodiment of Lennox's wrath.

Toying with the lighter, Lennox savored the mounting anticipation, each second stretched to its limit as he contemplated the act that would seal his victory. His finger hovered over the ignition. Hidden in that hallway, he was about to rewrite history and bring the operator to his knees.

All with a swipe of his thumb.

He readied the lighter.

Flick. Flick. Poof.

A one-inch flame danced into existence.

The inconspicuous fuse in his other hand was the final component. It waited patiently.

Lennox moved the lighter close to the fuse.

A foot of space separated the pair.

Now nine inches.

Now six.

The flame flickered a mere three inches from the fuse's end. This was where Lennox stopped, holding it there to savor the anticipation. The quiet of the hallway was profound, broken only by the faint sound of his breathing and the hiss of the lighter.

Enough waiting.

He lifted the lighter.

Just as the flame was about to kiss the fuse...

...everything changed.

A deluge of water cascaded from above, dousing Lennox and extinguishing the lighter. He was soaked instantly, the water pouring down from the ceiling in a torrent.

Lennox looked up, blinking as water pelted his eyes.

He realized what had happened. The building's sprinkler system had activated.

His gaze shifted from the now useless lighter in his hand to the drenched fuse.

The water continued pouring from the sprinklers. Lennox stood there, drenched, water cascading down his face, his entire body. His arms shook with both chill and rage.

This was no accident.

This was the operator.

42

Silence perched precariously on a folding chair, arm fully extended above his head, stretching his six-foot-three frame to its limits.

In his hand, Pushard's lighter flickered, puttering in the artificial rain. A moment earlier, Silence had raised it to the nearest sprinkler head.

The heat did its job.

The sprinkler system, old and neglected, had groaned into life, unleashing torrents of water. With any luck, that would have done the trick against Lennox's plan to ignite the gas cans.

He imagined it had. Fuses don't work so great when they're wet.

The water cascaded over Silence, rolling in sheets down his length. He tossed the lighter aside; it clattered away in a trio of splashes.

As Silence tried to climb down, his feet slipped, and for a moment, he was suspended in mid-air, a marionette cut loose from its strings, before he crashed to the concrete with a wet thud.

Pain shot through his back while numbing cold water poured over him.

Lying there, drenched and disoriented, Silence's vision blurred. The world around him warped into a hallucinatory carousel. Shapes twisted, colors ran, and for a moment, he was lost in a deluge of water and visions.

C.C.

Lennox.

Doc Hazel.

Lennox.

C.C.

C.C.

Lennox.

But this was no time for weakness.

With a grunt, he banished the spectral images invading his mind and heaved his battered body to its feet.

He lurched forward, rounding a bend. Through the industrial-style windows lining the main warehouse floor, he glimpsed the turmoil his actions had incited. Lennox's actors had snapped out of make-believe, now panicked at the notion of an apparent fire in the ancient building they were occupying.

Lennox was there, too, outside the door, drenched like everyone else, waving and screaming at the opaque windows. An explosion of frantic energy pulse through the mass of people as they surged against the door, their collective panic drowning out his shouted orders.

Then, with a resonate metallic groan, the sliding door yielded. The crowd had hurled themselves at it, wrenching it down with the kind of raw force only a panicked mob can muster. Silence observed as the door caved under their collective might, the actors spilling into the hallway in a flood of terror-stricken bodies.

Lennox freaked.

The man's usual air of control had crumbled, his face twisted into a mask of fury and disbelief as his carefully orchestrated scheme fell apart around him. He flailed his arms, desperately trying to stem the human tide, but they swept past him, heedless of his commands.

As Silence stumbled forward, the distance between him and Lennox dwindled. Now, closer, he saw that Lennox's face was a canvas of unadulterated fury. His eyes, usually so controlled and calculating, burned with untamed fire. His shouts and threats weren't the intimidating, charismatic snake venom of earlier; they were just the desperate cries of a man watching his plan crumble.

Abruptly, Lennox stopped screaming.

And spun his attention on Silence.

Streams of water cascaded over Lennox, tracing his scars.

He moved forward. Silence didn't divert his path. They came to a standstill barely a yard apart, enveloped in a synthetic downpour.

"You're wobbly, *Chad*," Lennox taunted, putting an odd emphasis on Silence's pseudonym. "It wouldn't be hard for me to take you out. You're vulnerable, disoriented. A sitting duck."

But Lennox made no move to attack. Instead, his next words cut deeper than any physical blow could.

"I know who you are, Silence Jones," Lennox hissed.

Silence felt his world tilt.

His name.

The name he had adopted when he joined the Watchers, a new name that signified the shedding of his former self.

It was a secret held close, known only to a select few.

"Or is it 'Jake Rowe'?" Lennox continued, giving Silence a wide-eyed shrug of feigned confusion.

Jake Rowe, his original name, the one given to him at birth.

The name tied to a past life, a different face, a different voice, a different identity.

The name of the man who'd won C.C.'s heart.

That name was meant to be buried, unknown to the world outside the Watchers. As far as anyone else was concerned, Jake Rowe no longer existed.

Silence stumbled. His foot splashed through a puddle.

Lennox clasped his hands behind his back and leaned in closer, blinking water rivulets out of his eyes.

"I have multiple names, too," Lennox said. "My real name is Brendan Keane. Does that ring a bell? It should. You assassinated my father."

Brendan...

There it was. The connection between the Code Red, the old mission, and Colin Lennox.

The angsty teen in the family photos.

He'd be a mid-twenties man now.

Just like Colin Lennox.

Silence was unsure if his drug-weakened legs could sustain him under the weight of such a revelation.

"You killed Richard Keane, staged his suicide," Brendan said. "Just another job for a killer like you, huh? To me, it was everything. You destroyed my world. Now, I'm here to destroy yours."

Brendan's grin was hideously triumphant.

"There is no Colin Lennox," he said. "Never was. These?" He gestured toward his scars. "Prosthetics. High-end prosthetics."

He dug his fingernails into one of the apparent scars, right into one of the trio of deep fissures, gripping it tightly. A sound like fabric tearing filled the air as he peeled it away from his actual flesh.

Silence saw a foam core structure.

Foam.

Like the inside of the prosthetic chin he wore in Montana.

"You know a thing or two about high-end prosthetics, don't you, Silence? Suppressor? Asset 23? You wore some just like this a few weeks ago."

Brendan continued pulling up on the neck scar as he spoke until a small black box appeared underneath. He wrapped his fingers around it and gave it a swift tug, ripping it off his neck.

He held it out for Silence to see, which was challenging as a fresh wave of dizziness made Silence rock on his heels. He squinted.

The device was small, roughly an inch and a half square and a quarter-inch thick. It was vented on the top.

"Voice modulator," Brendan said, sounding markedly different.

He no longer sounded like a snake.

He sounded like the FBI special agent from the VHS tape and the audio logs.

"This entire scenario," Brendan said, his new voice laced with a triumphant edge, "was designed for you. All for you."

He paced back and forth, his eyes never straying from Silence.

"My father was a data specialist and a computer whiz. That's why the State Department hired him and why the Watchers recruited him for their secretive agenda. Both groups misjudged his honor, the Watchers especially." Brendan paused. "But who doesn't want to make a few bucks on the side?

"The Watchers also misjudged how much of Richard Keane's tendencies he passed on to his son. I was raised around computers. A prodigy, people called me when I was young. When I got a little older, as a teenager, they labeled me a hacker.

"I've spent years plotting, trying to breach into the Watchers' databases. Fully infiltrated only a year ago. Excellent cyber security you folks have. That's when I made my presence known—only after I had everything in place for my grand scheme here in Indianapolis."

Brendan brought a hand up to his eyeball. Touched it. And suddenly, his eyes matched; both were now brown. On his finger sat a pale blue contact lens.

He grinned at Silence. "Don't ya just hate contact lenses? No need to answer that. I already know the answer. You bitched and moaned about wearing them in your Montana mission's AAR."

Brendan looked down at the lens on his finger, smirking. He rolled it between two fingertips for a moment, then flicked it away into the gathering water on the concrete floor.

"There is no Code Red, Silence," Brendan said. "It was all me. I hacked Doc Hazel's electronic devices, bypassed your boss, Falcon. Every piece of mission material Doc Hazel gave you, I fabricated. Every note, record, photograph, government document. Doc Hazel had no clue. Neither did Falcon." His smirk broadened. "For the last two weeks, I've curated all the Watchers communication you and Doc Hazel received, fabricating much of it myself. I even hacked your GPS tracking dot and disabled your phone to incoming Watchers calls. The Watchers think you're in Pensacola, Florida, right now tending to that neighbor friend of yours. What's her name? Rita Enfield?"

Hearing Mrs. Enfield's name, spat out by Brendan's sneering lips, sent a surge of heat through Silence. His blood didn't just boil—it ignited. He tried to lunge at Brendan but only lurched forward, plunging deeper into the puddle that was gathering around him, creeping over the soles of his double monks.

Brendan, with his usual lazy arrogance, shifted back a step. A smirk played on his face.

"I've enjoyed myself, toying with the mighty Suppressor, the top Asset, my father's murderer. I crafted a perfect Silence Jones mission," Brendan boasted, "one designed to break you, to humiliate you. Colin Lennox's suicide tape? Nothing but cheap Hollywood tricks—a squib, a blood packet, some phony teeth. The audio log? Just me dabbling in a bit of drama. I do have a flair for it, after all. Aside from computers and data, my other passion is storytelling—theatre, books, movies.

"I wrote you a masterpiece of a character to chase after: the poor unfortunate soul, Maya Fuller. Someone to tug at those big, long heartstrings of yours. I even spiced it up with a little family drama—the dead husband, the grieving brother-in-law, the naughty kiss ... oh no!"

He clapped a hand over his mouth, feigning shock.

"But there is no Fuller family. Mike played Nate, and played the role well. And Maya? That picture in your dossier was a damn *stock photo*, the kind you see plastered on real estate leaflets or lawn-care billboards. *Ha!*"

Brendan's laugh boomed, echoing as he smacked his thigh with a wet slap.

"I had a trail for you to follow: you were to use the mission materials to track Nate Fuller to his house, where he would flee. But, of course, you'd investigate, finding the brochure for the Steady Progress Summit. See, I timed everything around the convention. Made things legitimate. Made them real, no reason to think otherwise. When you went to the Steady Progress Summit, there was Fuller, ready to lead you here, where all my other actors were in place and waiting.

"I added a little extra flavor to the plot here—I scattered some Chinese documents around the office for you to find. A hint, a nudge. Led you to believe that ol' Colin Lennox was orchestrating this mass suicide charade to harvest organs for the Chinese black market. That's what you bought into, wasn't it?"

Yes, that was precisely what Silence had pieced together. But he wasn't about to give Brendan the satisfaction of knowing that.

Silence didn't respond.

"Of course, the climax was to have all those people go out with a literal bang," he said, pointing to the now-empty warehouse floor strewn with overturned folding chairs under a relentless downpour. "But you, in typical Suppressor fashion, had to play the hero. Oh, so gallant. You think I actually give a shit that they survived? They're not gonna pin anything on Colin Lennox. There is no Colin Lennox!"

He flicked the flap of loose scar tissue foam dangling off his neck.

"That part was just for my amusement—making you fail a mission, making you watch dozens of people get blown to smithereens on your watch. But there's a bigger goal to accomplish."

Brendan paused, his gaze drilling into Silence.

"*I'm bringing down the entire Watchers organization.*" He let the words hang in the air. "Remember, I cracked the Watchers' databases a year back. The dirt I've dug up—once it's out there, it's going to raze the Watchers to the ground. It'll send a good number straight to jail, while others will have targets on their backs. The mission of justifiable kills, disrupting terrorist plots, obliterating cartels, avenging the unavenged—all that's about to end. And you? You'll be right here, a stone's throw away, utterly powerless to stop it. Isn't that just delicious? Now, if you need me, I'll be in the control room."

With that, Brendan spun on his heel, radiating the smug aura of a man who had already won. He knew Silence was disoriented, unable to react, so he just strolled past him. His steps quickened, his figure blurring as he rounded the corner and vanished from sight.

The full weight of Brendan Keane's deception crashed down on Silence then.

The Watchers...

Their righteous mission.

Silence's righteous mission.

Silence tried to give chase, but his body betrayed him. He staggered sideways, wavered, held his ground for a fleeting second, then crumpled into the water.

43

Brendan Keane, the man many knew as Colin Lennox, was a shadow in the pulsing light of the warehouse's disproportionately high-tech control room.

He double-clicked the icon for his custom-made program he called *Doomsday*. The backend was all taken care of long in the past. Nothing was in the window except a giant, obnoxiously neon green *SEND* button. Brendan didn't even have to click it; all he had to do was press the *ENTER* key.

He raised a finger over the *ENTER* key. Let it twist and dance there for a moment. And retracted it.

It wasn't quite time yet.

Not yet. This was the culmination of years of planning, a moment he needed to savor. And he wouldn't do so without his special guest.

Which reminded him...

Brendan tapped a few keys and activated the control room's sophisticated lock system. The heavy deadbolt slid into place with a resounding thud in the doorframe behind him.

From the corner of his eye, he caught movement among the bank of small screens to the left of the computer monitor.

Silence Jones appeared in one of the black-and-white feeds.

The guy who killed Brendan's father.

Brendan leaned closer to the grainy image. Silence, the once untouchable assassin, the best of the best, stumbled like a fool through Brendan's hallways, doing so under the effects of the drugs that Brendan had tricked him into consuming.

Brendan snickered.

Silence was headed for the control room. Of course. That's why Brendan was waiting before sending the *Doomsday* materials. As with everything else, this was part of the narrative Brendan had crafted; it was, in fact, the climax, the moment when the anti-hero gets to witness his seemingly righteous—but in actuality *self*-righteous—organization get destroyed right before his eyes.

But with Silence's slow stumbling, it would be a few more minutes until he arrived. This gave Brendan a chance to reflect, to savor the details of what had led to this moment.

His mind drifted back to a different time, a different Brendan—an seventeen-year-old with a world of shock awaiting him.

His father was dead.

Overdose. Heroin. Suicide note.

The man had been dead for three weeks.

Brendan spent a lot of time in the family office during those weeks, right where his father had killed himself. His mother had removed the chair where Richard Keane's slumped body had been discovered, but otherwise Brendan spent hours sitting in the exact spot where his father had died—behind the desk, beside the computer.

His father had been a tech whiz. He'd passed that skill on to his son. That's why the desk had felt so comforting for three weeks.

The discovery had been accidental—in a moment of child-like grief, curling up beneath the desk where the chair was usually stowed away. That's where Brendan saw it: a 3.5-inch floppy disk taped to the underside of the desk. It held the weight of a devastating truth. His father, portrayed as a pathetic heroin junkie, was actually a victim.

A murder victim.

The disk's contents had been password-protected and encrypted, but even at that age, Brendan was a tech savant and had managed to access the disk.

Names, documents, cold, calculated strategies—it was all there. Materials related not to Department of State affairs but ... something different. Something illegal. It was a group known as the Watchers, a system of people embedded throughout U.S. government who took it upon themselves to correct errors in procedural justice.

They corrected these errors via their cadre of assassins.

Brendan dug further and further, peeling back the layers of his father's encryption. Richard Keane had been a member of the Watchers, but he hadn't been one of the assassins. He hadn't been among the higher brass, either. Richard had been a Specialist, one of the individuals who managed all the organization's detail work.

For Brendan's father, that detail work had been digital intelligence. Of course. Due to Richard's role in the State Department, most of the intel pertained to national security.

For some reason, though, his father started accessing Watchers databases for reasons wholly unrelated to national security, matters that weren't part of his pipeline within the organization. For a while, as he sifted through the information, this had puzzled Brendan.

But not for long. He soon saw that his father was selling secrets. Richard Keane had double-crossed both the Watchers and the United States.

At the same time, Richard had gotten too cocky with his encryption methods. He'd slipped up. The Watchers had found out.

And they sent one of their assassins to plug the leak.

A brand-new assassin, but one that the organization felt was their best recruit in years, perhaps ever.

Asset 23.

Codename: Suppressor.

Chosen name: Silence Jones.

Brendan's father's death hadn't been a suicide; it was a meticulous, calculated assassination.

Since Richard Keane had been a high-ranking State Department official, the Watchers couldn't simply eliminate him; his prominence demanded caution. So they'd opted for a bit of storytelling, staging a heroin overdose replete with a tearful suicide note.

The memories surged now, fueled by years of suppressed anger and pain. Brendan's transformation into Colin Lennox wasn't just a change of identity but a rebirth from the ashes of his shattered past.

When he applied the prosthetic scars—which he nicked from the Watchers, from one of their caches of advanced technologies—and slid into the persona, he became a man with a singular focus: to avenge his father and bring the Watchers to their knees.

Brendan spent years weaving an intricate web, staying hidden, staying patient. Now, as he sat in the control room, his plan was on the cusp of fruition.

Minutes away...

Movement on the surveillance monitors brought Brendan back to the present. Silence had stumbled off one grainy monitor and entered another.

A different hallway. A nearer one.

He was almost to the control room.

A smirk crept onto Brendan's face, a rare display of emotion in his usually stoic demeanor. He turned back to the computer and brought his finger to where it had been a few minutes earlier...

...hovering above the *ENTER* key.

44

Silence's world was a haze, a distorted reality filtered through the lingering effects of the drug coursing through his veins.

Each step was a battle, a struggle to maintain the clarity that had always been one of his greatest weapons. The warehouse walls loomed around him, all rusted metal, dripping pipes, and stained concrete, illuminated by the strings of flickering bare bulbs.

The pulsating shadows shifted and swayed. The horizon tilted, pitched.

And Silence stumbled. He caught himself, his palm slapping onto damp cinderblock.

Frustration mounted. This was not how he operated. Precision and control—these were tenets of his existence.

Now, he had neither of them.

He pushed himself off the wall. Took a turn to the right. Down another hall. A turn to the left.

And then he was there—back at the control room, the final barrier between him and Brendan Keane.

The door was a monolith of security—solid steel with a pane of glass—the ultimate example of Brendan's paranoia and cunning. This high-tech and substantial door looked oddly out of place on the stretch of rust-rotted corrugated wall that housed it.

So, too, did the cheerfully red fire extinguisher a few feet away on said wall, right there among Brendan's zig-zag pattern of strung-up lighting. It looked brand new. Through the window in the door, Silence saw an identical extinguisher installed on the wall inside the control room.

Clearly, Brendan was taking no chances with the electronics and their priceless information—information with the power to bring down the Watchers, stored on an expensive computer station in a building that looked ready to fall over at any moment.

Seeing Brendan through the window—the back of the man's head visible as he sat before a glowing monitor—brought a fresh wave of clarity to Silence's senses. He hurried.

In another fleeting moment of lucidity, Silence's gaze fell upon a small, rusted hole in the metal wall beside the door. It was barely noticeable, about four inches across, a minor imperfection in the warehouse's overtly decaying facade.

But to Silence, it was an opportunity, a weak point in Brendan's fortress.

Silence's mind, though clouded, began to calculate, to assess. He could widen the hole, breach the barrier that Brendan had so confidently erected.

It was a chance.

A slim one.

But a chance.

As he covered the last few yards, he watched through the window as Brendan rose and turned to face him, smiling. The younger man lifted a hand, fluttered his fingers at Silence in a playful wave, and then brought the hand down fast, going for the keyboard...

...but stopping short.

Brendan's extended index finger hovered there, right over the far right side of the keyboard ... where the *ENTER* key would be.

The indication was clear: Brendan was ready to send whatever transmission was required to destroy the Watchers. But the guy was waiting—waiting to drag out the moment as long as possible, the consummate showman.

Silence was to the control room. A few yards and an overbuilt door separated him and Brendan. They looked at each other. Face to face. Brendan smiled.

And Silence stepped to the side.

Gathering his strength, he aimed a kick at the hole in the wall, intending to tear through the corroded metal. But his typically precise coordination betrayed him, his foot swinging wide, connecting with nothing but air.

Another try. Another miss.

Frustration urged him on as much as purpose. But again, his impaired state turned what should have been a simple action into a nightmare. This kick went even farther off-course than the first two, skipping off the metal and going far to the left. It spun him around, nearly sent him to the floor.

And the hole remained stubbornly intact.

Silence moved back, taking a long breath. Not one of C.C.'s techniques. Just a good ol'-fashioned deep breath to steady himself.

It didn't work.

The drug was a shackle, chaining him to limitations. He was without his skill set. He was handicapped.

And he felt the seconds ticking away, each one a missed opportunity, each one another chance for Brendan to destroy the Watchers.

For a second, despair swooped in.

But only for a second.

Silence wasn't the desperate type; it was just the drugs talking.

He narrowed his gaze at the hole in the wall.

Drug cartels, murderers, serial rapists, human-traffickers—he'd tackled them all. He could handle a rusty fissure in the name of saving his organization.

With a resolve reborn and burning fiercely within him, he steeled himself for another go. This time, he was ready to shatter the obstruction, to confront the man hell-bent on destroying something decent in this world, something that made a difference.

Brendan, safely behind steel and fortified glass, watched Silence's faltering attempts through the window with a look of derisive amusement. He must have enjoyed what he was witnessing: the once formidable assassin struggling to land a simple kick.

"You honestly think you're getting through that?" Brendan said, voice muffled through the door and the corrugated metal wall. He stood with casual arrogance, his finger idly dancing over the *ENTER* key.

With a grunt of effort, Silence kicked again, his foot finally connecting with the corroded portion of the metal. The impact sent a jarring pain up his leg.

But it was a pain he welcomed. It signaled he was still in the fight.

He kicked again, harder.

The metal groaned. The hole began to widen.

Another kick.

Another.

Brendan laughed.

Another kick. Silence felt that one in his knee.

With a screech, the hole widened.

He kicked again, harder.

And the hole went a bit wider.

Still, both Silence and Brendan knew Silence would never widen the hole enough. It had started about four inches across; now it was quadruple that.

Sixteen inches. Nowhere near wide enough to accommodate Silence's broad, six-foot-three frame.

That's why Brendan's sneer hadn't faltered when the metal started to give.

But Brendan wouldn't have laughed if he knew what Silence was *really* planning.

The fire extinguisher. Mounted on the wall. Shiny red and new. Silence seized it.

In one fluid motion, he ripped the pin from the extinguisher and aimed it at the now sizable hole. He depressed the handle, unleashing a torrent of chemical foam that surged through the gap. It engulfed the control room, a white deluge splattering over Brendan and his precious equipment.

The banks of servers, the epicenter of Brendan's scheme, crackled wildly as the chemicals invaded their circuits.

Sparks flew from the largest monitor, flashing, filling the room

Brendan, now coated in foam, scrambled frantically, his earlier confidence evaporating into panic. His meticulously laid plans were disintegrating before his eyes, undone by a simple canister of fire suppressant.

Silence watched as the monitors died, their screens going dark one by one. The control room was a chaotic mess of flares and foam.

He looked at the sixteen-inch hole in the corrugated metal. The freshly torn sections were shiny and jagged.

There was always a way in. Always a chink in the armor.

Enraged and covered in a thick layer of foam, Brendan emerged from the control room. His eyes, wild with rage, locked onto Silence.

Silence knew it was coming.

It was inevitable.

Revenge is a poison. If it's not expelled, eventually, there will be an explosion.

Brendan exploded.

He charged at Silence, fists already swinging. But Silence, even through the drug's haze, was ready.

Bam!

They collided.

Silence's training kicked in, making up for his impaired senses, and he used Brendan's reckless energy against him, hip-checking the guy into the wall with a loud, metallic clang.

Brendan swung around, leaving his chest wide open, exposed, an absolute rookie mistake.

But Silence couldn't capitalize. When he lunged forward, a sudden wave of the drug's disorientation made him stumble to the right.

Brendan seized the opportunity, coming at Silence with a jab to the ribs. White pain flashed up Silence's side.

Fueled by raw anger, Brendan was relentless. He swung a looping right hook. But Silence was faster, even with the drugs doing their thing; he wouldn't make the same mistake twice.

He sidestepped, Brendan's punch whistling past.

Brendan, unbalanced by his missed strike, stumbled forward. Silence moved in.

A quick jab to Brendan's flank, precise and hard. Then a knee, lifted high and driven into Brendan's stomach. The air whooshed out of Brendan, a gasp of pain and shock.

But Brendan was surprisingly tough. He recovered, lunging again with a wild left. Silence ducked. The fist sailed over his head.

Silence's counter was a blur. An elbow strike to Brendan's jaw. A spinning back-fist. Each hit landed with a wet thud.

This pair of blows was enough to turn the fight definitively.

Brendan, desperate now, threw a haymaker. Silence caught the wrist mid-air. Twisted it. Brendan's face contorted in pain.

Then, Silence's other hand shot out. A palm strike. Straight to Brendan's nose. There was a sickening crack.

Brendan reeled back, blood spilling from his broken nose, streams of it spattering the foam on his shirt, going pink.

Silence didn't let up.

A taekwondo *yop chagi* kick, aimed at Brendan's knee. It connected with a snap. Brendan's leg buckled. He fell to his remaining knee, groaning.

Knees seemed to be the theme of the fight now.

So Silence brought a knee to Brendan's face, cracking his lower jaw into the upper one. Then a swift, hard elbow to the back of the man's neck. Brendan crumpled to the floor.

In the hollow nothingness that followed, there was only the heavy breathing of both men and the sound of falling water pattering on foam. Brendan lay motionless aside from the rising and lowering of his chest.

Silence stood over him, his own chest heaving. He stumbled to the right, his senses still clouded.

Regaining his balance, he knelt down and propped Brendan up at a convenient angle before putting his hands on either side of Brendan's head.

Brendan started to say something—perhaps "No," perhaps something venomous or retaliatory—but it didn't matter. Silence didn't give him the chance to speak.

He just broke his neck.

Silence released his hold, allowing Brendan's lifeless form to crumple to the floor. It made a wet *slap* as it fell into a puddle of foam and water.

The threat Brendan posed, the secrets he sought to expose, died with him. The Watchers' mysteries, their clandestine operations, remained secure, hidden from the public eye.

The Watchers' mission would go on. They would continue to right wrongs.

Silence straightened up and stood over Brendan, his breathing heavy, his body still reeling from the drugs and the blows he received and the exertion of the fight.

He thought of Brendan's photo on the shelf at the Keane family house. Years ago.

He thought of killing Richard Keane, hoisting the urine-soaked body, staging the man's suicide.

While he thought of these two things, he continued to look at Brendan's body.

After he was done thinking, he stepped over the body and left.

45

Silence navigated back through the labyrinthine corridors of the warehouse, his mind clearer than before but still clouded by the drug's residual effects. He found Malone right where he'd left him, slumped against the wall, on the verge of passing out. The broken ankle was really taking its toll now.

Of course.

It had happened hours ago. Malone's adrenaline had long since worn off. Silence was stunned that the guy was still conscious. Tough son of a bitch.

The distant wail of sirens pierced the air. Silence knelt beside Malone and pointed at the ankle. "Help's coming."

Malone's eyes flickered with recognition, then dimmed with despondency. "I'm no hero, Chad. I couldn't..." His voice trailed off.

Silence wasn't going to console the guy. Not now. He needed intel. And fast.

Because even though Lennox was dead, there was still more for Silence to do that night...

"Where in Insight Center..." he said and swallowed. "Can I find Radley and Perrine?"

"I wanted to help Taylor Perrine," Malone said. It wasn't an answer to Silence's question, but his gaze was so distant that, for a moment, it looked like he would finally lose consciousness. "I thought I could make a difference."

Shit. Now, if Silence was going to get the critical intel he needed, he *had* to console the guy. He pointed to the unconscious form of Michael Pushard beside Malone.

"Took action when it counted," he said and swallowed. "You *are* a hero." Another swallow. "Where can I find Radley?"

It took a moment, but Malone's glazed-over eyes finally met Silence's.

"Somewhere in the back of the facility. That's where Insight keeps the staff conference rooms, not the public ones." His voice grew increasingly despondent as his gaze shifted away from Silence, looking into the dark depths of the hallways. "Montoya has access to them. That's where he and Radley would have set up. Room numbers starting with A. Use my card."

Malone pawed dumbly at the keycard clipped to his belt but couldn't get hold of it.

Silence grabbed the man's arm, stopped him, and took the card.

He stood. Looked down at Malone. Gave him a nod. And left.

The night air had gotten foggy. And cool.

It tasted pure, even there in the middle of the city—devoid of Brendan Keane's incense and the shit it was laced with.

Silence began his half-drugged progress from the warehouse across the parking lot. But he didn't head for the Infiniti.

He couldn't drive. Not in this condition. Not half-drugged.

So Silence did the only thing he could do in this situation.

He ran.

Hell, it was only a quarter mile away.

Feet pounding rapidly.

Cutting a wobbly, side-to-side path.

Cars and trees and streetlights whooshing past in a blur. Skyscrapers lighting up the distant sky.

And straight ahead of him...

The Insight Center, glowing brilliantly, its massive parking lot still packed.

As he moved through the foggy night, a sense of déjà vu enveloped him. It reminded him of the recent mission in Montana, the confrontation with Hank Maddox at the foggy truck stop, Highway Haven.

A hallucination tried to surface, and he pressed it back.

He was done with hallucinations.

He nearly fell over. Didn't. Stumbled again.

But continued.

The Insight Center was right in front of him. Almost there.

His head was swimming. His stomach churned. And this wasn't his mission.

No involvement in local matters, Falcon would say if he could see Silence at that moment.

But that imperative didn't matter.

Silence needed to remedy one more issue in Indianapolis.

The foggy air did him well.

By the time he reached the Insight Center, his head had cleared somewhat, enough to walk a straight line.

Using Malone's keycard, Silence gained access to the back end of the building.

The transition was jarring.

He had just left the grit and shadows of Brendan Keane's warehouse behind, stepping into a world of bright lights and corporate décor. The hallway was deserted, the plush carpeting and tasteful art a contrast to the rough concrete and starkness of the warehouse.

He moved quickly, checking the doors as he went.

A101, empty.

A102, empty.

A103. He paused, his hand on the door handle. He heard voices inside, the murmur of a crowd. Taking a deep breath, he steeled himself for what was to come. This was it, the moment he had been working toward, the reason he'd just sprinted a quarter mile through both mental and literal fog.

He threw open the door and stepped into the room.

There were a handful of people there—including Taylor Perrine—a camcorder on a tripod in the back corner, and at the front of it all, the man Silence had seen talking to Taylor earlier, the pushing-fifty Asian heritage man in a sharp blue suit, no tie, dark hair trimmed and styled perfectly: Tom Radley.

Against the wall was a younger man of Hispanic heritage who shot up at the sight of Silence; this must have been Darren Montoya.

In the back corner—also starting at the sight of Silence, but doing so in an entirely different manner, her bright blue eyes flashing brighter, curly red hair bouncing as she straightened—was Kori.

The other people, Radley's audience, watched in confusion. The VHS camcorder was set up on a tripod in the back, just visible through a gap in a velvet curtain surrounding it.

Silence wasted no time.

"This man..." he said and swallowed, pointing at Radley. "Records private confessions..." Another swallow. "And sells them. Blackmail."

Silence wobbled slightly, caught his balance.

The room erupted into a cacophony of shock and disbelief. People began to rise from their seats, their expressions a mixture of anger and fear. Though no one acted out, no one stayed behind, either, despite Radley's protestations.

"Wait!" Radley said, waving his arms and leaving the front of the room to chase after them. "Folks, wait! You believe this man? Look at him. He's drunk!"

Still, no one turned around. The reality of Radley's betrayal sunk in, and they all fled.

Kori ran to her friend, ushering Taylor Perrine out with the others. Silence nodded at her as the pair passed. Kori smiled.

The room quickly emptied, leaving only Radley, Montoya, and Silence.

Radley's façade of calm crumbled, replaced by a look of desperation.

Montoya saw Silence's slightly unsteady stance and exchanged a glance with Radley.

"You stupid son of a bitch," Radley said to Silence. "What, you a cop?"

"Not exactly," Silence said. He stumbled again, caught his balance again.

Montoya stepped closer to Radley, jerking his head slightly in Silence's direction.

"Looks like our new friend's not playing with a full deck tonight," Montoya said, a hint of calculation in his tone.

"You're right," Radley said, looking Silence up and down. "Guy's probably a real beast on a good day. Might be our only shot. Let's not waste it."

Without warning, Montoya lunged at Silence.

But even in his impaired state, Silence's instincts were razor-sharp.

He sidestepped Montoya's lunging attack—a matador, using the man's own bullish momentum against him. Montoya fell face-forward.

Silence pivoted, his focus snapping to Radley. For a heartbeat, Radley froze, his eyes ballooning in terror. He looked like he wished the earth would swallow him whole, taking him far away from the fight he'd instigated and Silence's towering, unyielding figure.

But primal survival instincts kicked in. Radley's arm swung in a wide, reckless arc, his fist aiming for Silence's face. It was an amateur's punch, telegraphed and sloppy. Silence ducked effortlessly, the punch whistling harmlessly overhead.

His counter was a masterclass in controlled violence: a sharp jab to Radley's solar plexus, followed by a swift uppercut that snapped Radley's head back.

Montoya had gotten up, and he hurled himself back into the fray, fists flailing. Silence parried a wild left hook, spun inside Montoya's guard, and delivered a punishing elbow to his opponent's jaw.

Montoya's head rocked back, his body following suit, crashing to the floor.

The fight was over almost as soon as it had begun.

Radley and Montoya were crumpled on the floor, only a yard apart. Radley gasped for air, blinking up at Silence with more of that fear in his eyes. Beside him, Montoya was unconscious.

Silence leaned over Radley, looking straight down upon him. He pointed at the camcorder in the back.

"I think it's time..." he said and swallowed. "You confessed."

46

The next morning.

Avery sat alone in his kitchen, mechanically spooning cereal into his mouth. The taste was bland, dulled by the painkillers coursing through his system. Each bite was a reminder of his current state: numbed, both physically and emotionally. To his side, a shiny new set of crutches leaned against the counter.

He looked past the crutches to the small window above the sink, the morning light doing little to brighten the dreariness of his apartment. His mind replayed the scene from last night's hospital visit: the sterile smell of antiseptics and the sympathetic looks from the nurses as they tended to his broken ankle. They'd told him to take it easy, to take a few days off. But Avery had insisted on returning to work, volunteering for desk duty at the Insight Center.

What the hell else did Avery have to do?

As he sat there, his mind wandered down the familiar path of self-reflection, not for the first time that morning. He thought about the previous night's events, before the hospital visit, about the moment of chaos and clarity when he had found himself in the middle of a dangerous situation. For a brief moment, he'd been more than just a security guard;

he'd been a part of something bigger, a pivotal piece in a puzzle he barely understood.

But as the adrenaline faded, so did that fleeting sense of purpose.

Now, reality had returned in the light of a new day, in a cramped kitchen with peeling linoleum and sagging cabinetry. He was just Avery, the security guard. The heroism of last night was an anomaly, nothing but a momentary break from his true existence.

A loser. A man who'd reached the middle of his life with little to show for it. The stories of bravery and valor—the kind he'd heard at family get-togethers for years, stories of "Calvin the Cop" and "Flynn the Fireman"—seemed unattainable.

"Avery the Hero"?

Nah, it didn't fit.

He was just "Avery the Avoider" again—and now, a cripple as well, at least for a few months.

He pushed the bowl of cereal away and glanced at the uniform draped over the chair across from him. Today was simply another day, another shift at the Insight Center.

He couldn't complain. He *had* volunteered, after all.

The drone of the morning news broadcast filled the kitchen, a subtle background noise that Avery had grown accustomed to. It was part of his routine, a way to start the day with a connection to the world outside his small apartment. Today, however, the news anchor's words cut through the fog of his thoughts, snapping him back to the present.

"We're following up on last night's shocking events at the Indianapolis Insight Center, where a near-catastrophic con job involving socialite Taylor Perrine and other notable figures was thwarted at the last minute..."

Avery's spoon froze mid-air. He twisted toward the tiny television on the counter. While the anchor continued, the screen showed B-roll footage of the Insight Center. The image shifted to a video confession.

There was Tom Radley, his face ashen, panic in his eyes, a stark contrast to the man Avery had encountered just the previous evening, who'd looked composed and charismatic in his slick blue suit. This new incarnation of Radley was unraveling before the public eye.

"I ... I want to confess," Radley stammered, his eyes darting off-camera.

"Darren Montoya and I ... we planned to exploit people. We recorded their secrets during the therapy sessions, planning to blackmail them later..."

As Radley detailed his and Montoya's scheme, Avery watched, transfixed. The spoonful of cereal remained frozen mid-air. A smile crept onto Avery's face for the first time that morning.

The smile was one of realization. He'd deduced how this public confession came to be.

"Chad..." he said, shaking his head.

He lowered the spoon and set it in the bowl.

Chad had done it. Of course he had.

Chad the hero.

But also...

Avery had played a part, however insignificant. Chad had stormed into Indianapolis, into the Insight Center, and brought a pair of criminals to justice.

...but he couldn't have done it without Avery's help.

Avery grinned.

The sudden knock at the door made him jump, instantly wiping the smile off his face. Visitors were a rarity in his solitary world.

With a grunt, he maneuvered to grab the crutches leaning against the counter, then thumped across the linoleum, careful not to trip up his crutches on the curled edges.

He opened the door to find a sharply dressed young man holding a fancy envelope, an item so out of place in the surroundings of Avery's apartment that it seemed almost surreal.

"For Mr. Avery Malone," the young man announced, offering the envelope with a polite nod.

Avery took it.

"A telegram?" he said.

The messenger simply smiled, nodded again, and turned away, leaving Avery alone with the mystery. Avery closed the door and returned to the table.

His fingers trembled slightly as he broke the envelope's seal. Inside was a letter, its text elegantly written on high-quality stationery. The name at the bottom of the letter made his heart skip a beat.

Taylor Perrine.

The socialite. The woman whose face was showing on his television screen that very moment. The person he'd tried to help. The unwitting target of Tom Radley's scheme.

Avery's eyes scanned the words, each sentence bringing a growing sense of disbelief. Taylor Perrine thanked him, crediting him for his role in the previous night's events. The letter spoke of a semi-anonymous hero—a man who wanted to be called only "Chad" and disappeared before the authorities arrived—who had attributed the unraveling of Radley's scheme to Avery's bold actions and keen instincts.

But the most astounding part of the letter came next.

Taylor Perrine offered him a position as her personal security guard. The salary figure was written in clear, unmistakable numbers: $100,000.

The sum seemed fantastical, a figure that existed in daydreams and distant hopes, not in Avery's reality.

For a moment, Avery was motionless. His mouth hung open.

Then, "Chad … Thanks, Chad."

Avery eased back in his chair, the letter resting in his lap, grimacing as a bit of pain winked at him through the medicated numbness.

Things were finally changing—in rapid and dynamic fashion.

And maybe, just maybe, Avery *was* a hero.

For just a moment, anyway.

47

Three days later.

At least it wasn't a sex motel this time...

Silence was in a brand-new, one-room rental office, so new that he could smell the fresh carpet, paint, and furniture smells. The place was a study in sterile minimalism, the stark white walls interrupted only by a single abstract painting.

He wasn't happy about getting scheduled for another counseling session so soon after his last one, but the environment was infinitely cleaner than the previous session's setting.

And there was no sofa or bed onto which Doc Hazel could force him to lie down in classic clinical session style, as she so often did. That was good, too.

Doc Hazel wore cat eye spectacles and a skirt suit, navy blue. She was at the desk. Silence was on the office's only other chair—a metal job with a thin cushion—facing the desk.

Silence said, "Have something for you."

Doc Hazel's response was wordless. She simply raised an eyebrow. Her usually guarded demeanor was momentarily pierced by a hint of confusion and surprise.

Silence reached into his pocket and pulled out a small plastic sack with

Indianapolis Motor Speedway printed on it. From it, he withdrew a cartoonish, bright blue, two-inch, open-wheel race car on a keychain. He pressed a small button on the car.

VROOM!

The sound echoed harshly off the walls of the starkly adorned office.

On his way out of Indy, Silence had made a quick detour to the most famous motor speedway in the world with the sole intent of visiting the gift shop. He wasn't entirely sure if the car figure was of the same make as the one Doc Hazel had unintentionally revealed at the start of his mission, but he was pretty confident. It had the same obnoxious sound.

Doc Hazel was momentarily too stunned to reply or even move.

So Silence pressed the button again.

VROOM!

He handed it to her. Doc Hazel regarded the tiny blue car resting on her palm. For a moment, she studied it, her face unreadable, then she looked up.

"Thank you, Suppressor."

Silence nodded.

Doc Hazel scrutinized the toy one final time, then flicked off its power switch and put it in her attaché case.

Silence watched her. He would never know whether the car would end up with Doc Hazel herself or a child or a boyfriend or a husband. It didn't really matter.

Doc Hazel crossed her legs, placed a notebook on her knee with pen poised and ready to go in her hand, and said, "Close your eyes, please."

He did so. Knowing he would be instructed to visualize, he began looking into the pinkish depths in the backs of his eyelids.

"Describe your beach fantasy to me again," Doc Hazel said, her voice as sterile and clean as the surroundings.

Internally, Silence seethed at the repetition of this pointless exercise. Outwardly, he complied.

"Small. Isolated. Simplistic."

"And how about the interior? Is it cozy?"

"Cozy but chic."

"Of course it is. And the view?"

He was there. At the imaginary window. In the small home—humble on the outside, modern minimalism on the inside. He put one hand along the window frame, leaned closer. His eyes traced the palm fronds and foliage dancing in the strong breeze. A storm was coming; he could taste it in the air. But it wasn't there yet. Now, the sky was blue, the sun bright. Waves crashed against the shore.

"Stunning," Silence said.

"Very good, Suppressor. You may open your eyes."

Silence did so.

Doc Hazel leaned forward, crossing her arms over her knees. "Do you feel better about your identity crisis now?"

"Never had one."

Doc Hazel remained silent, her expression unchanging.

"I know who I am," Silence added, meeting her gaze squarely.

"And who are you?"

"Silence Jones."

Again, Doc Hazel said nothing. But this time, she raised an eyebrow.

So Silence offered an alternative response. "I'm a Watcher."

"Indeed you are. And have you come to a decision about the Watchers' offer of a one-year sabbatical?"

Silence leaned back, his eyes drifting away from Doc Hazel as he mulled over her question. His thoughts wandered to the very essence of his existence within the organization.

Without this life, he would be adrift, lost in a sea of normalcy that now seemed alien to him. He mused over his role, stopping people like Brendan Keane—it gave his life meaning and purpose.

Then, his mind shifted to his non-sanctioned endeavors, helping individuals like Taylor Perrine. *No involvement in local matters.* These weren't on the Watchers' books, but they were stitched into the fabric of the man he was. And without the Watchers—without their unwitting resources and funding—Silence wouldn't be able to complete this important side work.

Finally, his thoughts shifted to the indirect impacts of his missions, like the unexpected assistance he provided to strangers such as Avery Malone, someone who had unexpectedly become entangled in the Indianapolis mission. These unforeseen interventions weren't uncommon.

Returning his gaze to Doc Hazel, Silence's expression hardened.

"No, thank you, ma'am," he said.

"You're sure?"

"Don't need time off," Silence said and swallowed. "Like I said..." Another swallow. "I'm a Watcher."

TELL NO TALES
Book 12 of the Silence Jones Action Thrillers

A FORGOTTEN PAST. A DEADLY PRESENT.

When vigilante assassin Silence Jones hears of an old friend's death in his long-forgotten hometown, he expects to pay his respects and leave. But a dark truth lurks beneath the surface: his friend didn't just die—he was murdered.

Returning to streets he barely remembers, Silence is thrust into a shadowy world festering within a seemingly tranquil small city. His friend, it seems, had unearthed a secret too dangerous to know—a widespread network of corruption with far-reaching implications for both U.S. and international security.

To unravel the web of conspiracy and avenge the murder, Silence will have to retrace the footsteps of an ally who'd long ago become a stranger, clashing with both a ruthless enemy and the reality that in this game, the stakes aren't just personal—they're global.

The next standalone action thriller in the pulse-pounding series. Enter the world of Silence Jones. Hold on tight...

Get your copy today at
severnriverbooks.com

30% Off your next paperback.

SCAN ME

Thank you for reading. For exclusive offers on your next paperback:

- **Visit SevernRiverBooks.com** and enter code **PRINTBOOKS30** at checkout.
- Or scan the QR code.

Offer valid for future paperback purchases only. The discount applies solely to the book price (excluding shipping, taxes, and fees) and is limited to one use per customer. Offer available to US customers only. Additional terms and conditions apply.

SEVERN RIVER
PUBLISHING

ACKNOWLEDGMENTS

For their involvement with *In the Dead of Night*, I would like to give a sincere thank you to:

My ARC readers, for providing reviews and catching typos. Thanks!

ABOUT THE AUTHOR

Erik Carter tells high-octane stories filled with action, suspense, and just the right amount of chaos.

His background is as eclectic as his stories—he's a NASM-certified personal trainer, has taught college-level writing and film, worked for a history-based mobile app, co-hosted a TV show, and even created a top-ranked documentary on YouTube. He holds two master's degrees—one in Telecommunications-Digital Storytelling and another in Public History—because one just wasn't enough.

When he's not writing, Erik is passionate about fitness, classic sports cars, movies, and books. He lives in sunny coastal Florida.

Sign up for the reader list at severnriverbooks.com

Printed in the United States
by Baker & Taylor Publisher Services